GOING TO THE DOGS

GOING TO THE DOGS

Russell McRae

VIKING

VIKING
Viking Penguin Inc.
40 West 23rd Street
New York, New York 10010, U.S.A.

First American Edition
Published in 1987

LIBRARY OF CONGRESS CATALOGING IN PUBLICATION DATA
McRae, Russell.
Going to the dogs.
I. Title.
PR9199.3.M4247G6 1987 813'.54 87-40019
ISBN 0-670-81735-X

Printed in the United States of America by
Arcata Graphics, Fairfield, Pennsylvania
Set in Baskerville

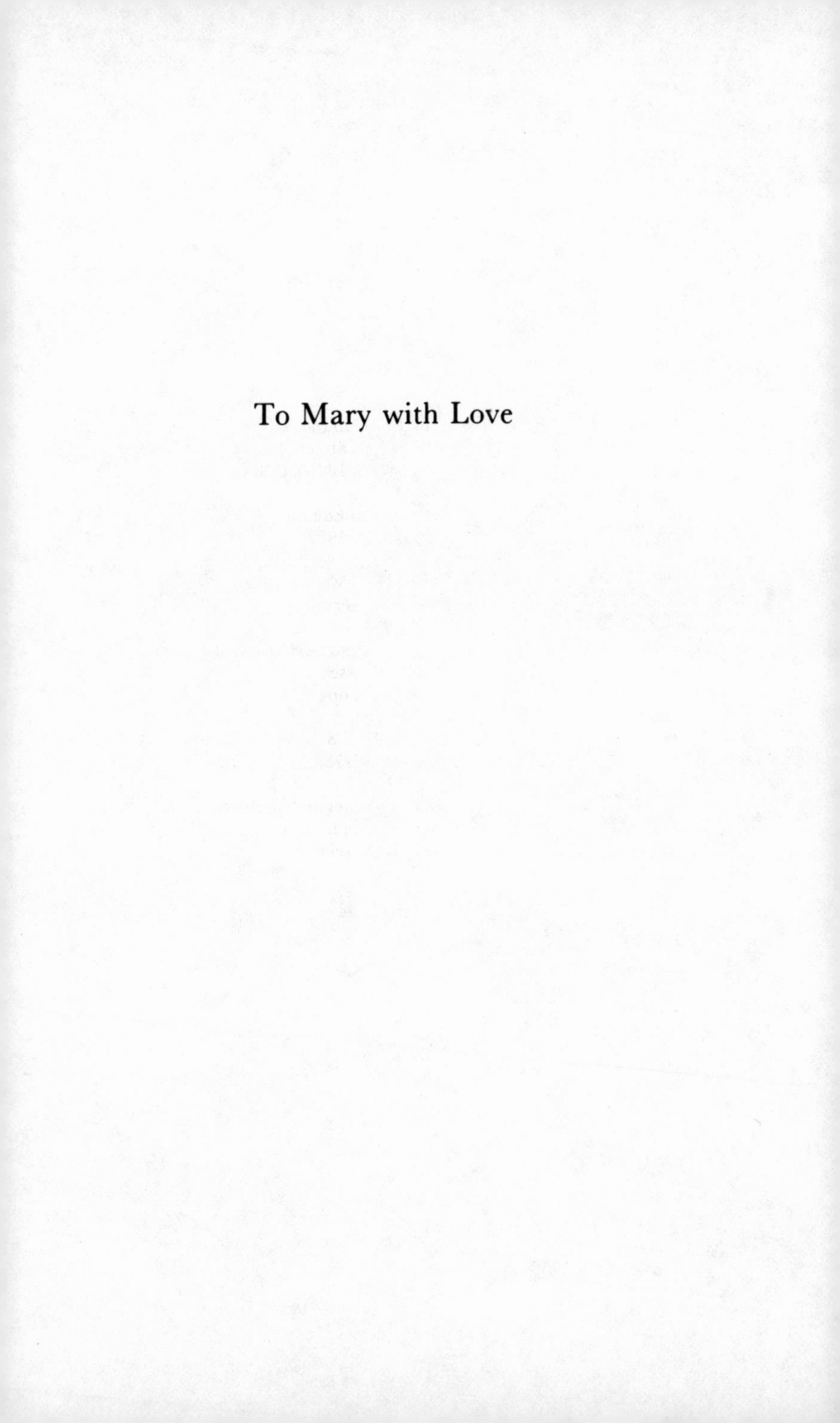

To Mary with Love

GOING TO THE DOGS

TEACHER'S REMARKS:

Billy is a lovely child! He is bright and quick to learn and a very advanced reader! Billy is cooperative, polite, and friendly with all his classmates, a pleasure to have in the classroom.

Promoted to Grade Two with Honors.

Mrs Betty Carlyle

TEACHER'S REMARKS:

It has been a real delight to have Billy this year in Grade Two! He is a very hard worker and has excelled in reading and composition. I wish there were more pupils as eager to learn as Billy.

Promoted to Grade Three with Honors.

Mrs Helen Jablowski

TEACHER'S REMARKS:

I will be sorry to lose Billy this year. Seldom have I had a more consistently pleasant and hardworking boy in my classroom. Billy is a great favorite with his peers.

Promoted to Grade Four with Honors.

Mrs J. Patrick Doyle

TEACHER'S REMARKS:

Billy excels in all his work and has a very creative imagination. His stories were always a pleasure to read! He is a neat and meticulous worker and always eager to please. A very popular boy!

Promoted to Grade Five with Honors.

Miss Florence Horwitz

TEACHER'S REMARKS:

Bill is a first-class boy in every respect. He is a very good sport and always plays to win! He is very competitive in games and has a great team spirit. Billy is a favorite with both boys and girls.

Promoted to Grade Six with Honors.

Jill Hill

TEACHER'S REMARKS:

Billy was my best Grade Six pupil this year. If it is possible, I would say he works too hard at his schoolwork, but it has certainly paid off! His notebooks are the best I have ever seen! I will be sorry to lose Billy!

Promoted to Grade Seven with Honors.

G. Smith

TEACHER'S REMARKS:

William is a quick learner when he wants to be. Let us hope he conquers his stubbornness and pride before they conquer him.

Promoted to Grade Eight.

Marjorie Copper

TEACHER'S REMARKS:

Billy is this year's top Grade Eight student and he should excel next year in high school. He goes out of his way to be kind at all times. He is especially considerate of those less gifted than he is at academic work, a real democrat. Teaching Billy has been a joy, not a duty! Good luck, Billy!

Promoted to Grade Nine with Honors.

B. F. Ornatowski

*

'That's me, ain't it,' said Rocky Barbizan one night years later when he and Billy were stoned on hash in Rocky's bedroom. Billy had come across his elementary school report cards by chance earlier in the evening, and brought them along for a laugh. Because Billy was so stoned, it seemed to take Rocky an eternity to read the damn things.

'Who's you?' Billy asked.

'Right fuckin' there,' Rocky said, pointing a grease-stained fingertip at the Teacher's Remarks slot on Billy's Grade Eight report card. 'Where she says "Billy is especially considerate of those less gifted than he is at academic work, a real democrat." That's me she's fuckin' talkin' about, ain't it? There ain't nobody as unfuckin' gifted as me.'

Rocky Barbizan used variations of the word fuck to give force to almost every statement he made. He used the word so often it was self-defeating – whatever shock value the word had left in the 1980s had no more impact in Rocky's conversation than a punctuation mark that made a noise. When he was with Rocky for a long time, Billy fell into the same habit.

Billy said, 'Yeah, that's you, Rocky. Mrs Ornatowski thought I cheated for you on your compositions.' He giggled to himself. 'I wonder why?'

Rocky laughed raucously. 'Fuck it, she couldn't fuckin' prove nothin'! Man, that shit you wrote for me sounded dumber'n the shit I wrote for myself.'

'Well, yes and no,' Billy said, remembering all the tactics he had devised to get Rocky passing grades and the countless hours he had poured into the project. 'What I aimed for was to make you sound very dumb, but also very lovable and trying hard to please. Teachers hate to fail the dumb but lovable and obedient kids. I also had to take out every appearance of shit, shitty, fuck, fucked, fucking, asshole, prick, and sucks. For one thing, you used to spell them wrong most of the time. Rocky, it took me three times as long to create your compositions as to write my own. First, I had to study the crap I forced you to do on your own, so I could see what mistakes you had made. Then I had to separate them into the mistakes you always made out of habit from the mistakes you made on the spur of the moment. I'm telling you, Rocky, it wasn't easy, it was hard work. I hated doing it, too, it turned my stomach. Your writing was gorgeous, it had a voice of its own. But I had to kill it to make it dumb but lovable. Every one of those fucking fifties you got was a labor of love.'

'Fuck it, Billy, I guess I know that. What can I say? I'm a lovable guy.'

'I guess you must be, to me anyway.'

Rocky grinned at Billy and said, 'Fuck, I bet you say that to all the boys.' Then the grin disappeared and he looked away from his friend and started beating out the rhythm of the music on his chest with his hands. 'Billy, do you really like me?'

'You know, you must have asked that question ten thousand times. When are you going to believe me? I love you, Rocky, you're my best friend. You're my only friend.'

'Hey, pass the hash, I'll roll another joint.' That was Rocky's habitual solution to the pain of trying to believe that anybody loved him.

The hash was expensive, but a few tokes produced a superb stone. When they had finished the joint, Billy got up to go home. He had a physics test the next morning.

'Shit, Billy,' Rocky protested, 'I don't want you to go home yet, I ain't tired. You know all that physics crap already. What the fuck are you going to fuckin' study?'

'I have to figure out what mistake to make,' Billy replied as he shrugged into his jacket, 'one that'll lose me about five marks or so. Cheating for myself is twice as hard as it ever was for you.'

'I don't understand why you lose marks on purpose when you could get a hundred.'

'Rocky, I've told you before, teachers pretend to be thrilled when you get a hundred but it really bugs them. Perfection has a backlash. It's best to always give them a little reason to feel superior, you know, so they can think, aha! I got him on the real toughie!'

CHAPTER ONE

More than anything else on earth, Billy Mackenzie aspired to freedom.

Consequently, he had learned early to want money, a lot of money, the more money the better. Money was the stuff that bought you power and freedom, which as far as Billy could see were one and the same thing, despite all the bullshit you heard and read in school about the inherent corruption of power and the precious heritage of democracy's freedoms. The only freedom he believed you could get was the kind that money bought, the freedom to buy your way out of circumstances like being born who you were.

More than once when he was stoned, Billy had seriously wondered if there were any crime short of murder that he would not commit for money, if the amount of money were big enough and he knew he wouldn't get caught. He excluded murder because his parents were the only people he had ever felt capable of killing, and that would have been an act of love for his sister, Anne, not out of greed.

Even before he'd begun thinking consciously about these matters, Billy had seemed to know them by instinct. As soon as he had the size and muscular strength to do physical work, he set out to accumulate money as a squirrel accumulates nuts. He mowed old ladies' lawns, he delivered papers, he baby-sat for neighbors, and, during the interminable northern Ontario winters, he shovelled snow by the ton. He had just turned thirteen when he began pumping gas at one of

Nugget's gas stations, and at nineteen he was still pumping it. During his sixteenth, seventeenth, and eighteenth summers, he'd made pretty good money as a lowly laborer at Universal Plywood in the nearby town of Lac du Bois. He got the job because he had smoked dope at a couple of parties Rocky took him to with one of the younger foremen and the guy had really liked him – Billy had made sure of that.

Almost all of the money he'd earned over the years had been put straight into the bank, and by the time he turned nineteen he would have over five thousand dollars in his account. He would have had a lot more but he'd spent over two thousand dollars on a 1978 Ford pickup so he could drive back and forth to see his girlfriend, Poppy Richardson, whose family lived in Lac du Bois. He'd grown bone-weary of sucking up to his parents every time he wanted to borrow their Datsun for a few hours. Apparently the driveway missed it when it wasn't there.

Billy's only other capital expense had been a cassette player he bought on sale – not the best but not bad, either – so he could listen to his modest collection of tapes. He had all of Bruce Springsteen and all of Mike Oldfield, both of whom he regarded as divine. He had the Rolling Stones' old stuff, what they had done before they knew they were the Rolling Stones, the Blues Brothers, some of the Eagles, and Barbra Streisand's rock tapes. He had tried and failed to make Rocky realize that Barbra Streisand had an angelic voice and that her prominent nose was immaterial. Personally, Billy thought she was beautiful.

His only other luxury was the marijuana he had been buying and smoking discreetly since he met up with Rocky in grade eight. Billy guessed he was an addict of some kind.

Dope was not the center of Billy's life, as it was for Rocky Barbizan who had started dealing in elementary school, but he liked getting high and saw nothing wrong with it. Being high eased his heart for a few hours and made him feel happy, chiefly because it evaporated the obsessive ideas that occupied his mind. Getting stoned was like escaping from a high-security penitentiary. He doped up regularly but seldom got wasted because he was too conscious of the money dope consumed. Even though he got his grass dirt cheap from Rocky, it was a costly indulgence. He always smoked a joint before he and Poppy made love because the sex felt freer and more real, and he smoked one nightly after he went to bed because sleeping came easier and sooner. Marijuana and black hashish were the only drugs Billy had ever used, whereas Rocky had tried snorting cocaine and dropping acid and was itching to smoke some opium as soon as he got the chance.

If Billy was a confirmed user, Rocky Barbizan was a devout believer. Among the members of the local drug culture – the size of which astounded Billy as he came to belong to it – Rocky was renowned as a true connoisseur of the various highs you could get from different combinations of drugs, beer, and hard liquor. He was also popular, of course, because he always seemed to have some quality stuff on hand for the right price for the right people.

In grade seven, Rocky had been suspended from the Catholic elementary school for smoking up at recess and passing joints around to the other kids, though they failed to prove he had actually been selling the joints. The kids who had been buying it were too scared to admit it – at fifteen Rocky had big fists and powerful shoulders. In grade eight, Rocky found himself transferred to the public school, and on his first day in class he offered to initiate Billy into the forbidden mysteries of smoking pot. After school that day, they went to Rocky's grandmother's house, where Rocky had lived since he was seven years old when his parents were divorced and disappeared like butterflies.

Billy never forgot that first experience of getting stoned with Rocky Barbizan. Six years later, he could still vividly remember the two of them howling with the most real laughter Billy had ever known and rolling around on Rocky's bed as his first true friend told him stories about his scholastic adventures with the nuns.

One young nun fresh from some convent had tried to bring Rocky to Jesus and teach him to read at the same time by forcing him to plow through a book of illustrated Bible stories. Her devout intentions came to a sudden end when they got to a centerfold reproduction of da Vinci's *Last Supper* and she asked Rocky to identify Jesus and His disciples.

'Fuck it,' Rocky had complained when he first described the event to Billy. 'All I said was they looked like a bunch of drag queens, and they did, too! So this nun starts blubbering and hauls me down to the principal. He says I have to say they don't look like drag queens, so I say they look like fuckin' drag queens to me. Then the nun pulls a fuckin' faint.'

Rocky got a strapping for that insolence. He regarded this as a heroic achievement.

'That fuckin' principal, Billy, he loved that strap! He beat the fuckin' shit outa me with his fuckin' whip! Both my hands puffed up and were dripping blood like crazy, but I foxed him. I grinned right through it and kept sayin', "More! More! I like it, I like it!" He didn't stop till he saw I was bleeding all over his rug.'

Since that time, Rocky had learned to read just fine as far as Billy could see, except when the reading had anything to do with a school. He had acquired a personal library on the general subject of drugs that was as comprehensive as he could make it in a town as remote and obscure as Nugget. He had collected paperbacks by the dozen from Thunder Bay bookstores, some of which he'd even paid for before walking out with them. He also had about three dozen hardcover books. These he had stolen from public and high school libraries in various northern Ontario towns and the city of Thunder Bay while he was on basketball tournament trips.

Several file folders sat on the bottom shelf of his dope bookcase. They were stuffed with newspaper and magazine articles by the hundreds.

Rocky was well on his way to becoming an amateur expert on drug lore, drug-producing nations, drug routes around the world, drug smuggling, drug laws and all the agencies that tried to enforce them, and the history of drug use as far back as it could be traced. He had been following the De Lorean case with intense interest ever since the celebrated bust of the failed automobile magnate in that Los Angeles hotel room. His favorite article Billy had found for him. It was headlined 'Street Fans Cheer De Lorean, Mob Christina'. The photograph under the headline showed a dense crowd of people waving placards and begging for autographs from the glamorous couple as they were escorted by some beefy-looking cops from the courthouse out to their waiting limousine.

'I love it!' Rocky had crowed when he saw the photograph for the first time. 'I fuckin' love it, Billy. They're like fuckin' movie stars, I bet they're more famous than Michael Jackson! This coke bust's gonna make them rich all over again.'

Billy suspected Rocky was dead right about that. The seemingly endless De Lorean affair struck Billy as more like the making of a highly publicized multimillion-dollar movie blockbuster than the sober proceedings of criminal justice. The screen rights alone would make De Lorean rich beyond Billy's wildest dreams, he had no doubts about that. And before the movie there would be the books.

Drugs had become a potent and enduring symbol of the age into which Billy Mackenzie had been born, a symbol that was fresh and rich with many mysteries compared with the stale specter of nuclear annihilation. Who needed or cared about bombs that might or might not fall when you could put yourself out of it on dope?

Billy's open intimacy with Rocky Barbizan had been his only

recklessness. Though it must have aroused suspicions, they had atrophied in time, and his otherwise exemplary behavior had preserved his reputation as a 'good boy'.

In elementary school, Billy had worked very hard and had routinely passed from one grade to the next, always at the top of his class. Until he got into grade seven, he'd assumed that was a plus for him. From kindergarten to the sixth grade, the chief pleasure he got from doing so well academically was showing off how much smarter he was than anybody else, though he hadn't realized it was vanity at the time. His naive delight in parading his intelligence came to an end during grade seven, when Billy was placed under the dominion of Miss Marjorie Copper.

Miss Copper apparently disliked Billy intensely. But he was so accustomed to assuming teachers liked him – why wouldn't they? – that by the time he understood the woman hated him, it was too late to do him any good. They were enemies. Only in hindsight did Billy realize that Miss Copper had started sending out hate signals on the first school day in September, when she called him William as she did the attendance roll call. All the other boys she addressed by their accustomed names. Rob was Rob, Jim was Jim, Jamie was Jamie, Bobby was Bobby, and Rick was Rick, but Billy was William.

'William Mackenzie?'

'Present,' Billy said, 'but everybody calls me Billy.'

'Present, *Miss Copper*,' Miss Copper reprimanded, without looking up from her list of names. Then she repeated, 'William Mackenzie?'

'Present, Miss Copper.'

Miss Copper addressed him as William for the rest of the year.

His eye-opening conflict with Miss Copper was engraved in Billy's mind as clearly as Miss Copper's meticulously scripted signature was later inscribed in his autograph book.

William, consider the humble stamp. It
costs but a few pennies, but it has the
ability to stick to one thing until it
gets there.

Marjorie Copper

Though his thirteenth birthday was still more than a month away at the time she smacked him with this lecture, Billy had recognized her message as a naked threat. And he knew he was intended to make the connection between the idea of being as dead but useful as a postage stamp and the idea of becoming successful.

Throughout the year Miss Copper had 'Williamed' Billy whenever she got the chance or could contrive one, and Billy dutifully 'Miss Coppered' her as often as he was compelled to. The only hint he gave that every 'Miss Copper' was an act of revenge was buried in the slight hesitations that preceded them.

'Thank you . . . Miss Copper.'

'May I please leave the room . . . Miss Copper?'

'The verb is part of the predicate . . . Miss Copper.'

Miss Copper was quick to catch on. She let Billy know she knew she had an unrepentant sinner on her hands by stealing his weapon.

'You're welcome . . . William.'

'Why do you wish to leave the room . . . William?'

'The verb is the *heart* of the predicate . . . William.'

Not until late in the month of May did the stalemate explode into open warfare. Miss Copper had appointed a certain Friday afternoon for the inspection and final grading of her pupils' language arts notebooks. Back in those days, Billy had taken great pride in his notebooks in every subject. He slaved over them late into the nights, copying and recopying page after page of notes, diagrams, drawings, charts, and maps as if they were destined to end up in famous museums. His individual specialty had been the imaginative decoration of every page with tiny, humorous cartoon figures. He wasted the greatest amount of time on the cute little men who appeared in the lower right-hand corners of every page, and whose pointed fingers urged the teachers to turn to the next page with the promise of further delights. He had always received the highest praise for his notebooks, as well as the highest marks.

On the Friday Miss Copper had set aside for the inspection, Billy had taken his two language notebooks home at noon for one last-minute perusal. Unfortunately, his mother's usual lunchtime distemper had climaxed that Friday in a physical attack on his sister, and his intervention on Anne's behalf had driven his mother even wilder. He and Anne escaped, but in the heat of the action Billy had forgotten to take his notebooks back to school.

Miss Copper refused to let him go back home to get them, and she also refused to accept them for grading the following Monday.

Billy was dumbfounded, and for several minutes he remained speechless. He could scarcely have given as his excuse that his mother had erupted into a vicious assault on his sister just because the seams had split on a new dress that was too small for Anne to begin with. That was a family secret. When he did speak, he told Miss Copper she was being unfair. Miss Copper told him the matter was closed, and when Billy persisted in his protest she sent him to the principal's office for insolence. When he refused to retract his condemnation of Miss Copper's action as unjust, and said hell would freeze before he would apologize to her, Billy was strapped.

During the first two weeks of June, Billy refused to write a word in his notebooks and sat out the days in obstinate silence. There had been strong words and many threats, and he was kept in after four o'clock on each of those ten days. Finally, Miss Copper telephoned Billy's mother, Agnes

Mackenzie, to come in for a consultation at which the principal would also be present, underscoring the dire seriousness of Billy's rebellious strike.

The night before the scheduled confrontation, lying awake in bed until three o'clock in the morning, Billy came to the conclusion that the only smart action was to appear to surrender unconditionally.

So he did. He also apologized to Miss Copper and caught up on all the notes he had refused to copy from the blackboards during his two-week insurrection. And on the last day of school at the end of June he had even asked the duplicitous old tyrant to write in his autograph book, because he figured if he didn't she might hold that against him as proof that his abject submission had been phony.

Miss Copper landed her last blow just before class was dismissed for the summer when she handed out the report cards in a ceremony of her own devising. Each pupil's name was read out in alphabetical order, each pupil walked up to her desk, received the report card, said 'Thank you, Miss Copper', and returned to his or her seat. This way the simple distribution of report cards became a slow and suspenseful torture. When he at last got back to his seat with his own report card, Billy found that Miss Copper had reduced his grades in both reading and creative composition to 'B+'s, which were and remained the only 'B's he ever received in school. Her comment in the space provided on the report card for Teacher's Remarks was anticlimactic – 'William is a quick learner when he wants to be. Let us hope he conquers his stubborness and pride before they conquer him. Promoted to Grade Eight. Marjorie Copper.'

It was the only time Billy had not been promoted with honors, too. But he didn't bat an eyelash, and when he felt tears coming to his eyes he bit on his tongue until blood filled his mouth. Then he concentrated with satisfaction on the fact that Miss Copper didn't even know how to spell stubbornness

– it had two 'n's, not one. He knew it was a cheap satisfaction but it helped some.

Billy Mackenzie never forgot Miss Copper's sermon in his autograph book on the virtues of transforming himself into a postage stamp; one reading burned it into his soul. Nor did he forget the way the old bitch had peeked at him like a satisfied rattlesnake from beneath half-lowered eyelids while he was looking at his report card. She couldn't resist the temptation, she wanted to devour and enjoy his pain when he saw the two 'B+'s and the promotion without honors, the punishments he'd earned for his stubborn pride.

To the day she died, Billy never failed to greet Marjorie Copper with a dazzling smile whenever he met her on the street, and in a town as small as Nugget that was often. The injustice of her conduct preoccupied his mind through the following summer. His first assumption was that she must have acted out of jealousy, precisely because he was so obviously proud of his natural intelligence and his scholastic superiority to the other pupils. Once he began to really think about it, though, Billy had to admit that he could justifiably be regarded as a showoff, although he had never thought of himself as conceited before. The fact that his hand was always the first to shoot up into the air to answer any and every question that was asked had been simply a fact of life in the classroom. But perhaps all of his teachers had thought of him as an arrogant and obnoxious know-it-all, and Miss Copper had simply decided the time had come to teach him a lesson.

In his heart, however, Billy never completely abandoned his belief that Miss Copper's capricious displays of power had sprung from personal envy and a meanspirited lust for revenge. She was wicked and lived on hate, and when five years later he read Muriel Spark's *The Prime of Miss Jean Brodie*, he thought back to Marjorie Copper as a sort of dumb Jean Brodie. In terms of the significance of the lessons she had taught him so well, Miss Copper was the most influential teacher Billy ever had.

From that year onward, he was careful to seem slower, less knowledgeable, prone to careless slips, and careful above all to make it appear that he had to work like a demon to excel. He systematically lied about the amount of homework he did and about the time he spent studying before tests and exams. In class, he frowned in feigned frustration while working out ten identically simple math problems. By the time he entered high school he had already converted himself into a conscious, calculating hypocrite, a consummate suckhole who never let a class go by without asking at least one question to which he knew the answer. Every once in a while he would make deliberate mechanical errors on inconsequential tests. He noticed, and played to, the complacent indulgence in the grins his teachers wore as they called his attention to the elemental stupidity of these mistakes. Billy never failed to reward them by groaning and pretending to be mortified by his own dumb carelessness. It worked like a charm, and Billy became a universal teacher's favorite – a smart boy, of course, but not as smart as they.

The price of success was high. School was no longer a natural pleasure, a playground for the mind in which the purpose was in the playing itself. In high school his only motive for continuing to do well academically had nothing to do with learning and everything to do with getting high marks, the stepping stones to what the guidance counselors referred to as positions of responsibility. Like ours, they meant, though they only admitted that with the expressions on their faces.

The only thing in high school Billy enjoyed was reading the few good books that somehow got into the English courses. His grade nine English teacher was Mr Sweet – a sumptuously funny name for a man whose highest marks, according to senior students, inevitably went to the best-looking boys in the tightest blue jeans. From Mr Sweet, Billy began learning that English teachers didn't enjoy the books, they merely taught them. Robert Louis Stevenson's *Kidnapped* kept Billy up all night in breathless excitement, lost on the stormy seas with David Balfour and plotting in the Scottish highlands with the mighty Alan Breck. But even *Kidnapped* wound up as a pile of dried shit on Mr Sweet's tests and exams. By grade eleven, having done time with each of the three English teachers, Billy had concluded that English teachers hated the stories they depended on. Nothing but pure hatred could account for the way they routinely beat them to death. Consequently, English classes became the most painful hours of all, daily visits to a slaughterhouse in which the heroes and heroines Billy adored were sacrificed like cattle or hogs. The fabled corpses lay hacked into anonymous hunks of meat on the floor, and blood flowed in rivers across the plastic tiles.

In grade twelve, through the enigma of timetable rotations, Billy was returned to Mr Sweet. By then no strategy was so low that he could scorn it, and he began wearing faded jeans he had outgrown and humping out his crotch. Mr Sweet launched the course by handing out copies of *A Streetcar Named Desire* and announcing that the author had been homosexual. Billy found this curious in view of Mr Sweet's reputation among the students, a reputation he maintained despite the fact he was married and the father of three grown-up daughters.

After Mr Sweet had eviscerated *A Streetcar Named Desire* by reading it aloud in class – he fancied himself a dramatic reader but the big performances used up a whole week of classes so no one complained – he distributed to the class Xeroxed copies of a snotty-sounding essay on Tennessee Williams's play by some critic. In senior grades, Mr Sweet was fond of such handouts, and their notebooks were stuffed with them by the end of the course. Billy presumed he liked them because he knew the kids would feel stupid as they strove to understand the unfamiliar terms and interminable sentences. The gist of the essay seemed to be that, because Williams was gay, Blanche Dubois was a homosexual in drag. Billy was bursting with outrage by the time he got to the end of it. It seemed wrong that anyone could say that in print and get away with it without being sued.

He put up his hand, aware that he was about to make his first dangerous move since Miss Copper had shown him the ropes. After ignoring Billy just long enough to show everyone who was boss, Mr Sweet acknowledged the raised arm with raised eyebrows.

'Sir, I guess I don't quite understand. Is this man—'

'Professor Ricardo?'

'Is Professor Ricardo actually saying that no homosexual can write about women, or is he only gunning for Tennessee Williams?'

'Gunning? How do you mean gunning?'

'Discussing, then,' Billy amended.

'What do you think, Billy?'

This was standard procedure in Mr Sweet's classes. He always pitched a potential impertinence back to the student who asked the question. Then he stared at the offender.

'Sir, I think if it were true of Tennessee Williams, surely it would have to be true of other gay writers, maybe all of them. But sir, he doesn't offer any proof at all for what he's saying, no matter who he means.'

'I think Professor Ricardo presents a very persuasive argument,' Mr Sweet said. Billy watched the students busily writing 'a very persuasive argument' into their notebooks. 'The play gains immeasurably in artistic magnitude, Billy. It enters another dimension and acquires a universal symbolism once we understand that Blanche is both a woman *and* a male homosexual.'

'But she *can't* be both,' Billy rushed on recklessly. In his voice he could hear the fatal conviction that the teacher was wrong. 'It's impossible. It sure does enter another dimension, but I don't think it gains anything! It's a horrible idea, it ruins the play. Good grief!'

Mr Sweet whipped his stare off Billy and lifted it into empty space above the students' heads. This signified that the issue was over and done with, and Billy was left with only his consciousness that his grievous lapse was going to cost plenty. The other students were now writing down 'artistic magnitude', 'universal symbolism', and 'another dimension' in their notes. Billy just kept quiet until the period ended, thinking to himself how right Blanche Dubois was – and how very lucky, too – that she was just passing through.

So was he, Billy decided, and he set about undoing the damage at once. He began wearing old shirts that were too small and left the top three buttons undone to display his summer's tan and his curly black chest hair. He rolled up his shirtsleeves almost to his shoulders to emphasize his tanned, sinewy muscles. Poppy Richardson objected to Billy's blatant exhibition of his body's contours and the baring of as much skin as possible.

'Billy, it's embarrassing!' Poppy had nailed him in a corridor between classes and backed him against the wall.

'It doesn't embarrass me,' Billy replied.

'Well, it embarrasses me! Those old jeans are too damn tight and you know it! They're so worn you could spit through them in some places! And you aren't wearing any undershorts, either, are you? Billy, it shows!'

'What shows?'

'It shows,' Poppy whispered, almost nose to nose with Billy as hundreds of students streamed along the corridor. 'It, it! You know what I mean, I mean anybody that looks there can see absolutely everything!'

'Honey,' Billy said as the bell rang, 'now we're late for class. Believe me, it's all in a good cause.'

'Oh? You look like you're selling it!'

'You're right, I am. What difference does it make? I've been whoring my mind for years. Now I'm dressing for the job.'

When he wrote the mandatory essay that proved Mr Sweet had earned his bread and butter, Billy began by stating that the more deeply one considered Professor Ricardo's essay on 'The Homoerotic Hero', the more logical his interpretation of the play became. The substance of Billy's own essay was given over to considering the near certainty that all the male characters in *A Streetcar Named Desire* were gay, even Stanley Kowalski and his poker buddies. Mitch, he maintained, was unquestionably homosexual; he was still in love with his mother and wouldn't come out of the closet until the old lady died. Once he had formed this intention, Billy was fascinated to discover how easy it was to find innumerable bits of dialogue to quote in support of his thesis. It turned out to be a damned good essay.

Like all Mr Sweet's senior classes, they were given many periods of class time in which to work on the essay in the school library. During these library work periods, Mr Sweet sat reading alone and waiting for any students to bring him their problems. Billy went as often as he dared, ostensibly to seek help with tricky points of sentence structure. And while Mr Sweet explained where he had gone wrong, Billy stood close with his hip cocked, his pelvis tilted, and his gut sucked in. He did everything but fondle himself suggestively to win back the man's favor. And he was rewarded with a big fat 96 on the essay, and eventually with the highest final grade in the class.

Aside from Mr Sweet, none of his other grade twelve teachers required any special forms of manipulation. He just slogged away using the same old bag of tricks. But he found to his surprise that his new *Playgirl* magazine beefcake look exerted a strong appeal on both of his female teachers, especially Mrs Doremus.

Mrs Doremus was his class's homeroom teacher that semester and also taught them mathematics in first period.

She had liked Billy back in grade nine, especially when he made one of his deliberate errors on a term test and she could laugh at him for it. But that year in grade twelve Mrs Doremus positively loved him. Whenever she gave back tests she always returned his last, and she managed to touch Billy a lot during the time she spent hovering over him and taunting him about his slip-ups.

'Billy Mackenzie, you've done it again! I was so darned *mad* last night when I saw you mess up this equation, I swear I could have wrung your neck!' Of course she was lying, but she didn't know it. She even gave a demonstration of her exasperation by placing her hands around Billy's throat and gently squeezing it as she pretended to growl.

'Not another one!' Billy moaned as he saw the 93% on his test paper.

'These things you do are so stupid, Billy! They aren't even mistakes, they're plain ordinary carelessness!'

'I know,' Billy said, 'I don't understand why I can't stop doing them.'

'Billy, Billy, Billy, Billy, Billy! For the last time, you have *got* to learn to keep your mind from wandering away as soon as you get near the end of a test!'

Mrs Doremus laughed lustily at the hopelessness of her task to cure Billy's flighty habits. Then she reached her right arm around his shoulders and pointed a finger at the next to last problem on the test paper itself. In order to stretch the tip of her finger onto the paper, she had to press a lot of Mrs Doremus against Billy's left shoulder and upper back. Billy could feel the heat of her body, and especially the warmth of her large breasts.

'Okay, look at this equation in question nine. What do you see *there*?' Mrs Doremus shifted her breasts to the right.

'$(x-y)^2$,' Billy answered in a puzzled tone.

'Now,' cried Mrs Doremus triumphantly, pressing against his back even harder in order to flip to the third page of Billy's answers and point her finger again. 'What do you see there, Billy?'

'Oh, my God,' Billy said, 'oh, Jesus—'

'The name of our Lord, Billy, is for prayer and prayer alone,' Mrs Doremus warned, as Billy had expected. He knew she was a devout Presbyterian; she was over at the church three and four nights a week for one reason or another. He sat back a little but Mrs Doremus didn't budge as his back crushed her Presbyterian breasts.

'Just tell me what you see there!' she ordered in little pants.

'$(x+y)^2$,' Billy read, banging his fist on his forehead and throwing back his head until it was touching her chest. Mrs Doremus's eyes were beamed straight down at Billy's crotch. He didn't even try to resist the temptation to spread his legs farther apart.

'And that,' Mrs Doremus shrieked in jubilation, 'that cost you *seven marks*!'

As she stood up her breasts dragged up his neck and brushed the back of Billy's head. He had lost seven marks, Billy thought, but the future looked bright.

Yet even little unexpected bonuses were no longer able to make the bamboozling fun. About the real purpose of schools Billy had lost all fine illusions, and it would take more than Mrs Doremus's breasts to fill that void.

School was an organized crime, designed to dissolve the individual spirit into habitual submission to authority. Orders were given; orders were obeyed. That was the essence of the process. Whatever the brainier kids absorbed aside from this secret curriculum was purely incidental. The hidden promise was never really in doubt – do what you were told long enough to prove you knew your place and eventually you might get to hand out orders of your own.

Nobody believed this false gospel more fervently than the nice kids who were neither bright nor abysmally stupid. The anguish of their ordeals as they floundered in the mystifications of physics, calculus, and the poetry of Alexander Pope was a horrifying thing to witness. It was always a relief when one of them gave up the dream and bailed out.

During that last semester in grade twelve even Billy's waning faith in the dogma that more and more years of education would, some distant day, bring financial independence dropped dead for good. Like all students shoveled into the academic stream – those who could read, count, and stay awake – Billy had been pulverized with propaganda about getting his university degree. The need to ensure admission to at least a fifth-rate university was the main threat used to get them to grind out hours of homework every night. The real reason was to provide teachers with filler for the next day's class. By the guidance counselors, university was extolled as the elite sanctuary where at long last you would be free to learn and do as you pleased, but Billy had never swallowed that lie. Back in grades seven and eight they'd been fed the same crap about high school.

His suspicion that universities were money-grubbing business corporations was annually confirmed when the university recruitment posters were stuck up on the painted cement walls of the main hallway.

Each colorful poster hyped one or another Canadian university as more fun, more in, more glamorous, more romantic, more promiscuous, and less work – none whatsoever, apparently – than any other. Many of the ads showed softly photographed lovers posed in romantic isolation on acres of manicured lawn. In others the lovers held hands in the shade of autumnal trees. Billy's favorite that year was a PR masterpiece. It featured five deliriously happy models, all with capped teeth and sun-lamp tans. All five were piled into an antique white Cord convertible, along with their tennis rackets, golf clubs, water skis, and surf boards. Clearly, scholarship was the last thing on their minds – they had gotten lost from a TV beer commercial. Besides, who had to study if they could afford to whiz around the campus in an automobile that would cost, according to Rocky Barbizan, at least half a million dollars, even if you could find one outside a museum. The big print trumpeted 'Come to Where the Action Is! – Come to New Oxford!' In other words, blow your borrowed money here, we're broke.

At the start of what turned out to be Billy's last guidance interview, Billy said he'd made up his mind. He wanted to go to New Oxford.

'New Oxford,' echoed Mr Carney, the head of the guidance department. 'Why have you chosen New Oxford? It isn't one of the better-known universities, Billy, have you thought about that?'

'Yes, sir, I have. But I like their poster, it appeals to me.'

'Which poster is that?'

'The one in the center hall, sir,' Billy said.

Mr Carney was frowning. 'That seems a peculiar reason for choosing one's future, Billy.'

'Oh? Then why are all the posters there? New Oxford looks full of opportunities for an ambitious young man. Maybe you've forgotten their poster – one look and you'll know what I mean.'

Billy stood up ready to go, and Mr Carney's curiosity brought him to his feet as well. Moments later they stood side by side before the five beautiful people in the white Cord convertible.

'See that car,' Billy said. 'It's a Cord. Rocky tells me it's worth half a million at least—'

'Rocky? Rocky who?'

'Rocky Barbizan.'

'Oh. Well, Rocky's a good basketball player, Billy,' Mr Carney said, 'but I don't think I'd let him decide what university I would apply to.' He laughed at the innocence of youth.

'Sir, one thing Rocky knows is cars. Those students must all be loaded with money. I figure I can make some good connections at New Oxford. And look, there isn't a book in sight. Mind you, books are hard to spot in any of the posters. So I may as well go where the money is.'

'Billy, it's just a poster,' Mr Carney said, 'it's only meant to draw your attention.'

'You mean they aren't real students?'

'I don't know who they are,' said Mr Carney irritably. 'Now, let's get back to my office for some serious talk. Have you studied your NDHS computer printout?'

'Oh, yes sir, I have.'

The computer printouts Mr Carney was referring to were produced by some outfit that was making a killing by feeding kids' dreams and fantasies. On the basis of information sent in by the schools on each student – their percentile scores on standardized brain tests and their high school transcripts of actual grades – the company sent back a list of careers and professions likely to make the individual successful and happy. Billy's printout had been seven yards long; he had measured it.

'Did it help you in your career thinking?' asked Mr Carney. 'Most of the students find it invaluable.' He sat down in his padded chair.

'No, sir, it didn't,' Billy said. 'Actually it floored me. Do you know it was seven yards long? That's true, I measured it. As far as I could see, I might as well toss a coin, it doesn't matter what I do.'

Mr Carney said he had to go for lunch and would see Billy again soon, but he never did.

Billy was certain by then that he would hate the only kind of life he could expect to get if he did adhere to the conventional propaganda. He knew that the Miss Coppers he'd been exposed to – and once he knew what to look for, he found her everywhere – were the model products of schools. He would never be happy in the sealed and dehydrated world where they shook their heads in unison at the troublemakers, dumbbells, and lazy bums who actually didn't want to get into the vanguard of civilization. As human beings went, most of his teachers had been harmless enough, as long as you always obeyed their orders, catered like a convict to their sense of rightful power, and bowed deeply and often to their transcendent intelligence.

But in their souls they were policemen who served the administration as a dedicated squad of spies and informers. Catching, reporting, and punishing malefactors for even the most trivial of infractions brought a gleam of moralistic pleasure that was repulsive to behold in their courtroom eyes. Billy didn't trust any of them; really, he didn't even like one of them. He had just learned to play their games more deceitfully than they played them themselves.

Due to the absence of other reasonable alternatives, Billy had plowed onward dutifully, while his true mind divorced itself ever more completely from what it appeared to be doing, or learning, or thinking.

At least half the hours spent in classrooms were consumed by repetitious reviews and sarcastic harangues directed to the indolent, the bored, the latecomers, the chatterers, the bubblegum chewers, and the slow-witted. Many teachers seemed to relish these sessions, maybe because they helped to use up time. Billy passed that time by pondering the riddle of contemporary education. Surely, modern, so-called democratic schools were the most fraudulent institutions ever conceived by the collective mind of man. Presented to the world as citadels of free learning and the hope of the future, yet regimented and policed with the ruthless efficiency of totalitarian prisons, as far as Billy could see they really functioned as crematoriums for the minds and souls of the young. Every burned-out case who graduated was called a success.

It was a testament to his strength of character that he had not only survived the monotonous mediocrity but also had continued to flourish. In a triumphant *tour de force* of manipulation, hypocrisy, and impenetrable cynicism, he comported himself like Miss Copper's postage stamp. And, as every June rolled round at last, he was licked once more by the long tongues of authority, stuck to the empty envelope of his own packaged future, and shipped upward like a piece of heavily insured, special delivery mail. He was always postmarked as the top-ranking flunky in his class.

To crown his reputation as Nugget District High School's most promising student, Billy was rivaled only by Rocky Barbizan as the star performer on both the junior and senior basketball teams. Twice he had served as the Secretary-Treasurer of the Students' Council. It was his good fortune, as well, to have matured into a tall, muscular, and handsome young man, and he was as popular with the run-of-the-treadmill students as the summer holidays.

Billy was aware that the paragon he had so artfully constructed was a weapon that might backfire at any time. Almost everyone he could think of could find at least one good reason for nursing a secret hope that he would fuck up his life.

His sister, Anne, and Rocky Barbizan were the only two people alive who knew Billy as he really was. Poppy Richardson knew a lot, but she didn't know it all yet. What she did know scared her.

Anne was happy to bask in the reflection of Billy's golden public image and also to be in on the secret of its delicious falsity. Rocky Barbizan had a keener eye. He described Billy as potentially the smartest fucking criminal who had ever walked the earth. 'I'm tellin' you, Billy,' Rocky liked to say, 'you got it made. You got balls to burn, and a brain like a fuckin' machine gun.'

Rocky talked a lot about Billy's brains, far too much as far as Billy was concerned. It disturbed him, because Rocky had been so callously victimized by the system he didn't even know he had a mind. The year Rocky's parents split and abandoned their son, he was stuck into remedial classes with the all-but-feeble-minded. He had never since been returned to the mainstream flow. Rocky had been remedied for ten years, remedied into a model of shame and defensiveness. In grades nine, ten, and eleven he had managed to skip classes when most of the half-dozen standardized tests were administered.

Billy never spoke truthfully of these feelings when he wanted to shut Rocky up. Instead he said things like, 'Rocky, will you shut up about my Goddamned brain? On the open market, I figure it's worth about as much as a pound of sausage meat. Now lay off it.'

Billy knew how clever he was – he didn't need to be told. He also knew cleverness alone meant nothing, that it could be easily neutered and defanged by its passage through the system. The only free minds he knew belonged to dropouts.

Billy didn't care at all how smart he was, had been, or ever would be. Smart wasn't happiness, smart was a dog's life. Love, and love alone, had made him happy once in a while – and freedom was the gateway to love. Unless he could somehow, someday, become free, love would hide its face from him forever, crouching in his hideaway heart. But freedom had been hunted down, chained, and price-tagged – by whom or why or how he neither knew nor cared. Billy loved his sister Anne, he loved his friend Rocky, and he loved Poppy Richardson. This much he thought he knew. The trouble was he didn't want to know it, he wanted just to feel it.

For the time being, Billy's freedom to lose himself in love had to be bought with dope.

Someday, Billy wanted to have it pure, just to see.

CHAPTER TWO

'Billy, why doesn't Mommy love me?'

That was the first sentence Billy remembered Anne speaking to him. He had been on his way back to school after lunch. Anne had already formed the habit of pretending she was going to school with him. Thinking back to that habit from the perspective of adolescence, Anne surmised that she had known even then that anything was preferable to being stuck at home with their mother. She was between four and five years old when she asked that question. Billy could never remember what, if anything, had happened to provoke the inquiry, nor could he remember his reply. But he assumed that back in those days he had tried valiantly to reassure her that Mommy did love her. He went on trying for another ten years or so, but he never succeeded.

He did, however, remember an incident that occurred when Anne was attending kindergarten in the mornings. She often brought home a rolled-up sheet of big paper covered with bright poster paints in cold, sweeping brush strokes. She would unroll the wrinkled paintings and tell Billy and Agnes Mackenzie what they were – houses, trees, sunny days, and flowers. But one noontime the painting she unrolled on the kitchen table was particularly arresting. Most of the large expanse of cheap paper was covered with a whirl of purple strokes that formed – more or less – a circular vortex with a smaller scarlet circle in the middle. Inside the red circle were blobs of other primary colors. The total effect was sensationally ugly.

'That's a scary one,' Billy said, pretending to shiver in fear. 'It looks like a big monster man.'

Anne said, 'It's Mommy.'

Until then, Agnes Mackenzie had been busy opening a can of something and heating it up on the stove, but Anne's revelation quickly brought her to the table. She stood behind Billy and Anne, looking down at the painting over their heads.

'See? . . . That's her mouth,' Anne went on, pointing at the red hole full of blobs, 'and those things are the noises jumping out at Daddy.'

Without saying a word, Agnes Mackenzie reached between Billy and Anne, snatched up the painting, crushed the paper into a ball with both hands, and threw it in the garbage.

Though that experience was etched vividly in his mind, Billy suspected it got there as recalled by Anne, not as a legitimate remembrance of his own. If it was, it stood alone. Just as he had been a saucer-eyed sucker in school until his abrupt coming-of-age under Miss Copper, Billy seemed to have drifted through his first decade at home in a somnambulistic coma. The amnesia of infancy had locked him into the inexplicable delusion that the Mackenzies were a happy family. Although she was almost three years younger than Billy, his sister Anne was the first to emerge from their common self-deception to realize they were the abused children of a spectacularly unpleasant marriage.

Anne was a quiet, gentle child who loved to read and was able to play quite happily by herself for hours, acting out her bizarre fund of fantasies. The most sinister of these – the fruit of Agnes Mackenzie's frequent complaints that Anne was too fat – required only a Sears Christmas catalogue and a black magic marker. Anne would turn to the many pictures of dolls for sale, decide according to her private formula which ones were too fat, and kill them by blacking them out of existence. By the time Anne was through, only the starved-looking model dolls – Barbie and her clones – ever survived the black plague.

Her favorite imaginary life was that of an army nurse like those who cavorted on M*A*S*H. For entire afternoons, Anne dedicated her life to looking after soldiers on the battlefield of Vietnam. Both Alex and Agnes Mackenzie were dedicated news freaks, corpse-counters who could and did stare at the same news four times daily on four different channels. Images of violent death and lavish destruction poured out of the TV into the small living room for hours a day like movies of the end of the world. Vietnam seemed just around the corner.

'Where are they killing people today?' Anne would ask solemnly as she tied on the voluminous white apron, complete with a big Red Cross symbol on its bulky bib, that Agnes Mackenzie often boasted making for her. The red cross was his mother's personal contribution to Anne's costume, sewn on against Anne's protests that none of the M*A*S*H nurses had red crosses on *their* uniforms. They didn't wear white aprons either, of course, but Anne accepted that deviation out of necessity, it was the red cross that bothered her. But Agnes Mackenzie's girlhood memories of the Red Cross field nurses in World War Two prevailed, and Billy's observation that Anne's toy nurse's kit did have a red cross on it almost reconciled his sister to the situation.

'Still in Vietnam,' Billy would say.

'In Saigon?'

'Sure, in Saigon. All over Vietnam.'

Then Anne would arrange in rows all the old towels and blankets she could scrounge up, each representing a wounded soldier. She bathed their hot faces with a cool, wet facecloth and gave them injections if they were in pain. Sometimes Billy used to get under a blanket and pretend to be a dying soldier whose legs and arms had been blown off in a bomb blast. When he died, as he was required to do, Anne sobbed in wild abandon as she pulled the blanket up over his face.

Though Billy was sure he must have loved his sister from the moment he first saw her in the hospital bed with their mother, he always traced his incorruptible feelings for her to the grief-stricken six-year-old nurse whose tears fell like big drops of warm Vietnamese rain on the eyes he had closed in imitation of death.

Anne had a natural sense of comedy, an observant eye, a remorseless memory, and an intuitive mind that moved with the speed of light to make sudden unexpected connections. Except for her demonic memory, all of these faculties naturally became liabilities as soon as she got into school. But by the time he was in his early teens Billy considered her his intellectual superior and suspected that Anne agreed with him. Anne's intellectual and imaginative gifts, nurtured by her sense of being unacceptable because she was fat, were fused early into an uncanny ability to see through people. They also bred her startling and precocious insights into the real nature of the conspiracy between their parents. Billy learned a lot from Anne – he learned who he was.

'It's not a marriage, Billy, it's a disease,' was how Anne unforgettably phrased it one Tuesday night when they had smoked a couple of joints and were high as balloons adrift in a summer sky. 'We're not children at all,' she added, 'we're by-products.'

They were eighteen and fifteen respectively when she said that. By that time they had analyzed their family's bizarre pathology so often and for so many hours that it had become boring, while at the same time remaining an irresistible habit, like an addictive drug. Almost all their conversations took place on Tuesday nights, the only night in the week when they were alone in the house for a few precious hours. Agnes Mackenzie played bingo at the Legion Hall and their father went to his Rotary dinner meetings.

As soon as they were alone, Billy and Anne retired to his room and stoned up. They made themselves comfortable on Billy's bed, pigged out on smuggled-in junk foods and candy, and laughed till they were sick. Most of the laughter was hysterical, and Billy thought of these weekly sessions as therapeutic orgies. Even into his late teens Billy had tended to insist that, underneath it all, their mother did really love them. But Anne was adamant.

'Underneath what?' she would demand. 'Billy, there *is* no underneath! And if there is, I hope to God it stays there, because what's on top scares the shit out of me.'

As for whom their mother loved, Anne had equally stubborn opinions about that.

'You, my dear, beautiful brother, are the only living creature that woman has ever loved – except herself, of course. Actually, our Agnes is still madly in love with you even though she knows you've been screwing girls behind her back. You should see the way she ogles your body whenever you strut around in those technicolor holsters you call underwear. I don't think Agnes quite knows what she really wants, but her eyeballs look like they're going to sprout fingers! Stop laughing, I'm dead serious, she wants your body, and it's time you admitted you know it. Billy, I said stop laughing! You're going to spill the chip dip. And—' Anne paused long enough to stuff some dip-coated chips into her mouth and wash them down with a slug of beer. '. . . And I might add that you exploit your secret knowledge with the cunning of an old whore. Why, it's just downright amazing, Billy, how often you just *happen* to saunter by a doorway or through the kitchen on your way to take a shower with your little bag of goodies so – how shall I put it, I wouldn't want to be crude – so professionally gift-wrapped! Not that it makes all that much difference when you do happen to be wearing some clothes. I mean, Billy, I know tight fits are in except for hopelessly fat slobs like me, but somehow or other, Billy, your tight fits are

. . . words fail me, I think, and God knows they don't fail me very often. Let me put it this way, you always look as if every seam is going to split wide open as soon as you sit down. You're so vain it isn't even disgusting, it's sort of endearing.'

'I am not vain!' Billy protested, but Anne ignored him.

'If I sound just a trifle on the jealous side, I can't help it, I am jealous. I think if I had a body as lurid as yours, I'd use it to torture everybody, too. Meanwhile, pass the caramel corn and get me another beer out of the freezer. I feel so good tonight, I could eat myself.'

Anne accounted for Billy's prolonged oblivion and belated awakening to the nastiness of the days put in by the Mackenzies by the fact that he had been born first.

'Let's face it, Agnes had you for three years all to herself before I came along to spoil the perfect couple. I'm sure that's why she's never liked me. Not only was I born alive, I was a girl too. So I was competition, even if I was, as I have been told and told and *told*, a fat lumpy thing even when I was in diapers.'

None of Billy's innumerable reassurances that her mother loved her had any effect on Anne except to make her cry.

'No, Billy,' she would say, brushing tears away, 'it's nice of you to want me to believe that, but it's just not true. Sometimes I think Daddy loves me, or at least he used to, but that just makes it worse. In doesn't raise anyone in Agnes's esteem to be liked by Daddy. In fact, it's the surest way onto her hit list.'

Anne once suggested half-seriously that their parents must have found one another through advertisements in the same bondage magazine. 'After all, Billy, you can't publicize these freaky cravings, certainly not in a dead-end, hole-in-the-wall town like Nugget. At least you couldn't back in the sixties. Her ad would read: "Beautiful bitch with steel tits seeks big dumb horsy to whip." Daddy's would be more discreet – "Mild male in need of firm discipline from severe and merciless lady. Object degradation." Imagine their surprise when they found out they both lived in Nugget!'

Billy was twelve years old before the first incident took place that he remembered having recognized on his own as proof that the marriage between Agnes and Alex Mackenzie was a fateful alliance between a morbidly unhappy woman and her chosen stooge.

One night, after having lain in bed for a while, Billy got up to go to the bathroom to take a leak. The kitchen and the narrow hallway through which he had to pass on his way to the toilet were both dark. His parents were in the tiny square living room, where the TV news from somewhere was blaring as loudly as usual. As he was about to switch on the bathroom light, which would have alerted them to his presence, he distinctly heard his mother say, 'Fuck off!' in an ugly, coldly brutal voice.

Billy was thunderstruck. It was the first time he had ever heard that word used in the house. He could not believe his mother had actually said it to his father. When he peeked cautiously into the living room to see what his father would do, his parents were engaged in one of their staring matches. Alex Mackenzie had put a hurt, yet curiously satisfied expression on his face. Apparently this irritated his mother, for without any warning she threw the contents of a steaming hot cup of tea she was holding into her husband's face. Then she burst out laughing and sat back down in her usual chair.

Alex Mackenzie stood his ground, looking martyred and superior in his suffering. The tea was glistening on his forehead and cheeks, and dripping from his eyelids, his nose, and his chin down onto his pajama top.

Agnes Mackenzie stopped laughing, poured herself another cup of tea, leaned back, and said, 'Either you get the hell out of the way so I can see the TV, or I'll heave this cup at you too.'

Burning with the shame he felt for his father, Billy backed

down the hall a few steps to Anne's bedroom door and ducked inside. He didn't want his father to know that his own son had witnessed his absolute humiliation or his cowardice. In the darkness of Anne's room, he realized he was crying.

Anne leaped up on her elbow in bed. She was wide awake. 'What happened after she told him to fuck off?' she asked in a matter-of-fact whisper. 'What made her laugh so hard?'

'She threw a cup of hot tea in Daddy's face,' Billy replied, as he brushed more tears from his eyes. 'That's when she laughed at him. She laughed right into his face!'

'What's so new about that? She laughs in his face all the time.' Anne bunched her pillow up and slid backwards to lean against it. 'What's so different, Billy?'

'She told him to fuck off!' Billy whispered angrily.

'She says awful things to Daddy all the time and you know it. She calls him a big dumb turd, she calls him an asshole, she calls him a wimp, she calls him a stupid bugger every day. I don't see why you're crying about it this time. So she told him to fuck off.'

Billy sat down on Anne's bed and leaned close to her. 'Because he just stood there with tea dripping off his face and let Mother laugh at him, that's why!'

'Daddy always just stands there,' said Anne calmly, 'and she always laughs at him. He's scared shitless of her, do you blame him?'

Billy sat in silence as fresh tears dripped from his eyes.

'Yes, I do blame him,' he said at last. 'I'm ashamed of him, I'm so ashamed of him I could die. He can't be my father, he's not even a man.'

Anne Mackenzie sat up straight and spoke fiercely in their father's defense. 'It's easy for you to talk tough, Billy Mackenzie! You're the one she loves! She doesn't treat you like a piece of shit, she lets you get away with murder! And she doesn't leave bruises on you, either! Look!' Anne held out her right arm. Even in the pallid light from the small window in the wall above Anne's bed, Billy could see the dark bruise on the flesh of Anne's arm.

'When did she do that?'

'In Mrs Beecher's store today, because I said I didn't want the blouse she'd picked out for me. It was ugly, so it was on sale for half price, and the one I liked cost three dollars more. Mother kept saying over and over how pretty the ugly blouse was, so of course I gave in. But she was already mad at me because Mrs Beecher was right there listening to me argue. So Mother had to pretend it wasn't the *money* she was thinking about! Oh, good heavens, no! We'd take the one I wanted even if the other one was prettier, ha, ha, ha. And meanwhile, she's pinching my arm so hard it turned black. Then I started to giggle. I thought it was so funny her standing there like that and twisting my arm in secret. So you know what she did? She started talking really loud so everybody in the store could hear how *hard* it was finding clothes to fit me. She made me sound like a baby elephant, Billy, and *Linda Beecher* was right there in the store helping her mother.' Anne flopped back onto her pillow and stared blankly up at the ceiling. Tears trickled, then streamed from her eyes. 'I think she's a bitch.'

Billy was shocked by Anne's use of the word bitch to describe their mother.

'She doesn't mean what she says, you know that,' Billy objected doubtfully. 'She's not a real bitch. Is she?'

For the first time in his life, Billy was fully conscious of having acknowledged that his mother was not a divinity.

He continued more hopefully, 'After all, Mother's the one we have fun with, you have to admit that.'

Anne bounced back up again, rigid with anger. 'You're a boy! And you're skinny, and you get the highest marks in school! She doesn't call you the Crisco Kid! She doesn't say you look like a sack of potatoes! You're just so used to her you don't even *know* what she's like, and I think she means every Goddamned word she says. Mother's idea of a good laugh is making fun of people, but her jokes aren't so funny when you're one of her victims. She's mean, Billy.' Anne lay down again and gazed up at the ceiling. 'I think she was always a bitch. Maybe she can fool you, but she doesn't fool me. I hate her.'

Back in his own bed, Billy lay sleepless, his imagination possessed by images of the horrific confrontation he had secretly witnessed in the living room, his mind amazed by Anne's violent denunciation of their mother. Before he was many months older, he would look back to that memorable night as the true beginning of Billy Mackenzie, the real birthday of his life. Everything before that experience came to seem like a long, mysteriously convincing dream. That night he began to think, and he was never able to stop thinking again.

The wholesale renovation of his assumptions about his parents proved to be a lengthy and extremely frustrating experience. In its logical and deliberate way, his mind launched confidently into its independent investigation of the past, but Billy soon realized that the past did not reveal its buried treasures just for the asking.

Night after night, he stared into the darkness as if it were the cloaked guardian of evil and unholy secrets. Looking backwards was like gazing into the farthest reaches of the universe; the years gone by were deep, black distances, lit up briefly here and there by sudden tantalizing flares. What he needed was a complete motion picture he could play in the theater of his mind; what he got were brief teasers like the little snippets of dreams you could remember in the morning. These were about as helpful as random snapshots stuck away in a drawer to be found years later and puzzled over.

Thinking critically about his mother was most difficult of all, because his knowledge of the intense and passionate love Agnes Mackenzie felt for her son made Billy feel like a traitor.

He was like a chained pet. He could dimly remember having idolized his mother as a very young boy, an enchantment that had ripened into the blind devotion of a slave. He could remember thinking she was the prettiest and most charming mother in the world, and even Anne admitted Agnes Mackenzie was pretty and could be charming. Billy could also remember thinking his mother was devastatingly witty and clever. During their almost daily walks uptown together to collect the mail, do the shopping, and pay the bills, Agnes Mackenzie had never tired of criticizing and mocking the town of Nugget as the world's supreme dump. For that particular practice, Billy could not honestly blame her. Nugget was a forlorn and dilapidated little town.

Billy had to concede, however, that Anne had scored heavily with her attack on Agnes Mackenzie's vindictiveness towards people. What he had regarded as his mother's killing sense of humor really did boil down to unkind and often vicious wisecracks about the physical eccentricities of other people's bodies. She was a wizard at doing imitations, and delighted in mimicking even those who were supposedly her friends. She even mimicked old Mr Popowski, who stuttered so badly it took him several minutes to say good morning and comment on the weather.

Unfortunately, Billy's new and distressing awareness that his mother's howling wit consisted of corrosive and malignant cruelty came too late to rescue his father, her most inspirational victim.

Under the hypnotic spell of his mother's vitriolic tongue, Billy had been innocently conscripted into her sour and angry world, and in that world Alex Mackenzie was the arch-criminal and the favorite target. She practiced on him. Unaware and wholly trusting, Billy had been saturated by his mother's sense of having been cheated by fate when she met and married his father. Never was she more rancidly entertaining or more irresistibly hilarious than in her murderously accurate takeoffs of Alex Mackenzie. She relished above all else describing what a hopeless sap, what a gullible flunky, what a boring drip her husband was. The job she did on him was beyond mere callous mimicry. It was an act of vivisection, pornographic in the clinical purity of its exposures, from which Billy Mackenzie's father emerged as sexless, mindless, gutless, and virtually pointless – the quintessential asshole.

One thing his mother had said stuck in Billy's mind like a bloodsucker. He could remember realizing at the time that she ought not to have said it, but then he had promptly buried it deep in the inaccessible recesses of his mind where it remained until he began the great excavation.

He had been taking a bath a few years earlier, before the shower was installed, when Agnes Mackenzie came into the bathroom, supposedly to get some painkillers from the medicine chest above the sink. Once in, however, she lingered to chat. Billy thought he must have been nine years old, old enough at any rate to feel very self-conscious about being naked in front of his mother. To help his shyness along, Agnes Mackenzie had observed that Billy was – as she phrased it – 'hung like a stud'. 'Christ, you're just a kid and you've already got more between your legs than your father. His looks like a shelled peanut, haw, haw, haw, haw, haw.'

True or false – and Alex Mackenzie was a modest man so Billy never got the chance to check it out – that image polished his father off once and for all. Billy decided he would rather be castrated than be like his father. He never changed his mind.

Despite the stupendously swift revisions in Billy's idea of his mother, he continued to sympathize with her in her bitter disappointment over her life. Her father, a carpenter by trade and an alcoholic by vocation, had emigrated from Scotland to Canada at the end of World War Two. He settled with his wife and six children in Nugget, where the three gold mines that had brought the town into existence were still operating in full force. Then he promptly died of a heart attack while walking home drunk and was found the next morning frozen stiff in a snowbank. His oldest daughter had been trapped there ever since. After years of working as a waitress, a store clerk, and a barmaid to bring in money that helped to feed the younger children, Agnes McKay had married Alex Mackenzie soon after he came to Nugget from the west to manage the Hudson's Bay store.

According to their mother, her future husband had led her to believe that he would soon be promoted to the management of a bigger store in a bigger town. Otherwise, she claimed furiously, she wouldn't have let him get to first base. Anne got a lot of mileage out of that metaphor on many a Tuesday night.

'She wouldn't have let him get to first base! Who does she think she's kidding with that bullshit! She let him play till he hit a home run, and I'll bet she hit the ball for him, too. Billy, I know it, you know it, probably half the town knows it – you, dear brother, were the biggest premature baby in the history of medicine! As well as the most beautiful, of course, that goes without saying! As does your flawless command of the English language when you stood up, cut your own umbilical cord, and thanked Agnes for giving birth to you. Not to mention your walk home from the hospital when you were six days old without getting lost once. How often must I remind you, Billy, that that woman was twenty-nine years old before she caught her man! Let me repeat that, she was *twenty-nine* when she was still protecting her first base so vigilantly. Now, I ask you, Billy Mackenzie, why? Why, oh, why was that succulent piece of ass, sweet Agnes of Edinburgh, the bonnie Scots lassie with the gorgeous gams and boobs like watermelons, *why* was she single until she was almost thirty years old? I will now explain that mystery for the umpteenth time. Because she had to wait for the right victim to materialize, one that craved the whip. And along came poor, innocent Daddy, ripe for his destiny.

The rest, unfortunately, is history, yours and mine. Roll one more joint. I am so tired of thinking about those people, why can't I stop?'

Since their parents' marriage in 1965, Nugget's gold mines had all closed down, and the makeshift boom town had degenerated into a stagnant outpost in the northern bush. The town had been kept alive by artificial respiration as the district headquarters of various government agencies, as the site of the district high school and the district hospital, and by the economic side-effects of the Kimberley-Clark and Universal Plywood plants in nearby Lac du Bois. Of course, the population declined rapidly with the exodus of all the miners and their families – an exodus commemorated now only by abandoned shacks that still sat rotting in luxurious weed jungles, so many monuments to Nugget's glory days.

But the Mackenzies were still there, too, rotting with the shacks. The promised promotion, legendary or not, had never materialized. What had materialized instead was a family Anne often referred to as the world's second Auschwitz.

Once begun, it was amazing how swiftly the upheaval in Billy's way of perceiving his mother brought about his fall from grace. Like Lucifer, he plunged directly into hell. It happened on the morning after Anne showed him the ugly dark bruise on her arm. As usual, Agnes Mackenzie had purposely waited until her husband had gone to work before she got out of bed. Billy and Anne were dressed and ready to walk to school together. Anne had stepped out onto the tiny porch that was parked like a podium at their front door, unattached to the house itself. Billy told her to wait a minute and walked back along the dim hallway. He had made up his mind.

His mother was in the kitchen in her housecoat, which she often wore until she went to bed at night. She was standing at the stove and yawning while she waited for the kettle to boil for the strong tea she drank by the gallon. She claimed it helped to prevent the development of the migraines from which she frequently suffered.

Billy asked her if she had seen the awful bruise on Anne's arm.

'What bruise?'

His mother poured boiling water into the tea pot and put the lid on it.

'The bruise she says you made when you twisted her arm in Mrs Beecher's store yesterday.'

Agnes Mackenzie turned and stared at him.

'She says what? What the hell are you talking about? You're going to be late for school, go on.'

'I'm talking about the big bruise on Anne's right arm,' Billy persisted, staring right back at his mother in a way he had never done before. 'You shouldn't hurt Anne like that, Mother. It's not right.'

'You shut your mouth!' Agnes Mackenzie ordered. 'You're quite the big shot today, aren't you? I've got a blinding headache, Billy, I want to sit down and drink my tea. Now go to school before I lose my temper.'

His mother had poured a mug full of black tea. She walked past Billy on her way to the living room as if he weren't there. Billy followed her along the narrow hallway and stopped at the archway that opened into the living room. His mother ignored him while she turned on the TV and switched channels until she found the show she watched every weekday morning. Then she sat down in her chair to drink her tea and light up the first cigarette of another day that would essentially consist of tea, TV, and cigarettes.

'Are you planning to stand there on duty all day long?' she asked finally. 'Am I under house arrest?'

'I guess Anne's a liar,' Billy said. 'I guess you didn't twist that bruise into her arm like she said, or you'd have apologized to her before now. I should have known you'd never do anything that's against the law.'

Agnes Mackenzie's eyes pointed at him like spears.

'What's against the law?'

'Child abuse.'

'I guess you got a pretty big mouth all of a sudden. It's gonna get you into trouble if you don't clear out of here, and fast, too.'

'Don't worry, I'm going,' Billy said. 'I don't want a mug of hot tea pitched into my face.'

Billy took off without waiting to see his mother's reaction. He knew he had scored a perfect bull's-eye.

Anne became quieter and quieter as she grew into her teens. She spent as much time as possible alone in her cramped bedroom with the door locked against intruders. She kept the room unnaturally neat and read obsessively late into the night. Though she was in fact a very pretty girl, she believed she was ugly and hated looking at herself in mirrors because she could detect similarities between her own features and her mother's. Billy often thought that if she could Anne would have blacked herself out of existence as she had blacked out all the fat dolls in the Sears catalogues.

At school, her caustic wit and her sharp tongue made enemies of the teachers and drove away any and all candidates for friendship among girls her own age. It was heartbreaking to watch, but Billy found he was powerless to arrest Anne's determined descent into the loneliness of an isolation in which she at least felt safe. By the time she was thirteen, the Tuesday nights she spent stoned with Billy were almost the only times Anne emerged from her self-imposed seclusion. Every once in a while, Billy suggested they invite Poppy Richardson or Rocky Barbizan to join them. But Anne pleaded against anyone's interfering in their weekly communions.

'Billy,' she said one Tuesday night after he had hung up the phone on Rocky, who had called looking for something to do. Billy had lied that he had too much homework. 'I know you think I should try to be more social, and you're right, I should. The truth is I can't, because I'm terrified of everybody, so everybody's terrified of me. I see to *that*! Ha ha! Nobody ever gets a chance to hurt me, you see, because I hurt them first. The awful thing is I know what I'm doing to myself. I used to make promises to myself every morning, "Today I'll be different!" But of course I never was. And now it's too late to change, Billy. I don't even make the promises any more.'

'Hey, don't cry,' Billy said, 'I'm happy just with you.'

'Really?'

'I wouldn't say it if I didn't mean it.'

'Guess what? You're the only person on earth I don't feel fat with.' Anne looked away from him. 'You're my paradise.'

CHAPTER THREE

After the alliance between Billy and Anne became an acknowledged fact, and he had consciously assumed responsibility as her champion and protector, the Mackenzies' domestic machine began to lurch, then slide, then hurtle downhill like a runaway truck. Its mature phase was a pantomime of congealed frenzy. Through it all, Billy clung stubbornly to his magical belief that somewhere behind them in the rubble there must have been happy, or at least happier, times. This possibility Anne continued to dismiss as a pipe dream.

Over and over again, Anne produced details by the hundreds from her computer-bank memory to prove that Billy's versions of family experiences were fanciful and wholly untrustworthy.

'Boy, did Mother do a number on you,' Anne would sigh with an incredulous shake of her head. 'It was not Mother who got us safely into the car that day, Billy, it was Daddy. I admit, there isn't much to be said for the poor bugger, but fair's fair!'

On that night, they were doing an autopsy on an aborted blueberry picking expedition of some years back.

'Mother did everything she could,' Anne went on, having paused to light the joint she had just rolled, 'and I do mean everything, to terrify that poor bear into attacking us. As soon as she saw it, she screamed like a banshee, dropped her pail of blueberries, and hightailed it through the bush in the wrong direction. If we'd followed her we'd still be running across the tundra! It was Daddy who collected you and me and put us into the back seat of the car. And then he had to go back into the bush to hunt Mother down. Mind you,' she giggled, 'Daddy did rather spoil the heroism of it all by crapping in his pants so that Mother could goad us into laughing at him all the way home. For ages, she called him Diarrhea Dick, which wasn't really necessary, now was it? And she promptly told everybody in town about how Daddy was so scared of the damned bear he'd shit in his pants, while he stood there trying to pass it off with that little-boy's smile. Even back then, I knew that was wrong. If he'd had any sense at all, he'd have left Mother out there with the bear and started praying it did go for her. It might've, too, just to shut the bitch up.'

Despite his striking lack of success, Billy persevered for a couple of years in his campaign to persuade Anne that their mother had, in fact, loved her when she was a little girl. But even he could hear in his voice the gradual erosion of his former conviction and the gathering forces of disillusion.

'You're sweet, Billy, you really truly are, no wonder everybody likes you so much,' was typical of Anne's perfunctory responses. 'I think it's nice the way you want things to be different than they are. I guess if you could you'd make the whole world happy, wouldn't you? You make me feel like a spoilsport, the poop of all poops.'

For Billy, their Tuesday night summit conferences came to mean the surrender of one cherished illusion after another. Where had he been all his life?

'Billy, I'm curious,' Anne said once after a long silence. 'Have you never wondered *why* you ran away from home so often? Not every little boy starts running off from home as soon as he knows there's somewhere to run to.'

Billy objected. 'I don't think I was really running away, Anne.'

'Oh, yes, you were! They had to call in the police every time. The first two times you ran away I was too young to know what was going on, but God knows I've heard the stories often enough. Mother actually brags about your flights, Billy, she's proud of them – her son, the fearless adventurer! She doesn't appear to realize that when a little boy runs away from home, he is running *away* from something. The first time you were only four years old, for Christ's sake, and you actually hid out overnight up in the old Buchanan mine shaft. It was November, Billy, *November* – you nearly froze to death! And the next time, you walked all the way out to Highway 11 and were more than halfway to Lac du Bois before some truck driver reported you and the cops went out and brought you home in the middle of the night. Billy, that's more than ten miles! And how come the cops hadn't spotted you, hmmm? They'd been on the alert since late in the afternoon – what did you do? Hide out in the ditches?'

'I don't remember,' Billy said. 'I don't remember any of it.'

'That's a bit odd, isn't it? There's something weird about the way your mind works. If it was unpleasant, it didn't happen. I guess I have that backwards, it's me that's weird. Those are the things that stick in my head like glue. The third time I *do* remember. It was the day after your tenth birthday, so I was seven years old. And that time, by God, you meant business. You hid in the back of that big delivery truck down at the store and rode all the way to Thunder Bay. Half the cops in northern Ontario were looking for you! Mother, naturally, was doing the frantic mommy routine – I remember her raving *on and on* about how some pervert had picked you up on the highway and they'd find your corpse in a ditch somewhere all chopped up in pieces. Boy, did she lay on the sobbing and screaming! Oh, I tell you, Billy, she put on quite a show, very dramatic, smoking cigarettes and gobbling up codeine pills. She had me so terrified I went hysterical, and the doctor had to come and give me a needle to put me out of it. She had me utterly convinced you were dead and cut up in chunks. Daddy did his best to shut her up, but Agnes was enjoying herself too much. Needless to say, she'd conveniently forgotten it was all her fault. That's a detail she always leaves out when she gives her version of that particular story. She concentrates on what a bold, adventurous son you were!'

'It was her fault?' Billy avoided looking directly in Anne's eyes. 'I remember going off in the truck but I don't remember why.'

'I'm not surprised,' Anne said, 'not at all. Billy, you don't seem to remember anything you're not supposed to remember according to the Gospel of St Agnes! It most certainly was Mother's fault. It was the day after your birthday in August. Mother had given you a beige-colored sweater, she probably got it from Sears in a back-to-school sale. You insisted on wearing it the next day, even though it was hot as hell outside. On the way home for lunch, you bought a Fudgsicle or something. Whatever it was, it dripped a few spots down the front of your new sweater. Mother was out on the front stoop looking for you. She went berserk when she saw the stains and hit you so hard you actually fell down the steps and almost split your skull open on the sidewalk! She was screeching about you buying a Fudgsicle when it was lunchtime – I think that was supposed to explain how mad she was. You got up and took off the sweater and threw it at her. Then you marched off down the street with blood streaming down your face from a cut over your eye. For God's sake, Billy, you've been looking at the scar in the mirror ever since! And we didn't see you again until they found you two days later at that shopping center in Thunder Bay. The cops sent you home on the bus – COD. Or maybe it was DOA, now that I think of it.'

Billy had rolled another joint and they smoked it. Then he got the last two beers out of the freezer, where they put them as soon as their mother and father left on Tuesday nights to get them cold fast.

Anne giggled to herself as she sipped her beer.

'The reunion was priceless,' she said. 'It gave Mother another golden opportunity to throw an exhibition, and the scene she caused down at the old bus stop was gross, double-gross! Mr Grimsby was supposed to be there to take a picture for the paper, but he was a few minutes late. You'd already got off the bus. He was going to take the usual hugs-and-kisses picture, but the bus was still taking on passengers so Mother made you get *back* on the bus and come down the steps a second time! And when you did, Mother laid it on for Grimsby with a trowel. Oh, God, my baby, my baby, oh God, my little boy, look everybody! Hear me sobbing as I crush him in my arms! See my tears? Feel my suffering? Et cetera, et cetera, et cetera. It was revolting. You were almost as tall as her.' Anne burst into cackling laughter. 'God, what a farce. I wonder if Daddy was embarrassed. I don't suppose so. You were nice to me, though. As soon as you could get away from Mother, you came over to where I was crying and told me you were sorry you'd left me alone and promised you'd never do it again.' She smiled at Billy. 'And you didn't. After that, you started to change. I wonder why?'

The last of Billy's gallant attempts to retouch Anne's grimly hilarious portrait of Agnes Mackenzie, to soft-focus her through a filter of normal motherly instincts, made a powerful impression on Billy's mind. For the first time in his life, he began to dimly realize what being crazy must mean.

Indeed, Anne made him think he had been heading in that direction.

Billy had brought up the Red Cross nurse's uniform Agnes Mackenzie had made for Anne as irrefutable evidence of natural maternal affection.

Anne gaped at him in astonished silence.

'You really are loco,' she said finally. 'Mother didn't make that damn white apron I had to pretend was a nurse's uniform, Billy. You made it.'

'Anne, come off it,' Billy challenged cautiously. His mind had been bowled over by Anne so often by that time that he no longer opposed her with even a pretense of confidence. 'That isn't true.'

'You bet your life it's true, Billy Mackenzie! It was your idea, too. You took the idea to Mother, but she didn't have time. So you made it yourself, out of an old see-through sheet she grudgingly gave you after you pleaded until she lost her temper. You spread the sheet out on the grass and drew a picture of the apron on it with a crayon. You drew it all in one piece and three times too big for me, it was absolutely huge! Then I said a nurse's apron would have to have pockets, so you drew a couple of big squares and cut them out, too. You insisted on using that ancient sewing machine to sew the pockets on and make a hem. All Mother did was show you how to operate the machine, and she even bitched about that. She was probably watching one of her bloody babble shows on TV. You nagged and nagged at her until she finally dragged herself away and showed you how to use the machine, snapping at you about what a pest you were. Then she broke the needle because she was so angry. That made her even crabbier, because she had to hunt in all the little drawers for another one. It only took you a few minutes to learn how to run that machine – you were proud as punch about that. All Mother did was criticize your crooked seams and say it was no good anyhow without a red cross on it. I said I didn't want a red cross on it, but you gave in. You *always* gave in to Mother. The only red thing you could find was an old polyester skirt of Mother's, and she wouldn't let you have it. She hadn't worn the damn thing for years because it had a cigarette burn in it, a real *hole*, but she said it was a perfectly good skirt and she could repair it in no time. Needless to say, she never did. About a year ago she tried to palm that skirt off on me. For some reason, nobody would notice the hole if I was wearing it. I don't suppose you remember how I did end up with a red cross on that apron either, do you?'

'No, I don't,' Billy admitted in a resigned, stoned stupor.

'Actually, it was quite funny. Do you remember the policeman's wife, Mrs Lattimer? They had just moved in next door. Mr Lattimer used to show you his gun collection.'

Billy did remember the Lattimers and the gun collection. Twice Mr Lattimer had taken Billy along with his own son out to a remote garbage dump in the bush and let them fire a handgun.

'Well, the next afternoon, I was out in the back yard, nursing away like mad with this gigantic apron wrapped around me like a shroud. Mrs Lattimer came over and talked to me, she said I would be a very good nurse when I grew up. You weren't there. You were probably mowing somebody's lawn, you nearly always were in those days. I was so proud to tell her my *brother* made my uniform! Then out comes Agnes, and what does she do but launch into how *she* made me the apron! Then she went on about how she'd wanted to put a nice red cross on the bib, but she didn't have a thing around the house she could use. Right away Mrs Lattimer said she was sure she had some old red thing she didn't want, and back she came in no time flat with a red table napkin! So there was Agnes, trapped by her own big lying mouth. She had to go in and sew on the damned red cross then! You know, I used to wonder who Mrs Lattimer thought the liar was, me or Mother. Not that it matters.' Anne looked at Billy with sad shiny eyes. 'But you did make the apron, Billy. It's true, you really did. And you don't even remember! Isn't that awful! It meant so much to me. It still does.'

Then Anne had begun to cry. She wiped away the tears and said, 'I just realized something. That was the same summer you ran away to Thunder Bay in the truck. I got that nurse kit for my seventh birthday.'

'Anne,' Billy wondered aloud, 'why did I think Mother made it? I honestly don't understand – it makes me think I must be crazy the way I have everything screwed up.'

Anne smiled and then wriggled down on the bed and sighed. 'It must be nice to just think it. When you know you're crazy you don't seem to feel it, at least I don't. Maybe you can't do both at the same time.'

'Don't say that, you're not crazy at all.'

'Don't bet on that, I don't tell you everything. Billy, I think you thought Mother made the apron because she ought to have made it. She ought to have done lots of things she didn't do. What you do is make things be the way you think they should have been. You've invented a mother who was never there. But I don't think that's crazy. It was just something you had to do, because—because you were always, always such . . . always such a *nice* little boy. You still are. And it might have worked for you, too, if I hadn't come along to fuck up everything and break the enchantment. Who knows? You might have been quite happy just not to be crazy. On the other hand, you might not. We'll never know. And this way, even if we're both absolute basket cases before we escape, at least we'll have company in our straitjackets. I mean, if one of us does go round the big bend some night and takes an axe to both of them, at least we'll have each other as character witnesses, whether they believe us or not.'

So, in the end, Billy had capitulated entirely to Anne's conviction that Agnes Mackenzie had been deranged long before she had even met their father. In doing so, he also subscribed to her theory that what they had experienced, and were to continue to experience, was not a transformation for which Alex Mackenzie was in any way responsible. He was merely the booby who walked into the trap.

Soon, it no longer seemed to matter whether the memories Billy had dredged up for Anne to demolish in her businesslike way were fantasies or not. Nor did it matter whether Anne's version of things was entirely dependable. Both points were irrelevant. Whatever their mother may once have been, she had long since become a destructive and unpredictable woman, a creature of sudden black moods and inexplicable tempers, a witch who could turn her emotions on and off like light bulbs. Zap! – and you were plunged into darkness and stony-faced disfavor.

This simplication did not bring happiness to Billy, but it did bring relief. Like Anne, he now knew where he stood. On shaky ground.

Their mother began to refer to the headaches from which she frequently suffered in the singular form, as The Migraine, as if the pain were a demon with a will of its own. Though Billy did not actually doubt the reality of the excruciating pain his mother claimed to endure, both he and Anne came to realize that Agnes Mackenzie's affliction was a supremely effective tool in the tyranny she exercised over his father and themselves. Anything one of them said or did to thwart her capricious will, any argument lost, any pigheaded difference of opinion inevitably triggered a threat of The Migraine. If the delinquent stood firm and The Migraine was allowed to triumph, Agnes Mackenzie took to her bed and lay moaning in the dark. When this happened, whoever was trapped at home – preferably Billy – had to keep her supplied with cold facecloths for her throbbing temples.

Anne grew increasingly more skeptical about these attacks. 'You must admit,' she said more than once, 'it is distinctly odd how these Goddamned migraines seem to skip her bingo nights!'

During his early adolescence, Billy himself began to suffer from inexplicably severe headaches. They struck randomly and without any warning, and he attributed them to anxiety and tension. But his mother immediately appropriated them as incontrovertible proof that her own migraines were a curse that ran in the blood. This convenient explanation of The Migraine did not, however, prevent her from using its attacks as a means of punishing whomever she was determined to punish at the time. In effect, as soon as she vanished into the dark bedroom and the moaning began, everyone was punished no matter who the guilty party might be.

'That fucking migraine stalks us like Jack the Ripper,' Anne complained angrily one night. 'Night after night, she keeps us awake with those bloody news shows, but I couldn't watch *Gone with the Wind* even though I had the volume turned down to where I couldn't even hear the *commercials* more than three feet away! I had to lip-read the movie. God, she's been eating that fucking codeine like popcorn all day long, anybody else would be comatose.'

Agnes Mackenzie's contempt for her husband skyrocketed during her middle years. She openly despised him as an impotent weakling and took an increasingly flagrant delight in humiliating him in public. Their father spent as many hours as possible at work and stopped coming home for lunch, and Billy was sure he dreaded the sight of his wife coming through the doors of the store. The only times Alex Mackenzie was safe from personal annihilation were those when his wife's malevolence was directed at one or both of their children. Then, in a delirium of relief, he became his wife's suckhole, slave, and grateful accomplice.

Alex Mackenzie, though too unimaginative to be the brains behind any operation, was a natural spy and stoolie. Even though Billy's and Anne's comings and goings after school never involved anything more exciting than drinking coffee and smoking cigarettes in the Fleur de Lis restaurant to postpone the return home, their father faithfully reported everything he saw or heard of their movements to headquarters.

Occasionally, he struck gold. Billy once made the mistake of buying a copy of *Penthouse* from the magazine rack in the Hudson's Bay. He hid the *Penthouse* inside one of his school binders, but the girl at the cash register must have joked about it to his father.

For the first time in years, Agnes Mackenzie expressed an intense interest in how things were going at school, and as soon as he got inside the door, she asked him to show her his notebooks. Billy pretended not to have heard her and made straight for his bedroom, but his mother followed him and he knew then that she had been told about the magazine. As she flipped through its pages, pausing briefly to throw an accusing stare at Billy when she came across the more salacious photographs, he felt guilty and dirty-minded, and angry with himself because he felt guilty.

'This is what you're learning from that Rocky Barbizan brat, is it: I've told you to stop hanging around with that doped-up bum, and I mean it!'

His mother confiscated the *Penthouse*, turning in his doorway on her way out of the room to shake it at him. 'The next time one of these filthy magazines shows up in this house, I'm going to march you straight back to where you bought it and make you get the money back. Three dollars and fifty cents! Big spender! Huh!' She slammed the door behind her.

Billy didn't blame his father. Even though he had no respect and felt no love for him, he did sympathize with the man. He accepted the fact that groveling in abject servitude was less painful than public persecution.

'She didn't throw that *Penthouse* out, you know,' Anne told Billy a few weeks later. 'She hid it in her underwear drawer. I caught her reading those phony letters to the editor the other day when she was supposedly in bed with The Migraine. Interesting, eh?'

The beginning of Billy's real sex life – sex that involved the bodies of girls, not just his own – also took place in grade eight, thanks to Rocky Barbizan's enthusiastic tutelage, and introduced a new and highly explosive element into the Mackenzie family equation. Because he had failed twice in his remedial classes somewhere along the way, Rocky was sixteen when he joined Billy's class at Nugget Public School, where the policy was to keep those branded as slow in with the regular kids. Rocky had already screwed two girls, not once but many times. Once revealed, this fact introduced a competitive urgency into Billy's already obsessive need to lose his virginity as soon as possible.

Basically, Billy thought of his father as a eunuch, and because of this there was something coldly mechanical in the way Billy set out to get himself laid, as if he wanted to prove a point and develop the habit before it was too late. Billy did not know if there was any substance to Anne's later assertion that his mother found him sexually stimulating, but he learned in grade eight that the idea of his being with a girl, any girl, drove Agnes Mackenzie to distraction.

Rocky talked about his own two conquests, but one had moved out of town and the other had left school and gone on to higher things. She was sleeping around only with older guys who owned motorcycles. Billy had to start from scratch.

By that age Billy had begun baby-sitting, and he was often successful in persuading a girl pointed out by Rocky as a likely prospect to join him after the people he was baby-sitting for had left the house. On other nights Billy sneaked into the houses where the girl was baby-sitting, or joined her in her own home when her parents had gone out.

'First one, then another,' Rocky advised. 'Make 'em jealous and keep 'em guessing.'

But none of the girls succumbed to Billy's seductive advances throughout the long winter, and he began to fear that he wasn't as sexy as Rocky Barbizan. Then one night he persuaded the girl he was with to smoke a joint with him;

Rocky had said if you could get a girl stoned, you nearly always got fucked. Maybe that was true, because that night Billy got laid for the first time. Hallelujah!

Once Agnes Mackenzie discovered that her son had skipped secretly out of his room not once but several times, she zeroed in on this new form of dereliction like a guided missile. When Billy got home from his mysterious expeditions, his mother was always waiting to interrogate him about where he had been, with whom, and why. As often as not, Billy was stoned as he reeled off his elaborately prepared lies, the most frequent of which had to do with spending the night hours with Rocky Barbizan, here, there, and everywhere. His mother suspected Billy was lying, but just the fact of his defying her demands that he should end his friendship with Rocky was almost guaranteed to convert her suspicions into fury about his disobedience. As soon as this diversion had taken place, Billy's defense of Rocky would start a fight and he would be off the hook.

But one Friday night when he arrived home – he was fifteen and nearing the end of the tenth grade – Billy discovered he had been under surveillance ever since he left the house after the evening meal. It was a quarter to two when he sneaked in the front door and the little bungalow was in darkness. He was slipping in his socks along the hallway towards his bedroom at the back of the house, when suddenly the light from the floor lamp in the living room burst on.

'Phone the police, Alex,' he heard his mother say. 'Tell them we have a burglar in the house. Or could it by any chance be our fifteen-year-old son, who we thought was sound asleep?'

Billy felt like applauding; his mother's timing had never been better. He had to clamp his teeth together to stifle the laughter that rose in his throat, but he managed to present a face both straight and innocent as he looked through the archway to see his parents seated in their usual chairs.

'Gee whiz, you scared me,' he said. 'What goes? Did you really hear a burglar?'

'Gee whiz, Alex, we scared our little boy, the one we thought was tucked away for the night. How come you're carrying your shoes?'

'Just in case I might wake you up,' Billy explained. 'Why are you sitting here in the dark anyway?' he asked as his mother lighted a cigarette and stared at him.

'It's a surprise party,' she said.

Billy could hear Anne giggling helplessly in her bedroom a few feet away.

'Don't just stand there,' Agnes Mackenzie continued, 'the night is young, it's only two o'clock in the morning. Sit down and tell us what you've been doing for the last eight hours. That's the surprise we're waiting to celebrate.'

'Nothing worth celebrating,' Billy replied, faking a yawn. 'I pumped gas till quarter past ten, the place was really busy tonight—'

His mother looked at his father.

'He pumped gas till ten-fifteen, Alex, did you hear that?' She looked back at Billy. 'Don't you usually quit when Chuck Courtis collects the cash from the till, puts it in the safe, and turns out all the lights? He did that at nine-thirty.'

'Was it only nine-thirty? Boy, it felt like midnight.'

'It felt like midnight. So what'd you do when it felt like midnight?'

'Rocky picked me up and we went over to his place. I did some homework and then I helped Rocky study for a test tomorrow morning.'

Tomorrow morning was Saturday, Billy instantly realized, but he knew better than to correct the lie. Knowing he'd been watched had unnerved him.

Agnes Mackenzie looked at her husband again and said, 'He went over to that bum's house and did homework and then helped the bum to study . . . for a Saturday morning test.'

'God, you're right, it's Friday, I guess his test's on Monday.'

Agnes Mackenzie stared at Billy as he spoke. 'It must be hard doing homework in the dark,' she said when he had finished. 'Your father and I went for a long walk tonight and ended up down where the bohunks live. Maybe we were looking at the wrong house.'

Billy shrugged. 'Okay, so I've been lying. So we watched a couple of movies on the Betamax and drank a few bottles of beer. Is that satisfactory? Or do you want to test me on the lie detector? I'm sure you've got one.'

His mother nodded her head and looked back at her husband. 'They watched a couple of movies on the Betamax,' she reported, 'and drank some beer. It's good to hear the truth, isn't it, Alex? I guess we'll have to invest in one of those video machines. Then our son can watch his movies at home; maybe he'll even let us watch the movies with him.'

Inspiration struck. 'Not these movies we couldn't,' Billy said, trying to sound as well as look guilty. He'd had plenty of practice at both. 'We were watching a couple of porno movies.'

Behind him, down the hallway, he heard the infinitesimal click as Anne opened her door so she could hear the latest battle of wits more clearly.

'Ooooooh, *porno* movies.' Agnes Mackenzie repeated, lifting her eyebrows and letting out a cloud of smoke. 'In grade ten, our son is into pornography, Alex. Hard-core pornography? Or just *Penthouse* stuff in motion?'

'They were both pretty raw, I guess,' Billy confessed, softening his voice into shame and lowering his eyes in abasement. 'I'm sorry, Mother, I really am. If it makes you feel any better, I was disgusted with myself for watching them. I feel dirty just telling you about it.'

'He feels dirty,' his mother relayed to his father. 'Tell me, I'm curious, did the old lady watch these porno movies too?'

'Don't be silly, Mother, of course she didn't. She was already in bed when we got there.'

Agnes Mackenzie nodded some more and remained silent for so long that Billy thought the inquisition was over. He was about to head for his bedroom when his mother resumed speaking.

'What about those two girls that went into the house? Did they watch those porno movies with you, or did they just go to bed like the old lady?'

'Mother, for Christ's sake—'

Alex Mackenzie spoke then for the first time. 'Don't you dare talk to your mother like that!' he ordered.

'I'm sorry, I shouldn't have said that. Mother, you must have been passing the wrong house. Maybe you were on the next street over, those funny little streets are confusing. Because the girls I hang around with don't sit and watch dirty movies with guys, that's for sure!' Billy sighed and shook his head in consternation that his mother would even imagine him knowing *that* kind of girl.

'Well, I'm certainly glad to hear that. We must have been looking at the wrong house, Alex, I guess he's right.' Though she had addressed his father by name, Agnes Mackenzie's eyes were drilling into Billy's like pile-drivers into cement. 'A couple of slutty-looking bitches went into the house we were watching at about ten-thirty. Then this loud music came on and all the lights went out. I guess they were dancing in the dark. Dancing or something. What do you think, Billy?'

Billy was thinking his mother had Bette Davis eyes like the girl in the song. There seemed to be no end to the subtle variations she could infuse into the basic inquisitor's stare. *All the boys think she's a spy, she got Bette Davis eyes* – the song might have been written about Agnes Mackenzie.

Any further pretence that his parents had been spying on the wrong house was futile. Rocky's blue and gold Trans-Am had been parked in the gravel that surrounded his grandmother's old miner's shack. Agnes Mackenzie was obviously saving that. He pictured his parents lurking for hours in the scrub bush across from the shack or behind one of the trucks or cars parked out on the roadway. Billy lounged against the archway and stuck his hands into his back pockets, trying for a casual look to throw her off guard. He didn't want his anger to show.

'I would imagine they were doing something,' he said with deadpan deliberation. 'I also think you're very lucky none of the neighbors phoned the cops to report a couple of peeping Toms. Who knows? Maybe they were all doing something, and something is something people like to do in private. I also think that from now on I'll keep my eyes open. I don't like being spied on and followed, especially by my parents. That's too . . .' He paused and shifted his left hip against the archway '. . . too kinky for me.'

Alex Mackenzie came suddenly to life and bounded across the living room until he was face to face with his son.

'Are you calling your mother kinky?' he shouted. 'Eh? Eh? Are you calling your mother a peeping Tom?' He clenched his hands, his eyes glowing.

Little flecks of his father's foamy spit sprayed Billy's face, and he wiped them off with the back of his hand. 'I'm calling you both kinky,' Billy said, 'and I'm telling you to stop spitting in my face, I don't like that either. I do hope those aren't fists I see, Father, because if they are, I should warn you that I'm boiling mad at the moment.'

'You are, are you?' Alex Mackenzie shouted wildly. 'Did you hear that, Aggie? He's boiling mad!'

To Billy's utter amazement, his father had assumed a crouching position and was dancing like a boxer from bare foot to bare foot in a sort of hippity-hop war dance.

'Go on, go on,' he urged, out of his mind with excitement at the very idea of socking his wife's favorite. 'Did you hear that,

Aggie? You heard him! Now he wants to hit his father! So hit me, go on, hit me! Oh, just try it, just try it, you little son of a bitch!'

'You said it, not me,' Billy grinned.

By that time, Anne had been lured out into the hallway by this unprecedented development. The sight of Alex Mackenzie bobbing around and pumping his fists in the air like a boxer was too much for Anne. She burst into loud peals of laughter and collapsed against the wall.

Alex Mackenzie spun crazed eyes on his daughter. 'Are you laughing at me?' he demanded. 'I'm funny, am I? Funny? Funny? I'll show you how funny I am!' And all of a sudden, while Billy had turned his head to look at Anne, his father actually did pop his right fist off Billy's chin.

Billy let out a whoop of laughter and ducked his father's second attempted jab at the other side of his jaw. His father's fist slammed into the wall, which was only a quarter inch of fake maple paneling over empty space. The paneling bounced and a small picture fell to the floor. The glass smashed.

'What are you laughing at?' his father hollered, more spit hitting Billy's face. 'You wanted to hit me, didn't you? So hit me, hit me! Go on, hit your own father!'

He was still hopping from one foot to the other and plunging his fists back and forth like pistons when he knocked over the floor lamp with an elbow and sent it crashing to the floor. The shade flew off and rolled across the rug. The heavy glass bowl that sat on top of the lamp hit the edge of the coffee table. This time a lot of smashed glass flew up in a fountain and showered the rug in every direction.

Agnes Mackenzie jumped to her feet with a cry of alarm.

'For Christ's sake, you fool, you broke the Goddamned lamp! Watch out, you'll cut your stupid feet! Be careful!' she screamed.

But his wife's warning came too late. Alex Mackenzie had already tripped over the fallen lamp post, and toppled backward to land with a resounding thud on the floor. Agnes Mackenzie sat down again, doubled over with laughter in her armchair. Alex Mackenzie, on his hands and knees, glared at his wife balefully. Then he transferred his glare to Billy and said, 'I hope you're happy now.'

'Oh, shut up, you big jackass,' his wife commanded, 'it's a damn good thing Billy didn't slug you, you'd be out cold.' She glanced at Billy knowingly and jerked her head at Alex Mackenzie, still on the floor, as she stood up. 'Mighty Mouse,' she said ironically. 'Who'd you think you were all of a sudden, Muhammad Ali? Get up! And clean up all this glass before you come to bed!'

This cruel betrayal of her ally should have marked the end of the hostilities. But that night held one last surprise.

Above the sofa, hung on two hooks attached to two adhesive patches that were stuck to the paneling, were Agnes Mackenzie's most prized household decorations, a pair of green Javanese dancers in stylized postures. Abruptly, the male dancer dropped from the wall and smashed on the floor behind the sofa. All eyes were immediately riveted on the wall where he had hung. Not even the adhesive device remained. Dried out by years of electric heat, it had apparently lost whatever grip it had left as a result of the reverberations from Alex Mackenzie's crash landing. Even as they watched, the female figure took her own fatal plunge and was shattered out of sight with her mate.

In the silence, Agnes Mackenzie looked at her husband. 'Now see what you've done with your jumping around like a maniac? I want them replaced, understand? I hope you're pleased. I feel The Migraine already.'

Their mother stalked into her bedroom, and Billy and Anne took the opportunity to slip off, too, leaving their father still seated on the floor. He looked as if he might start to cry. In the belief that they were for once real allies in the cause, he had risen pugnaciously to his wife's defense. Now he found himself abandoned as the usual joke. It took him a long time to vacuum up the thousands of glass splinters.

Nothing changed, of course. By the next morning things were back to what passed in the family as normal. The Javanese dancers were replaced by two similar green figures made from the same cheap ceramic stuff. The Mackenzies continued to live like a houseful of secret agents, of spies and counterspies. His mother's animosity to any girl Billy had anything to do with was instant and implacable, and the few girls he did become involved with in imitation romances soon learned to avoid Agnes Mackenzie at any cost, even the cost of giving Billy the heave-ho.

Once, when Billy was eighteen and had already been going steady with Poppy Richardson for more than a year, his mother found a condom in a pocket of his blue jeans when she did the washing.

'I did the washing this afternoon,' she informed him portentously when he got home from pumping gas at the Texaco station. But she said nothing about the condom he had so carelessly forgotten about.

When Billy had washed the oil and gas stink off his hands and sat down to supper in the kitchen, the condom was staring up at him from the middle of his plate, its circular form showing clearly through its paper enclosure. Billy looked at it for a while. Then he covered it up with spaghetti and meatballs and ate it, paper and all.

It was Anne's opinion that, jealous as Agnes Mackenzie manifestly was, she in fact took great pride in what she imagined to be her son's insatiable sexuality.

'I know it's supposed to be the father who's proud of his son in that particular respect, Billy, but let's face it – Mother's taken over the man's role in this outfit. If this is an example of the nuclear family, then God help us, something went wrong with the atoms. You know, it wouldn't surprise me at all if she has one of those monster dildoes buried away somewhere, the kind you can strap on.'

'Anne,' Billy said, 'who gives a shit?'

It was almost eleven o'clock on a Tuesday night, and any minute one or both of their parents would be home. He was happily stoned, and had put Mike Oldfield's *QE2* on his cassette player. He wanted to listen to the music, not Anne. He felt like a traitor, but he was weary of Anne's inexhaustible preoccupation with their parents' queerness. It was like an emotional thumb she couldn't stop sucking. Billy was beginning to fear his sister could never be weaned, that she would suck that thumb forever.

Anne's smile brightened and froze. 'I'm boring you. I suppose that had to come, didn't it?'

'I'm not bored, Annie, just tired of it.'

'I don't believe you,' Anne said, 'but I'm going to pretend I do. I know how boring I am, Billy. I must try to manufacture some new material, my act is wearing thin. I promise I'll work on it.'

She got up to go, and Billy reached to hold her back.

'Annie, I'm never bored with you, you know that.'

Anne sat down again and lighted one of Billy's cigarettes.

'Maybe it's me who's bored with myself,' she said, smiling back when Billy smiled at her. 'I wish you didn't have to go out tomorrow night. I don't know what to do with myself when you leave me alone on Tuesday nights, I'm addicted to them. Sometimes, I really do think if it wasn't for my weekly communions with you, I'd . . . but I know you have to go.'

Billy had been invited to Poppy Richardson's home for dinner the next day. It was her parents' wedding anniversary and Edgar Richardson had planned a secret extravaganza celebration at the White Birches. Only his wife thought they were eating at home.

'Believe me,' Billy sighed, 'I'd rather stay home with you.'

'Is that really true?' Anne asked.

'You know it is, Anne. I'll just sit there at the White Birches waiting for it to end, then I'll sit over at the Richardsons' and wait some more. I can't even have a cigarette, and they don't drink, either. Mr Richardson has a nose like a bloodhound, and when I sneak out to my truck for a smoke, he can smell it as soon as I come back into the damn room. And I can't stand Poppy's brother, Jack, and his wife. I wish she'd have that damned baby and get it over with. For months I've been feeling it kick inside her belly.'

'Well,' Anne said, 'I can practice my oboe without listening to Mother gripe about it. I can't really blame her, it must get tiresome.'

Billy said, 'I like listening to you practice. In fact, why not practice your solo in here while I'm doing my homework?'

Anne went to get her instrument. She had been in the school system's music program since grade seven, and Billy thought she sounded pretty good on the oboe after only three years of effort. His sister seemed to have a natural feel for music, and he knew she loved playing in the school band. Anne herself was driven to disparage her talent, and scorned any suggestion by Billy that perhaps in the oboe she had found more than just a school credit. Even his assurances that Mr Perrine wouldn't have given her an oboe solo in the band's version of 'You Light Up My Life' if he didn't mean the praise he expressed, Anne dismissed as crap.

'So I play the oboe better than Linda Beecher, so what,' Anne had said. 'The only reason I'm better is that I practice a lot, and I practice a lot because I have nothing else to do. I don't have dates and nobody asks me to parties. Besides, Billy, there's something comical about a fat lady playing an oboe. Sometimes I have to stop practicing and giggle when I think of that. And anyhow, I'm terrified of doing the damned solo, I wish it wasn't in the score.'

Nevertheless, and despite Agnes Mackenzie's complaints about how irritating it was, she had practiced it to near perfection, and she practiced it for an hour and a half that night in Billy's room before she packed the school's oboe away in its case. Billy could tell his sister was happy with the sounds she had made, so he refrained from saying how pretty it was. If he praised her, Anne would be compelled to belittle herself. He suggested they have a smoke together to make up for his absence the following night. Anne rolled the joint while Billy shot home the bolt lock on the door into the kitchen and opened the door into the back yard. Cold air rushed into the tiny room.

The Jamaican pot he had at the moment was potent; the shared joint was enough to give them both a high. They didn't talk. Billy played Mike Oldfield's *Tubular Bells*, which Anne loved, and they listened to it in an easy silence. 'Isn't it pretty,' Anne said at last, sounding almost happy, 'he must be a genius.' Then she got up to leave Billy to finish his homework.

'There's always next Tuesday night, isn't there,' Anne observed as she prepared to open the door into the kitchen and head for her room. 'Come to think of it, I guess one-seventh of my whole life will be Tuesday nights, won't it? What on earth will I do with all of them after I don't have you? I must give that one some thought.'

Anne never had to play her oboe solo in an assembly, and Billy didn't have to go to the Richardsons' thirtieth anniversary party after all.

That night, Anne Mackenzie swallowed every painkiller she could find in the bathroom medicine chest, including a new prescription for a hundred Percodans, and approximately two dozen of her mother's sleeping capsules just to make sure. Billy found the envelope containing the long letter she had written to him as soon as he got out of bed in the morning. She had slipped it under his door. He was not surprised by the envelope, and certainly not alarmed. Anne had often sent

Billy little messages this way, things she thought of to say to him late at night after he'd fallen asleep.

He opened the envelope and unfolded the sheet of lined paper that she had ripped from a school binder.

It began: *Billy darling, my Tuesday man. I don't want anyone else on earth to see this, though for the life of me I cannot imagine why I care. One of my eccentric whims, I guess, but you must promise to keep it. I don't actually know why I've done what I've just done—'*

That was as far as Billy got before he started screaming Anne's name, running for his sister's room. The door was locked. But Anne often locked it when she went to bed or wanted privacy. Billy braced his back against the wall of the hallway and kicked the door open.

Anne's body was on the floor beside the bed. As soon as Billy took her into his arms he knew she was dead. Her corpse was heavy and cold.

Billy heard his mother out in the hallway, shouting, 'What the hell is going on in this house?'

In the doorway of Anne's room, Agnes Mackenzie started screaming and came towards him where he held Anne in his arms. Billy folded his sister's naked corpse even closer to his own body. He looked up at his mother, hating just the sight of her.

'Don't touch her,' he warned, 'don't even try. If you do, I'll kill you.'

Later, he went to his room, locked himself in, and read Anne's letter.

Billy darling, my Tuesday man, I don't want anyone else on earth to see this, though for the life of me I cannot imagine why I care. One of my eccentric whims, I guess, but you must promise to keep it. I don't actually know why I've done what I've just done, but it's done now. I only know I do not look forward to the rest of my life as a shy, fat loony, certainly eccentric and perhaps a little mad, who plays the oboe instead of living. I can smell it coming, I have a nose for things like that. I would not write this at all except to say that I do love you, and I know that you love me, and to say that you must not feel guilty. (I know you *will* feel guilty, but truly you aren't.) I am sure Mother will do her best to turn my funeral etc. into a production number. My advice is that you let her run the show while you just sit back and enjoy the spectacle. I certainly would if I could! Don't put your foot down even if she orders fireworks, and if she tries to throw herself into the grave, give her an unobtrusive shove if you can for me! Be nice to Daddy, Billy. I still think he could have been a different man, though I probably made him up out of thin air the way you made up another Agnes. Please, please, know how much I have loved you.

Anne

PS I am enclosing a little gem I came across in the Thunder Bay paper an hour ago that strikes me as some kind of last straw. What interests me is that I identify with the poor woman. It is the rest of the people, the normal ones, who seem very odd and callous to me. I especially like the young man who heard a 'whoosh sound' and saw 'a pillar of fire hit the floor'. And I do like the idea that some friendly bystander may have actually set her ablaze. I can hear her turning to the nearest person and saying, 'Excuse me, but do you have a match? I want to set my head on fire.'

Annie

ANTI-PORNOGRAPHY PROTESTER BORROWS
MATCH TO IGNITE GAS-SOAKED HEAD

Cincinnati (AP) A woman carrying leaflets reading 'Stop Porn Now' poured a gallon of gasoline over her head in a bookstore and apparently set herself ablaze yesterday in what may have been a 'dramatic protest' against pornography, witnesses and authorities said.

Lena Mancusi, 27, of Cincinnati, suffered third degree burns over seventy per cent of her body, said a nursing supervisor at the County Medical Center, where the woman died early this morning.

'I felt a sudden blast of heat and heard a loud whooshing sound and when I turned around, she was on fire,' said Rosita Rodriguez, 23, who was standing near the woman in Lovenut's bookstore. 'I turned around just in time to see this pillar of flames hit the floor like a ton of bricks.'

Store clerks and customers attacked the human torch with fire extinguishers and tried to smother the fierce blaze with carpets, witnesses said.

Ms Mancusi told nurses she set herself on fire, but investigators have not confirmed that, said Angie de Salvo, a city fire battalion chief who responded to the call.

She said nothing and did not cry out while she was on fire, but a stack of singed handwritten leaflets saying 'Stop Porn Now' was found among assorted fireworks and gold-colored bullets that had spilled from a backpack she had been wearing, witnesses said. Several fireworks exploded and showered the store with sparks. At least two rockets hit the ceiling.

'I walked in the door and it looked like the Fourth of July,' said one witness. 'Rockets were zooming all over the joint, it was absolutely amazing.'

The city has been divided in a violent controversy over pornography, and the city council has considered several proposals to control pornography through civil rights legislation. A council member said Ms Mancusi may have been involved in recent anti-pornography demonstrations at City Hall and various bookstores.

Mitzi Manning, a clerk at Lovenut's, most of whose shelf space is reserved for adult books and magazines, says she noticed the victim enter the store. Several minutes later, Miss Manning saw the woman pour gasoline over her head at the rear end of the store. 'Of course, I didn't know it was gasoline,' she said, 'I mean who goes around setting themselves on fire?'

An unidentified customer gave the woman a match according to some witnesses, when her cigarette lighter failed to ignite. She was immediately engulfed in flames that shot several feet up in the air. 'She looked like a bazooka,' said one witness, 'then all them rockets started whizzing around.'

Police are searching for the man who may have lent Ms Mancusi a match after she had soaked herself in the gasoline.

Billy went down to the bank as soon as it opened and rented

a safety deposit box. He couldn't think of any other way to make absolutely sure that nobody got to read Anne's epitaph but himself.

Of course, Billy didn't kill his mother, though her outlandish conduct during the next few days made him realize just what Anne had meant when she had said so often that Agnes Mackenzie would be easy to kill. Anne's prophetic anticipation of her funeral didn't begin to do the actual event justice. Agnes Mackenzie seemed convinced that she really meant her fantastic charade of grief and all her histrionic sobbing and wailing. Certainly, she convinced the mysteriously large throngs of people who hung around the house for days as her audience of her sincerity. Neighbors who had never known Anne virtually moved in. Mr Popowski, the high school principal, and the music teacher, Mr Perrine, both hustled over on the first afternoon, outdoing one another in their emotional displays of grief. Grade ten students who had been in this or that class with Anne came to cry, as did a couple of dozen students who played in the school band. Not one had been a friend of Anne's. And, though neither Billy nor Anne had ever been sent to Sunday school or taken to church, and though to Billy's knowledge his parents had never been inside a church since they got married, somehow or other the Presbyterian minister got into the act and was employed to conduct the funeral service.

At about three that first afternoon, Billy locked himself into his room and got stoned. He was nearing the end of his supply, and got in touch with Rocky to ask for more. His friend showed up in fifteen minutes and got stoned with him. Lying on his bed, Billy kept hearing Anne say, 'I don't believe it!' But Billy did. It was almost six o'clock before he decided he had to go back out into the action, so Rocky Barbizan went home, having cried the only sincere tears except Billy's own.

Great developments had taken place during his absence,

which didn't appear to have been noticed by anyone. The kitchen was crammed with women preparing trays of cold cuts and pouring coffee out of a giant coffee pot he'd never seen before. As Billy neared the living room, he heard his mother's voice.

'—rine's bringing the whole school band over to the church in one of the school buses. They're coming early so they can get all set up before the service starts. They're playing 'You Light Up My Life', the song with Anne's oboe solo in it . . .' Agnes Mackenzie paused for a sob and some gasping. 'Only there'll be silence instead as a tribute.'

'Mother,' Billy interjected, all eyes turning toward him, 'why in God's name would the school band play at Anne's funeral service?'

Agnes Mackenzie stared at Billy in the archway. Her face had assumed the formality of a Greek mask of tragedy, a plaster cast face, and Billy saw that she was deliciously deep into the murky regions of inconsolable sorrow.

'What d'you mean "why"?' she asked. 'Because she was in the band, of course. Mr Perrine says all the kids in the band are breaking down, he couldn't hold a class all day long.'

'That's right, Billy,' Mr Popowski said solemnly.

Billy hadn't even looked to see who was in the room. Not only was the principal back, this time with his wife and two of his three sons, but two of Anne's teachers were there, five students, the Presbyterian minister and his wife, and three women who worked under his father at the store. The adults were all standing with styrofoam cups of coffee in their hands. The brokenhearted kids were sitting down.

'It's been a sad, sad day at Nugget High,' Mr Popowski continued in the same mournful, sing-song voice. 'A lot of the students had to get out slips and go home, and I think you can expect a big crowd of Anne's friends at the service on Thursday morning.'

Billy shut off his mind before he got sick. Twice before he

had observed such travesties, both for guys who had killed themselves in car accidents on icy highways when they were drunk. Dozens of kids had broken down completely and had been forced to miss as much as a week of classes before they could return to school. When they did show up, they had paraded their anguished faces around the halls until the first dance or party they wanted to go to lifted them abruptly out of their distress. The administration and the teachers colluded with the dissemblers in these exhibitions. Tests were cancelled and assignment due dates were postponed for the most sensitive sufferers.

'I hadn't realized Anne had so many, many friends,' Billy said, glancing around at the five students in the room, none of whom he could recall ever having heard Anne refer to by name, except Linda Beecher. And, as far as Billy knew, the only time Anne had spent with Linda Beecher had been in school. 'I guess I didn't know my sister as well as I thought I did,' he added.

He caught his mother checking out his face for signs of sarcasm.

'Anne was a quiet girl,' Mr Popowski conceded, 'but she was very well liked. I do hope the weather holds, Mrs Mackenzie, it will be touching to see the band marching in their school blazers in front of the procession to the cemetery.' Mrs Popowski nodded her assent.

Billy closed his eyes and begged God for rain.

Agnes Mackenzie started sobbing, touched by the mere idea. She interspersed her seizures with cries of 'Why? Why?' The temptation to give his mother an honest answer to her 'Why? Why?' was difficult for Billy to resist.

But the reverend had picked up his cue. He had no difficulty coming out with the answer to 'Why? Why?'

'These are mysteries known only to God, Mrs Mackenzie,' he intoned, in a preview of Thursday's oration. 'We know what we need to know, that He has taken Anne to His heart, to a house in which there are many mansions.'

It was time Billy went back into hiding. He backed up a few steps until he was out of sight, and then returned to his room and locked the door again.

Billy got through the rest of the black comedy by keeping himself delicately stoned twenty-four hours a day. He seemed to be observing every ludicrous detail through Anne's sardonic and – he no longer doubted – undeceivable eyes.

Thursday was cool and windy, but sunny, and the school band did march in their orange-trimmed blue blazers at the head of the procession to the cemetery, which was a clearing in the bush out behind the hospital. Several band members caved in as they were playing 'You Light Up My Life' and were forced to abandon their instruments and sit down. But they all recovered in time for the death march. During the ghastly silence that symbolized Anne's oboe solo, heads were bowed dutifully.

Alex Mackenzie functioned throughout the entire spectacle as the stoic, husbandly comforter. He had little choice, since his wife frequently folded at the knees and would have fallen down in the ecstasy of her grief had she not been propped up. In the church, she confined herself to noisy, tasteless sobs, but as they lowered Anne's casket into the hole in the ground at the cemetery, Agnes Mackenzie pulled out all the stops, screamed to the heavens, and fainted.

Billy was grateful she had chosen that climax because she had to be loaded into the limousine and carted away. He was able to stand beside Anne's grave until the last car had disappeared along the pot-holed gravel road toward the hospital.

Everybody was gone.

Billy waited a long time for the tears to fall, but none came. And truly, he decided at last, he was glad.

CHAPTER FOUR

Anne was buried on the last day of April. Billy returned to school the next day, although everyone expressed shock and amazement that he hadn't taken some time off. Poker-faced, Billy explained that he thought it was wiser to get right back into his routine life. The truth was that anything was preferable to the prospect of staying alone in the house with his mother, but he couldn't say that. Another more threatening truth was his fear that if he stayed away at all he would never go back. So he pitched himself into grinding out homework, he pumped gas for four hours a night and all day on Saturdays at the Texaco garage, and he spent most of the little time that was left with Poppy Richardson.

He saw very little of Rocky Barbizan, who had quit school earlier in the year after he was caught smoking a joint and drinking a can of Budweiser in a motel parking lot during a basketball team trip by Mr Cartwright, the phys ed teacher.

Mr Cartwright was a fanatic opponent of tobacco, alcohol in any form, and, above all, drugs, as were nearly all the teachers. When he saw Rocky Barbizan sneaking out the back door of the motel after one-thirty in the morning, he followed him and caught him red-handed, sitting on the gravel and leaning against the bumper of a car while smoking the joint and guzzling the beer. The coach followed his customary procedure and sent Rocky home on the next morning's bus. A letter of explanation was sent by the principal to Rocky's grandmother, who couldn't read in any language, to inform her that her grandson had been punished with the regulation punishments. These included being suspended from school for ten days, being kicked off the basketball team, and being barred from participation in all other school athletic activities. Since soccer, basketball, and track and field were Rocky's only reasons for being in school at all, he quit.

Without Rocky's knowledge, Billy begged both Mr Cartwright and Mr Popowski, the principal, to modify the punishments and make an exception for his friend's sake. He spoke as eloquently as he could of the barren lovelessness of Rocky Barbizan's life, and of how he had lived alone with his old Pope-crazy grandmother since his parents deserted him when he was seven years old. He stressed the fact that Rocky's participation in the sports he loved was his last solid connection to the social system, and pleaded with them not to sever his friend's sole remaining link to the world most people lived in.

But both men were adamant. Rules could not be broken.

Billy was so angry as he left the principal's office that he almost wished he could have informed Popowski and Cartwright that, while they were busy protecting the student body against the wickedness of Rocky Barbizan, two enterprising grade eleven boys were running their third or fourth hash oil lottery. First prize in the draw was ten grams of oil. It cost five dollars to join by signing your name to the foolscap sheets that were clandestinely circulated during and between classes. Though Billy had refused again to sign his name, and had warned the boys to be careful, it hadn't surprised him to see at least a hundred and fifty student names on the lists.

In approaching the teachers, Billy had been acting partially out of guilt. The only reason he hadn't been busted with Rocky that night was that he'd spent most of it sitting on the toilet with a severe case of diarrhea. He had pleaded with Rocky to take the suspension and stay in school, but Rocky was too proud.

'Fuck 'em,' was all he would say. 'I'm not gonna get no diploma anyways, Billy, and you know it.'

Billy did know it. After three years of high school remedial math, remedial English, and remedial science, Rocky had managed to accumulate only eight of the twenty-seven credits required for the ordinary General Level grade twelve diploma.

Without Rocky's effervescent companionship, school became an even emptier and less interesting exercise in endurance than it had been before. The game of basketball also became boring without Rocky as his teammate, and so, after two weeks of brooding, Billy both quit the team and dropped the phys ed course. He had only enrolled in it so that he could spend one period a day having fun with Rocky, he didn't need the credit.

Mr Cartwright was enraged, but concealed his fury by pretending a solicitous understanding of the misplaced loyalties of youth.

'Billy,' he said, 'I know why you're doing this, and I want you to know I admire you for it—'

'Thank you,' Billy stuck in.

'—but it's a pointless act of protest and it won't change a thing. I shouldn't be telling you this, but I'm nominating you as this year's Athlete of the Year—'

'Well, I guess you'll have to find somebody else,' Billy interrupted. 'It's no fun without Rocky.'

'Don't you feel any loyalty to the team?' Mr Cartwright inquired. 'Now that we've lost Rocky—'

'You lost him by choice.'

The rage glittered momentarily in Mr Cartwright's eyes, then vanished. 'Billy, you know as well as I do that you were Rocky's only competition on the court. Without you, the team doesn't stand a chance of even getting into the finals. And in track and field, you're my only good high jumper and distance runner. I think you owe that much to the school, don't you?'

'No,' Billy replied, 'I don't. I thought I was making a

pointless protest, sir, but you seem to be making a lot of points on my behalf.'

'If you don't feel any loyalty to the school, Billy, I've always thought you felt a certain loyalty to me. I suppose I've come to think we're pretty good friends, even though you are my student.'

Mr Cartwright was now wearing the I'm-Deeply-Disappointed-in-You look. For years Billy had been amazed that all teachers looked alike as soon as they put on one of the wide assortment of professional faces they had at their disposal for problematic situations. He had even imagined a teacher training course in Manipulative Faces and Voices. As an experienced teacher, Mr Cartwright had had countless opportunities to practice the various faces. His fusion of blighted expectations and personal sorrow was nearly perfect. Only his pursed lips betrayed his exasperated hatred.

'I'm not doing this to hurt you, Mr Cartwright,' Billy explained, 'or to hurt the team. It's just the way I feel. Anyway, I've made up my mind and that's that.'

Mr Cartwright continued to say hello to Billy whenever they passed in the corridors of the school, but Billy knew his former teacher and coach had become a dangerous enemy.

During the long weeks of grade twelve that had to be gotten through after Anne's suicide, Billy managed to keep his mind more or less away from that subject until he climbed into bed. But he slept badly when he slept at all, and often lay in the dark for hours waiting for oblivion even after he'd smoked a joint.

Night after night, memories of Anne's brutal and hopeless interpretations of the Mackenzie family as a mechanism of pain and torture reverberated through his mind. Comments which had seemed mordantly funny at the time, and which had often reduced him to tears of laughter, now struck Billy as advance warnings he should have recognized as such. He wept often as he repeated aloud to himself, 'I should have known, dear God, I should have known'.

In the mornings he frequently woke up suddenly out of unrecapturable nightmares and began sobbing into his pillow so his parents would not hear him. How? how? how? he questioned himself without mercy, how could he learn to forget her lovely face, her pretty and bewildered eyes? Billy had never revealed to Anne the incoherent fears he had about their respective futures, fears that scared him shitless. Whenever he had tried to form specific images of what was or might be coming, he would be overwhelmed by vague premonitions of impending doom. Now, one of them had been given a name, for Anne had achieved her destiny. As the weeks went by, this knowledge inflamed Billy's desire to escape at any cost the fate the past had forged especially for him.

Billy did well on his examinations, and the year ended with his acceptance of his grade twelve Honors diploma and the Outstanding Student Medal at the annual graduation exercises. Agnes Mackenzie was still playing the bereaved mother who was rising above her tragedy, but in the end she showed up at the ceremonies with his father. Despite her many declarations that she couldn't, simply couldn't possibly endure the pain of the evening, Billy had known she would never deny such a large audience the chance to revive their sympathetic emotions.

And Billy enrolled to return the following September to Nugget District High School for grade thirteen, Ontario's unique fifth year of secondary education, which still served as a prerequisite for university. He felt no desire to return, he felt no wish even to try out a university on an experimental basis. He confidently expected what they called higher education to be more of the same thing – propaganda and indoctrination. But the stored momentum of the years and the seductive logic of his impressive academic record exerted powerful influences.

Billy simply couldn't think of anything else to do with himself.

The summer was helpful, if for no other reason than that it wasn't winter. During the long and bitterly cold winters, you could often drive around town without spying a human being anywhere – it was just too damned cold. For at least six months, and possibly more, the people lived indoors and Nugget looked like a settlement on the Antarctic icecap.

Usually there were six weeks that you could call summer. Sometimes in July the sun shone in more or less cloudless skies for days on end, and, since the northern days were so long, the nights were insufferably hot when the sun finally sank below the horizon. The grass turned green, flower gardens bloomed, and the citizens voluntarily spent as much time as possible outdoors. Children rode bicycles and tricycles, skipped rope, pulled wagons, and got into fights. And every summer, on the very hot days, an enterprising few set up little cold-drink stands along Main Street. Billy and Rocky always stopped to pay a quarter for a glass of Kool-Aid, but Billy had never seen anyone else stop and had always wondered why they didn't. It seemed mean.

Motorcycles of every size and description, many of them extremely expensive, roared up and down the paved highway that served within the town limits as Main Street. It was the only paved street in the town, the rest were gravel. Young people in cars drove back and forth along the main drag from one end to the other, windows opened, radios and cassette stereos blasting heavy metal rock. Most of the more costly cars were owned by the banks and were repossessed when government invented summer job programs came to an abrupt end. Billy's favorite car that summer was an old repainted Chevy lovingly decorated with two slogans. On the hood the curlycued message was Dope Is Hope, on the lid of the trunk it was Street Is Neat.

Young men, many of whom spent the long winters pumping iron in the Weight Club, paraded their muscles and rapidly acquired suntans along the paved shoulders that functioned on Main Street as sidewalks, and drank thousands of gallons of beer in the bars to quench their thirst. They drank just as much, or more, during the winter months, but without the same excuse. Young girls showed off their golden skin in the shortest of shorts and the skimpiest tops they could find. They walked up and down the paved shoulders, usually with no destination in mind, hoping to get picked up by any of the guys who were out cruising in cars. Summer romances bloomed and withered from one week to the next. One night stands were readily available from girls who had joined the summer flesh pageant in too many Julys and failed to snag a husband. Rocky seemed to have fucked them all.

'I had that one two years ago,' he would say to Billy, or, 'I fucked those two back in grade ten. The one with the limp fucks anybody, even Indians.'

The people with children who owned summer cottages on one nearby lake or another disappeared for a couple of months, and the public beaches were jam-packed on week-ends. After the bars closed down at one in the morning, impromptu beach parties materialized on these public beaches and often lasted till dawn – if the cops didn't show up to spoil the fun.

After the sun had retreated into the west, the middle-aged and older people who were stuck in town sat out on their porches to enjoy the cooling air and summer breezes, or went for walks after the kids were in bed. Gardens were nurtured to weedless perfection and lawns were mowed far more often than necessary to make the summer seem longer than it ever was. The sunsets were glorious, and also the signal that drove people indoors because the insects took over with the darkness. But for a couple of months, give or take a week or two, Nugget actually looked alive much of the time.

Billy began seeing a lot more of Rocky Barbizan, and that too helped to cheer him up.

Rocky had gotten his pilot's license and was working for an American-owned hunting and fishing lodge that flew rich sportsmen to inaccessible lakes and out again. He had paid off his loan on the Trans Am, including the down payment he had borrowed from his grandmother. He spent his nights off drinking and doping up in one bar or another, whichever had the loudest band as far as Billy could see, and trying to get laid as often as possible. Billy accompanied him too often. He knew that because the cops began stopping him in his truck when he was returning from a visit to Poppy in Lac du Bois. Except on those nights, Billy walked.

The cops had launched an all-out crusade against impaired drivers, and the courts cooperated by handing out huge fines for first offenders, doubling those fines the second time around, and throwing three-time losers into jail. A new law had been passed that legalized police harassment of virtually anyone on the street.

Like almost all small northern towns, Nugget was policed by the local detachment of the Ontario Provincial Police, and a gang of young and ambitious recruits was brought in to terrorize the town, under the puritanical leadership of a new sergeant. It was said he had vowed to clean up the town as he claimed to have already cleaned up half a dozen others. Sergeant Brandt kept a double shift of his most zealous young cops on duty from ten o'clock in the evening until four in the morning. Never had so many police cruisers, three of them to all intents and purposes unmarked cars, patrolled with such obvious relish the mile-long stretch of a single street. Billy thought that, during the six hours of this double shift, Nugget must without any doubt be the most fanatically policed town of its size on the face of the earth. Road blocks were set up on Friday and Saturday nights. Cruisers lurked in back lanes and in the dark gravel lots of closed-down businesses.

Soon the large number of young men who spent their nights in the bars began to leave their cars at home. Those who had driven straight from work to the bar of their choice and were still there when the bar closed down walked home and came back the next day to pick up their vehicles after they had pissed the alcohol out of their blood if not out of their heads. Rocky Barbizan, a known dope dealer, was, of course, a prime target. Rocky had always hated the police, and after a few weeks of this new regime Billy understood why. Because of his long-term and very well publicized association with dope, the cops repeatedly hauled Rocky over onto the paved shoulders of Main Street and searched both his Trans Am and his body for drugs. Every time, they made him blow into the breathalyzer. And every time, Rocky was cold sober.

'They've turned the whole fuckin' town into a big fuckin' school,' Rocky complained accurately during the first week of July. 'But they ain't gonna get me, the fuckin' sons of bitches! I know every one of their tricks, I didn't go to school for nothin'!'

A couple of weeks later, Rocky's hatred had spiraled.

'Eight fuckin' times in twenty-two days they hauled me off the Goddamned road to search my car,' he complained loudly and bitterly to Billy one night in the bar of the Gold Fever motel, 'and I only had ten nights off work! Eight fuckin' times they did everything but stick a flashlight up my asshole. You wanna know what that Sergeant Brandt is? I'll tell you what he is! He's a motherfuckin' Nazi, that's what he is. The whole fuckin' town's a Goddamned concentration camp!'

Billy tried to soothe his friend's rage by rambling on about how it was the same everywhere, but Rocky was too belligerent to listen. He wanted to kill.

'Oh yeah? Oh yeah?' Rocky banged his beer bottle down on the table so hard the ashtrays bounced. 'Then how come we got more impaired convictions than Thunder Bay? How come, Billy? How come? Just how come we got more impaired than a place with fifty times more people? Fuck you, man, that's fuckin' crazy and you know it.'

Billy was rolling a joint out of Jamaican Redhair as he tried to come up with a rational answer. By the time he had lighted the joint and passed it to Rocky, he had decided there was no rational answer. It was fucking crazy.

'You know what they're doing now?' Rocky went on. 'They're charging for impaired walking! Them fuckin' cops sit out there and memorize whose cars are parked outside the bar for how long, then when they see one of the drivers start for home without his car, they nail him for impaired walking!'

Billy knew this was true, so he just sat and listened for a while to his friend's fantasy of finding a secure vantage point somewhere in the bush along the highway and picking off cops with a high-powered semi-automatic rifle. As the Jamaican grass took effect, Rocky finally cooled down.

'Fuck 'em. They won't get me. I booked a room in the motel so all I have to do is get from the front door to my room.' Rocky laughed and emptied his beer bottle. 'Hey, Billy, can they bust me for impaired sleeping?'

Because of the prevailing police clampdown and the outrageous harassment condoned by the new laws, Billy thought Rocky's comparison of their hometown to a concentration camp wasn't far off the mark. Drunkenness, impaired driving, impaired walking, and petty narcotics charges now kept the little Baptist church that served every other Monday as Nugget's courtroom packed to capacity. This scourge of injustice and punishment came and went like a traveling carnival act.

It was probably thanks to Rocky Barbizan that Billy got once again the job he had had for three summers at Universal Plywood. Buck Slade, the young foreman who had taken a liking to Billy three years earlier, was getting married the first Saturday in July. Billy went with Rocky to a couple of stags thrown for Buck. Buck lived in Lac du Bois, so Billy only saw him during the two summer months. He had to make sure Buck Slade remembered how much fun he'd had with Billy when they went drinking and got stoned together. He knew too much about stoned crushes, which seemed sacred while they lasted, to expect them to endure for ten months without reinforcement. Often, they didn't survive a few hours of sleep.

Prior to the first stag, the familiar, wistful pipe dreams circulated about importing a stripper or a prostitute from Thunder Bay for the night. But, as always, the fantasy died unrealized. Instead, the first bacchanal was staged at some guy's parents' cottage in one of the several summer colonies that lay nestled in the sheltered bays along the serpentine shores of Lac du Bois. A sauna had built out on the edge of the rocks so that you could go in one door, torture your body until your nipples seemed about to ignite, and then open the door at the other end to plunge into the icy waters of the lake.

Aside from that, the stag was the customary ritual of beer, booze, a lot of dope, a lot of loud, stoned poker, and continuous pornographic movies played through a Betamax on a huge TV set. Billy wouldn't play poker because of the amazing amounts of money you could lose – the stakes rose to dizzying heights on the wings of intoxication – and poker bored Rocky, so instead they got high on grass, drank enough beer and liquor to excite the hearts of the entire police force, and stared at the sex movies for hours.

Rocky Barbizan had seen all four of the movies before and seemed to have memorized them. He kept up a running commentary on what was going to happen next.

'Now watch this! She gives a blow-job to the President at the Inaugural dinner right under the fuckin' table! Then she does his wife with a vibrator.'

Billy had never before given sustained attention to porno movies, but that night he found himself studying them. All four were new acquisitions, products of the billion-dollar pornography boom, lavishly produced and slickly photographed in color. The stories were laughable. For one thing, everybody in the new pornography appeared to be rich. They consumed cocaine as if their supplies were inexhaustible, and moved from one mesmerizing sex act to another through settings of opulent splendor.

The underlying message to the viewer was the same as it always had been: your own life, buddy, is boring, lonely, broke, frustrating, and futile, but you can pep it up by ogling the experts getting fucked in technicolor. It was taken for granted that in real life happy sex was inconceivable, which could be true to judge from the local popularity of video sex movies. One day at school, Billy had observed a crowd of grade nine kids gathered excitedly around a magazine called *Porn Superstars* at a table in the school library. They were hypnotized by a centerfold picture of Long Dong Silver's freaky penis. Seated at the next table doing algebra, Billy had been astounded to hear several of the kids – both boys and girls – bragging about the hard-core porn movies they had watched at home. He had wondered if they watched them with mom and dad.

Recently, Billy had read with interest several articles in both the Thunder Bay and Toronto newspapers on the menace of the pornography explosion. He had learned that hard-core porn movies were the single biggest-selling video cassettes in the world. Instead of discussing why so many millions needed to watch them, the reporters listed the ways and means by which governments planned to censor porn out of existence. In the personal columns of their want ads, the same newspapers ran advertisements for XXXXX rated videotapes placed by outfits with names like Red-Hot Video.

Rocky Barbizan punched Billy's shoulder hard.

'Now watch this! She meets the biggest fuckin' nigger you ever saw, Billy-boy, and gets it up the ass on a TV talk show!'

He was right.

The movie actress heroine, who was very rich, very bored, and very famous, too, got it up the ass on a late-night TV talk show with a host that looked remarkably like the most celebrated talk show host of them all. The actress was singing to a world-wide audience while a black stud with a mouth-watering body fucked her from behind. Her facial expressions reflected not the emotions of the song she sang, but the effects of the thrusting, off-camera cock, shot in mind-riveting close-ups. After three orgasmic seizures, timed to coincide with climactic moments in the song, the viewer was given to understand that the black stud's cock was too much even for the actress to take. Her face convulsed in wild sexual alarm as the man's penis, thanks to special-effects photography, rose out of her throat and ejaculated. Semen spurted up, up, up, in slow motion, then plopped down onto the singer's shuddering body.

She got a standing ovation.

'Beat that for a cum shot, eh,' Rocky exclaimed, punching Billy's shoulder again. 'I got a hard-on like fuckin' steel, Billy. Let's go back to town and see what's going on at the Gold Fever. Maybe we can get laid.'

'Let's not, and say we did.' Billy had a hard-on, too, but it was only something that had happened to his body, not to him. He didn't feel sexual at all. The movie came to an end a few minutes later, and Billy went for another sauna and a swim in the now frigid waters of Lac du Bois. The stars looked close enough to grab if you jumped high enough. He lay floating on his back, and found the Pleiades, Orion, the North Star, and both the Big and Little Dippers. Try as he might, and Billy tried his damnedest, he could not deny that, revolting though the movie was, the TV talk show fuck was witty social criticism. That was more than you could say about any TV shows he had seen lately. Maybe people bought the stuff because it made them feel alive.

Somehow, Billy remained conscious until dawn, when

Rocky drove him home in his Trans Am. He had a colossal hangover when he came to in the late afternoon, but he didn't care. He figured the release had been good for him. He made himself a pot of killer coffee and lay in bed drinking it until supper time.

His mother had developed a collection of subtly different silences, the meanings of which had to be inferred from the looks on her face. That Saturday night she used the one that meant My-Son-Is-a-Worthless-Bum. She maintained the silence until Billy pushed himself up from the table and said he would wash the dishes and clean up the kitchen.

'No thanks,' Agnes Mackenzie said, looking through him, 'I just watched a special news report on herpes.'

CHAPTER FIVE

Billy expected the second stag, planned for exactly one week after the first, to be anticlimactic – more beer, more booze, more dope, more poker, and another hangover. Instead it turned out to be one of the more interesting nights of the summer.

It began to get interesting when Rocky Barbizan phoned him at about seven-thirty to insist that Billy should drive them to the party in his truck and to tell him to pick up his friend at the Gold Fever. Rocky *always* drove when they went places together now that he had the blue and gold Trans Am, partly to show off the car and partly because he figured he was the world's champ at outwitting cops.

An hour later, when Billy pulled off Main Street into the gravel parking lot in front of the motel, Rocky was waiting for him outside the door that led directly into the bar. At first, Billy didn't recognize his friend leaning against the fake stone wall. Rocky was duded up in black leather stovepipe pants and a black leather jacket. He paraded over to the truck and posed. Billy rolled down the window.

'Flashy,' Billy said, grinning, 'very flashy. You look good. Where's your whip?'

Rocky laughed. 'Inside my pants, Billy-boy. Hey, seriously, I don't look stupid, huh?'

Billy knew his friend's concern was genuine. 'You look terrific. Nobody'll know you're stupid.'

'Can you tell it's real leather, not that fake stuff?'

'Definitely, definitely,' Billy assured him, and at last Rocky ran around the front of the truck and hopped up onto the seat.

As soon as Billy put the truck in gear and pulled out to the edge of the gravel, Rocky flashed a small paper packet at him and did a Groucho Marx with his eyebrows.

'Cocaine, Billy-boy,' he announced, as Billy turned into the southbound lane. 'Otherwise known as Miami snow, white lightning, dust, nose candy, or the Lady herself! Tonight, you and me and Buckie Slade are gonna blow our lids off. But keep it to yourself, this is all I got left from last night. And stick to the speed limit, ninety kilometers all the way. I'll watch for the fuckin' cops.'

'Oh, I'll stick to the speed limit,' Billy assured him.

A little thrill of fear had shot through Billy as soon as he saw the packet of cocaine in Rocky's large hand. He had had many chances to try cocaine before, and always declined, but he knew he was going to try it this night. At last, he was going to find out what all the fuss, frenzy, and publicity was about.

'Where'd you get the cocaine?' he asked.

Rocky hesitated for a few seconds, then he said, 'For your ears only, Billy, I got it from Charlie Buchanan.'

'Charlie Buchanan! Is he in town?'

'Just to pick up his old lady, he's taking her on one of them big cruises. This time it's Egypt and India. He's got himself married again, and she is one fuckin' beautiful woman, too. She must be half his age, and she looks just like her name, Sugar – no kiddin', that's her real name, I asked. They'll be gone by now, they left this morning for San Francisco. What a life!'

Charlie Buchanan was Nugget's most notorious former citizen. Indeed, he was its only former citizen who had ever been heard of again. He was the second son of old Charlie Buchanan, who, after a decade of prospecting in the northern Ontario bush, had discovered in 1936 the gold that accounted for Nugget's sudden materialization in the swampy and mosquito-infested muskeg that surrounded Reed Lake. The lake was renamed Nugget Lake, after old Charlie Buchanan's corporate name, Nugget Explorations Incorporated. The mine itself was ten miles north of the town on higher, dryer land. Why any one had chosen to settle the town in the swamp remained an unsolved mystery.

Around 1950 the Buchanans got divorced. Old Charlie had started whoring around, and his wife got tired of it. Then old Charlie moved away and married again; the elder of his two sons went with him. The young Charlie chose to stay with Mrs Buchanan, who for some unfathomable reason had elected to stay on in Nugget as the town's first lady and social queen bee. As soon as she was rid of old Charlie, Mrs Buchanan spent a bundle of money on the enormous, sprawling log house her husband had built for her on a rocky point of land that jutted out into the lake off the southern shore of the narrows. Once she had had her palace renovated, furnished, and polished to perfection, Mrs Buchanan had reigned in unchallenged pride over what she regarded as her principality for twenty years or so. Now, severely crippled and deformed by arthritis, and unable to move except in her wheelchair, she had become a recluse in her pain. She was cared for by an aging Finnish couple. The woman looked after Mrs Buchanan and the housework, and her husband served as gardener and general factotum and handyman.

As a teenager, young Charlie Buchanan had been a legendary hellion, famous for wrecking expensive cars and girls' reputations. Three of his alleged children still lived in town, but none of the mothers had been able to prove Charlie was the father. He quit high school without getting a diploma, buggered around for a while, bought a plane and learned to fly it, and then took off for the United States. For a decade, he more or less disappeared, except for the two or three times a year when he returned to Nugget to visit his mother and accompany her on luxurious long cruises to exotic places.

Then, in 1973, young Charlie once again became big news, and not only in Nugget, when he was sentenced to seven years in a Federal penitentiary following his conviction on cocaine smuggling charges in Florida. The mystery was solved – Charlie Buchanan had become a big-time dope dealer, big-time in Nugget anyway. After his release from the penitentiary, Charlie had resumed his two or three annual visits to his mother, and had taken her twice around the world, as well as on numerous shorter cruises. He kept a beige Mercedes permanently in the garage at Buchanan Point, as his mother's plushy residence was known, a car he used perhaps six times a year to drive his crippled mother around the decaying town. Other than these tours, Charlie never went out during the few days he spent visiting the old lady before they were whisked away to cruise one or more of the seven seas. Charlie seemed to have no old friends he cared to look up, and all anybody ever saw of him was a brief glimpse of a smooth-looking rich man at the wheel of his expensive automobile. He remained a local legend whose only virtue seemed to be that he loved his crippled old mother. It was assumed he had money to burn, and many suspected he was still a dope magnate. As Rocky Barbizan said, what a life.

'How the hell did you meet Charlie Buchanan?' Billy asked as they were crossing the long bridge that spanned the reed-choked narrows of Nugget Lake.

'Shit,' Rocky said, 'I didn't even know who he was. He just walked into the bar at the Gold Fever about midnight last night with this chick hangin' onto his arm, looking around for a place to sit down. The joint was packed, but I was sitting alone so he asks if they can pull up a couple of chairs. I said sure, so they sat down. I figured they were American tourists. We introduced ourselves but only first names, you know? He bought me a drink and asked me what I did, and when I told him, what does he say but he just bought the lodge I work for from those two guys down in Wisconsin. He asked what they pay me, and when I told him, what the fuck does he do but double my salary on the spot—'

'He what!'

'Hang on, there's more. So he doubles my salary and I'm sitting there with my mouth hangin' open, and this Sugar chick says to him, nobody can live on that kind of money and what's he bein' so chintzy with his money for. So what does he do? He triples it!'

'He tripled your salary just like that?'

'Just like *that*! I said, man, you're the boss, and shook his hand and that's when I find out he's Charlie Buchanan.'

From the middle of the long bridge, you could see the cedar-shingled gables of the Buchanan home above the old birch trees and thick shrubbery that concealed the house itself from view. Two big, expensive motorboats were tied up to the dock, and Charlie Buchanan's Beechcraft, a new acquisition, was floating and rocking on its pontoons.

'What'd you talk about?' Billy asked. 'Or did he just bring out the cocaine?'

'We left and went over to Charlie's place, Sugar said she'd seen enough of that dump. The only reason they came is she's bored stiff, but she says she might as well be bored stiff in a soft chair at his old lady's house. On the way, Charlie stops the car halfway along the road out to the point and, Billy, that's where we snorted the coke and Charlie started talkin'. Man, has that guy been around the dope circuit! You name it, he's been there – Colombia, Bolivia, every place! He even knows the Golden Triangle, for fuck's sake, he used to fly in and out of it back before he did time. And Billy, he says he might be able to use a good pilot when he gets back from this trip with his mother.'

'Rocky, what's he want a pilot for if he isn't back in business? He's been flying his own planes for more than twenty years. He used to buzz the high school for kicks until the cops stopped him back in the fifties.'

Rocky Barbizan shrugged. 'Who knows? He was just makin' talk.'

'Making talk,' Billy said, while he gave a wave to a passing jogger he knew. 'If he makes any more, don't listen too closely. You could end up dead.'

'Fat chance.'

'Fat enough for my money,' Billy said as he stopped at the intersection of the two highways and then turned left onto Highway 11, towards Lac du Bois. 'What else did he have to say?'

'Nothin'. He just told me what it was like in the pen. He thinks the RCMP's still got the whole place bugged. Sugar wanted to dance so she put on some music, then Charlie made her turn it down so it wouldn't wake the old lady up and she got mad and went to bed.'

Billy said, 'He thinks old Mrs Buchanan's place is bugged.'

'Yeah, from one end to the other. Down at his place in Florida, he says they even got bugs hidden inside the big rocks out in his garden, no shit. He says if he cleans out the bugs, they'll figure he's back in business, so he leaves 'em there.'

They had just passed the Sleeping Beauty motel and restaurant and Rocky swung around in his seat to look back.

'Watch it, Billy, there was an OPP cruiser hiding behind the motel and here he comes, right behind us, just out of sight.'

'I saw him,' Billy said.

'Torture the bastard, slow down to seventy-five until he gives up.'

Except that it was held in some guy's basement recreation room, that night's stag was a duplication of the first, but the host's wife kept coming downstairs to tell the men to quiet down, they were waking up the kids. About eight of the guests, the younger, single men who were on the prowl for women, left around midnight to hear the band over at the White Birches bar. They promised to come back but none of them did. After their defection, the stag lost its energy and quickly wound down into boredom and weekend weariness. Rocky got Buck Slade to go out to Billy's truck and they snorted the cocaine.

Billy had read a lot about the cocaine high, mostly in paperbacks borrowed from Rocky, but the experience itself was like nothing he could have ancitipated. After that night, he understood the scenes at the end of *Scarface* that showed Al Pacino burying his face in the mound of cocaine on his big fancy desk like a pig. It might or might not be physically addictive – you couldn't trust what anybody said – but Billy decided it could sure as hell become an irresistible temptation in no time flat. He remembered reading in a newspaper that Peru had legalized cocaine toothpaste, cocaine tea, and cocaine chewing gum. He howled with laughter as he imagined millions of people packing their pockets and purses with toothpaste and toothbrushes, tea bags, and chewing gum by the pound before they left for work.

Early in the morning, as the eastern sky was just beginning to lighten and glow, Billy, Rocky, and the prospective bridegroom took off from the swiftly dying party and drove almost fifty kilometers to the public beach on the west arm of Nugget Lake. Rocky sat by choice in the back of Billy's truck with his new, portable stereo tape deck operating at full volume. About halfway to the beach, he scared the wits out of Billy by suddenly standing up stark naked and stretching out his arms to balance himself. Billy had almost floored the accelerator, but he slowed down gradually as Rocky began dancing to the music and waving his black leather jacket above his head. He was relieved when he saw in the distance the sign at the corner of the gravel road that wound south through the bush to the beach.

Just before they reached the turnoff, Buck Slade started laughing.

'Shit, Billy, that crazy bugger's dancing back there with a

hard-on, and there's a car behind us with two dames in the front seat watching him – Jesus Christ!' Buck was finishing the joint he and Billy had shared and was somewhere beyond stoned.

'Here's the beach road,' Billy said, 'maybe if we wave at them they'll follow us in.'

He flicked on his left-turn signal and slowed to make the sharp turn. They both waved like crazy but the car shot past them with a long, loud honk of its horn, and the girl who was driving gave them the finger.

At the beach they swam naked in the cold, shallow water, and then smoked a few more joints sitting on the coarse sand. After that, both Buck and Rocky fell sound asleep, immune to the cool air. Billy was still wired up and had never felt more wide awake. He sat on the beach as the cool breeze dried his skin and raised goosepimples. He watched the sky open up into the universe while the sun rose over the calm lake. He thought of Apollo, the majestic sun god who drove his mighty chariot and brought the splendor of light to the world every morning. The sunrise was beautiful. Buck Slade and Rocky Barbizan were beautiful, sprawled carelessly on the sand like sleeping gods themselves.

'I am beautiful, too,' Billy said aloud. 'And Poppy is beautiful.' Then he heard his voice saying, 'Anne was beautiful,' and tasted the salt of his own tears. He waded back into the cold water and lay down in it on the hard, rippled sand. Beauty didn't count.

'I am perfectly unnecessary on the earth,' Billy thought, 'and so is everybody else, but why must I be one of the ones who knows it? It must be so nice the other way, not knowing it. I guess that's what happiness is, thinking that you matter, that somehow you make a difference.'

Then he started to shiver, so he went back to the shore and got dressed. He waited until eight o'clock before he tried to wake up his sleeping friends. Neither wanted to be woken, so

Billy leaned over to shout into Buck Slade's ear, 'Hey, Buck! Aren't you getting married today?'
That did it.

CHAPTER SIX

The work Billy did at Universal Plywood was easy yet curiously exhausting. The labor didn't tire your body, the monotony and repetitiousness ate up your spirit. The men were in the habit of interrupting their boredom by going to the toilet, where they hid in the stalls and smoked two or three cigarettes. Quite a few of the younger men who didn't smoke tobacco doped up in the can instead.

But that summer Universal Plywood clamped down and instituted a new toilet policy. Any man who went to the toilet had to sign off the minute he left the job and sign back on when he returned.

This toilet-training regulation released a flood tide of hostility and immediately became an issue in the current contract negotiations between the union and management. Lunch breaks and after-work bar binges were filled with rebellious talk of a strike. The middle-aged men especially resented this imposition – it made them feel like they were back in school when most of them had kids who were already in high school. The company position was firm. The men had been abusing their toilet privileges and had to be punished for this abuse. The men were right, they were back in school. All the revolutionary grumbling pepped up the summer, but Billy felt sure the company would win. To him, the toilet discipline seemed a logical extension of another company policy to which the men had become inured. Records were kept of the minutes missed on the timecards of those who had punched out a few minutes early when they were going off shift. These minutes were added up, and when they totalled sixty the man was docked an hour's pay.

Basically, the men were trapped and they knew it. They hated the company but they needed it, and the company didn't need them. After five or six bottles of beer, the impulse to revolt subsided into talk of weekend fishing escapes.

The drive to and from Lac du Bois added at least another hour to the working day for those who lived in Nugget. When he did get home, Billy ate and slept and that was about all. If he was working the day shift, he usually toked up in his room after supper, and then forced himself to watch a little TV with his parents, although Agnes Mackenzie always had a caustic comment ready. 'Well, well, Alex,' she'd say, 'it looks like we're to be honored again tonight, Mr High and Mighty's here.'

Now that the Canadian government had abandoned as futile its nationalistic vendetta against the evils of US television, small northern towns got the major US networks via satellite, as well as an assortment of channels from the east coast to the west coast of Canada. Alex and Agnes Mackenzie could watch news broadcasts almost twenty-four hours a day if they cared to. They watched the six o'clock evening news at six o'clock, seven o'clock, eight o'clock, and nine o'clock. They watched the late-night news at ten o'clock, eleven o'clock, and midnight. In between, there was always a news documentary special from somewhere.

For his parents, the news of the great world seemed to function as a sort of soap opera or a mini-series that never came to an end, something to be a part of. During the past few years, they had stared with obsessive fascination at the seemingly endless chaos and terror of blood-drenched Lebanon, the gory bombings and slaughters of Belfast, the peculiarly surrealistic British hijinks in the Falkland Islands, the Russian invasion of Afghanistan, the dust-blown, body-littered streets of assorted Latin American hot spots, all terrorist bombings, murders, massacres, hijackings and kidnapings, and the dizzyingly opaque reports on the ups and downs of the world's whimsical economies. That summer, starvation in Africa seemed to Billy to be getting the most hot air time. Depending on who was doing what to whom and where, Agnes Mackenzie often made remarks to her husband that the spics, Micks, wops, nips, chinks, krauts, or niggers were at it again.

Shortly after eight o'clock, Billy would begin yawning ostentatiously so that he could get up soon and head for bed. He never got out of the room without another observation being passed by his mother. 'I guess we should be grateful, Alex, Mr High and Mighty gave us an hour and a half tonight.'

On the afternoon and night shifts, Billy virtually never saw his parents except at random meals. And as July progressed, Poppy asked him more and more frequently to stay over for supper when he was working the day shift. His mother took to calling him the Invisible Man. She sullenly resented the nights on which he went out on the town with Rocky and was bitterly hostile about the amount of time he began to spend with the Richardson family or with Poppy herself.

The evenings spent with the Richardsons were all the same. Instead of staring at TV after they had eaten supper, the Richardsons played Trivial Pursuit in deadly earnest, and whoever was there was expected to play as well. Every time it dragged on as long as a Monopoly marathon. On several of these occasions, Poppy's older brother, Jack, was there with his wife and the baby girl to whom she had at last given birth. On those nights admiring the new baby also consumed a lot of time.

Jack Richardson had never liked Billy, and Billy often turned his head unexpectedly and caught Jack studying him as if he were an object of legitimate suspicion, more than a bit on the flaky side. He assumed Jack must have heard things about him that he didn't approve of. Like his father, Jack disapproved of so many things it was hard to stay in his good books. Poppy's brother regarded himself as the family's Trivial Pursuit champ, and Billy got a cheesy satisfaction out of beating him twice. To his amazement, Jack was genuinely disturbed by these defeats.

Edgar Richardson, Poppy's father, was opposed to both alcohol and tobacco. After his first experience of waiting ten minutes for Mrs Richardson to hunt up an ashtray while Edgar lectured on the subject of non-smokers being more endangered than the smokers themselves, Billy had given up smoking in the house. He would go out to his truck to smoke, slug down a couple of beers, and get mildly stoned before the Trivial Pursuit got under way.

Ellen Richardson had caught Billy unawares one night and trapped him into going on the traditional family picnic on the first Sunday in August. They wanted Billy to come over early so they could use the back of his truck, and he was there as ordered shortly after eight o'clock in the morning.

Never had so much stuff been required for one day spent at an isolated beach.

'Jack discovered this spot when he was a kid,' Edgar Richardson informed Billy proudly, 'so we call it Jack's beach. Nobody goes there, we'll be all alone, just the family.' That seemed to include Billy.

Billy's share of the load included the Richardsons' spanking new propane gas barbecue, the Richardsons' old baby carriage, four air mattresses, four foam mattresses, six cumbersome folding wooden patio chairs, a folding table, four cases of tinned pop, two five-gallon water containers, a badminton net, and picnic hampers and cardboard boxes filled with enough food to keep them all alive for two weeks if necessary. There were also three polyethylene coolers packed with bags of ice cubes, none of which contained any beer of course. Billy had come prepared; he had a twelve-pack of Budweiser hidden under a blanket behind the driver's seat.

He soon found out why nobody else ever went to Jack's beach.

When the caravan finally got moving, Jack led the way in his station wagon – part of the tradition. He was followed by a little Toyota loaded down with Cheryl, the oldest of the Richardsons' four children, her husband, Andy, and their three kids. Mr and Mrs Richardson and Rachel, their youngest child, drove behind the Toyota and hauled the aluminium boat on its trailer. Billy brought up the rear.

Fifty kilometers east of Lac du Bois down Highway 11, Billy asked, 'Where the hell is this lake anyway?' Poppy said to be patient, they'd be turning soon.

About eight kilometers further east, the caravan turned north onto a long-abandoned logging road and proceeded to wind its way into the bush for more than thirty kilometers over the worst road Billy had ever seen even in northern Ontario, and that was saying a lot. The potholes were deep enough to stop anything but a tank, and they had to slow down first to ten, then to five or six kilometers an hour. They couldn't open the windows because swarms of monster mosquitos clustered outside the glass. When at last they arrived, the lake turned out to be no different as far as Billy could see than any one of thirty or fifty thousand others lost in the northern wilderness. Jack's beach was soggy mud and you sank in up over your ankles when you waded into the water. Fortunately the sun was high and hot – and as long as you stayed near the water, the insects were endurable.

'Jesus Christ,' Billy said to Poppy, 'it's nicer in your own back yard.'

'Do you think I don't know that? Just be nice about it and tell them how beautiful it is, and remember to call it Jack's beach.'

After they had set up all the equipment, Billy spent a fair portion of the day dreaming up excuses for going back to his truck so he could sneak a warm beer and toke up. The rest of the time he did what was expected of him. Several hours were used in preparing for the two meals and cleaning up after them. In the afternoon, Jack, Andy, and Edgar Richardson went fishing while Billy and Poppy went swimming with the kids. The oozy mud bottom of the lake turned out to be so unpleasant that Billy found a place down the shore where the water was deep enough to dive into from a high ledge of pink rock nicely heated by the sun. He was just congratulating himself that the afternoon wasn't going to be so bad after all, when a bloodcurdling scream from Rachel brought the swim to a sudden end for the kids. She had discovered two fat black bloodsuckers fastened to her inner right thigh. The other three children started screaming and plowed through the mud to the shore of Jack's beach with their arms waving wildly above their heads.

Next, Billy tried to set up the badminton net but one of the standards was broken and wouldn't stand up. The kids got cranky and bored and whiny because they had nothing to do.

Billy and Poppy started on a walk down the road, but as soon as they were out of the direct sunlight mosquitos and black flies drove them back. Then they went up to the ledge of rock to lie down on a couple of foam mattresses in the sun, but the kids followed them. A fight began between Andy's and Cheryl's two boys, and one got pushed off the ledge into the deep water. Cheryl had a fit and Billy had to dive in to bring the boy out against his will.

By the time they started on preparations for supper, it felt to Billy like ten thousand hours since the day had formally begun when he pulled his truck into the Richardson's driveway and heard Edgar Richardson hollering, in his practiced, production manager's voice, 'Okay, everybody, let's get this thing organized and load up!' But it was actually only twelve hours later before it neared its end with Edgar Richardson saying, 'Okay, everybody, time to go, so let's get organized and pack up all this stuff.'

On the long trek out to Highway 11, Billy drove too fast over the potholes. He and Poppy were bouncing on the seat and banging into the doors, but he got a good head start. He popped open a can of beer and rolled some down his throat, then handed the can to Poppy to hold for him while he lighted a cigarette. They bumped along in silence until they reached the highway and turned west toward Lac du Bois.

'I wish you liked my family,' Poppy said suddenly in a quiet voice as Billy accelerated. 'Even just a little bit.'

'I do like them,' Billy protested insincerely. 'I think they're very pleasant people.'

'Don't lie to me, Billy, I know you don't like them. They bore you to death.'

'It's not that they bore me,' Billy explained after a moment. 'It's just that they don't interest me. They never talk about anything, they don't seem to think except when we're playing Trivial Pursuit. They never read anything, either – I don't think I've ever seen any of them reading a book.'

'And you hate Jack. I can see it in your eyes, in case you think you're concealing it, so don't say you don't.'

'Let's put it this way,' Billy said grimly, 'I could dislike Jack, I could definitely dislike Jack. But while we're on the subject, Poppy, your brother's not exactly fond of me. You know what he actually said to me today after dinner? He comes to stand beside me where I'm looking out over the lake from up on the rocks, so I figure, what the hell, tell him what a pretty place it is. But Jack beats me to it and says, "You know, Billy, a lot of these types you hang around with are pretty wild characters from what I hear." They're not men or guys, please note, they're types and characters. So I ask, "Oh, what have you heard about these types, Jack?" or something like that. And Jack says, "You know what I mean, impaired driving convictions, dope smoking, hanging out in bars and picking up any slut they can find to screw for the night." I couldn't believe my ears, Poppy. What is he, some kind of fucking watchdog? It so happens I like these men I'm working with over at Universal. Some of them are very interesting men, a hell of lot more interesting than Jack is. And a lot more fun, too.'

'What did you say to him?' Poppy asked cautiously. 'Did you have a fight?'

'No, what's the point? I said, "Heavens to Betsy, I'll have to tell them you're put out with them." That was the end of the conversation. You're right, I don't like you're big brother at all. The last guy I know that got an impaired conviction is Pierre, and he'd had exactly three bottles of beer two Fridays ago after work before he went home to his family. Now he can't drive for six months. Poppy, you know what Pierre does with his days off and his vacation? He goes into the damned bush and cuts down trees and saws them up into firewood and sells it, because he can't live on the money he makes at Universal. I guess Pierre is one of the *types* your brother disapproves of.'

After another silence, Billy went on, 'You know, Poppy, I am not exactly the best candidate you could have chosen to fall in love—'

'Chosen!' Poppy cried. 'That's a funny way to—'

'No, let me finish,' Billy interrupted. 'I've been wanting to get this said for a long time. If you're waiting for me to fit in with your family, you'll be waiting a long, long time. I do find them tiresome, I have to admit it. As I said, they never *talk* about anything. I'm so sick of that Goddamned Trivial Pursuit game I feel like smashing it when they haul it out. It's worse than TV. Don't they ever just *sit*? And if they don't, why can't I just sit? Twice I've said I don't feel like playing, both times I felt like a fucking criminal. I spend half my time wishing I could just sit on my ass, smoke a cigarette, and drink a Goddamned beer without having to sneak out to my truck to do it. But don't get me wrong, I know they're very decent people. They're what are called good people. On the surface, it's a real nice family, sort of the perfect family, the kind you see gathered around the Christmas tree on the cover of the Sears Christmas catalogue.'

'You've made your point,' Poppy said. 'Do I get a turn now? Isn't it possible, Billy, that you're not the world's best judge of families? You aren't, I hope, using yours as a comparison?'

'Christ, if I was, I'd *have* to rank yours as divine! What family isn't compared to mine? On the surface, that is.'

'What do you mean, on the surface?'

'I mean on the surface. The Mackenzie family doesn't have any surface. I have an idea that my family's a very accurate blueprint of families in general. To tell you the truth, I wouldn't change my parents or my life even if I could, not even to bring Anne back. At least in my family what seems to be going on is what's really going on. It's been an educational experience, you might say. I realize I may just be prejudiced, but I've developed a very cold eye when it comes to families. If it's such a sensational invention, how come they have to sell it so hard? So far, every so-called happy family I've gotten to know has turned out to be a myth, the same damn myth every time, too.'

'They can't all be myths,' Poppy argued.

'Oh yes they can,' Billy insisted. 'I don't know what families were like back in ten thousand BC, but I can sure see what they've been converted into. What they are now is murder factories, revenge machines so all the mommies and daddies can play house and do unto others as they were done by.'

'Billy, you scare me to death when you talk like that, I can't stand it.'

'Exactly,' Billy said. 'It's not your family that's your

problem, Poppy, it's me and the way I think. I'm all wrong for you, and the thing is, I don't even want to be right for you.' He paused a moment to light another cigarette. 'What I'm trying to say is you ought to be thinking about all this.'

'I know what you're trying to say,' Poppy said irritably, 'you're saying I shouldn't be in love with you. What's the point in saying that now, Billy? I'm already in love with you.'

'You think you are, anyways.'

'Please don't tell me what I think I feel! After listening to you sound off on that subject so often, I don't like being told what I feel any more than you do.'

Poppy angrily rolled down the window, and the dark night air rushed more noisily past the speeding truck. She stared into it at the wall of trees. 'I don't want to go home now, Billy. I wish we could go someplace and be by ourselves and make love.'

'You *wish*,' Billy said, stressing the word nastily. 'But what would Mommy and Daddy and big brother Jack say? I guess we know what Jack would say, he'd say some of the *types* you're hanging around with are pretty wild characters.' His laugh was nasty too.

'I can't help it if I love my family!'

'Neither can I if I don't. Now we've started this, I should be honest. With the exception of your mother, who seems sort of stunned to me, I loathe the sight of them. You say you *wish* we could go somewhere and be alone and make love. Why can't we? Why don't we? I don't understand that, Poppy. I don't understand why you don't just say the hell with it, let's go and do what we want.'

'I wish I could say it, I wish I could be like that, but I can't.'

'I know you can't,' Billy agreed, 'that's what I mean when I say you've got a problem. I can't stop you from loving me, but I want you to know what you're . . .' Billy hesitated. He rolled down the window beside him and cool air bathed their faces.

Poppy had leaned her face forward into her hands.

'You want me to know what I'm what?'

'I'm thinking, I'm trying to figure out what to say, or how to say what I mean. I guess I mean it's going to be expensive. It's going to cost you plenty, more than anybody should have to pay for falling in love. I am different, Poppy, I know it and you know it, and different people are expensive to love. They never go on sale for half price. It's as if I were protecting something. I don't even know what I'm protecting. But I know I'd sooner die than give it up, just like Anne.'

'Don't say that,' Poppy whispered, 'you mustn't say that, Billy.' She placed a hand gently over his lips.

Billy looked at her. 'It's true. Why shouldn't I say it?'

They were back at the Richardsons' home on Pine Point Crescent. Billy backed his truck into the driveway between the high cedar hedges and turned off the engine. 'Tell me,' he asked, 'what would you do, or what would you say, if we slipped into your bedroom now and were right in the middle of a terrific fuck and your parents barged into the room and turned on the light?'

'I would just die.'

'You see – I'd tell them to get out and shut the door behind themselves.'

Billy pushed open the door and got ready to jump down to the paved driveway. Poppy yanked at his arm.

'Kiss me good night, Billy.'

'I don't want to,' Billy said. 'I'm hostile and hateful now, so it wouldn't mean a thing anyway because I wouldn't be feeling it. Besides, the production manager would probably drive up in the middle of it and shout, "Let's get organized!" I want to unload all this bloody crap and get out of here before he gets the chance.' Billy pulled his arm, but Poppy grabbed it more tightly with both hands.

'Don't run away from me.'

'I'm not running away. Jesus Christ, I presume you noticed

that we never got a chance to be alone today for five consecutive minutes!'

'We can be alone now,' Poppy pleaded. 'Please? Leave the truck for my father to unload. That's the sort of thing he's good at, he won't mind. Besides, he knows where it all goes. Let's walk down to the dock, we can be alone there. Please, Billy? It's almost dark, and I love it down by the water then. We can sit on the dock all by ourselves and talk.'

'Being alone. I must admit that sure is a luxury in this family.' Billy looked at Poppy with a knowing smirk on his lips. '*Mother*, Billy's in his truck smoking *another* cigarette and drinking *another* can of beer,' he said in a high-pitched whine. Then added, in his normal voice, 'It's a good thing she doesn't know a joint when she sees one.'

Poppy urged him softly with her voice and the pressure of her body. 'Come on, let's go, please? They'll be here any minute. Please, Billy, for me? Don't be mean.' He looked over his shoulder and she smiled at him.

'I am being mean,' Billy admitted. 'Geeeeee whillikers, do you think maybe I could dare take the three cans of beer I have left down to the dock with us? Or will they smell it from up at the house? And maybe we should leave a note on the front door so they won't send out a search party. Something short and simple like gone for a fuck.'

'Billy, you've made your point too often, and you haven't said a thing I didn't already know. I've lived with them all my life, I know what they're like. I am not my family, I'm just me. That's how you wanted me to think, and now I do. Can't you be happy with that? If you want to bring the beer, bring the beer, but let's go.'

Just as Poppy finished speaking, they saw the Richardsons' car turning the corner onto Pine Point Crescent. Billy picked up the three cans of beer that were left and they walked quickly into the darkness past the enormous garage that was attached to the house.

The Crescent was the oldest and swankiest address in Lac du Bois, and most of the big shots at Kimberley-Clark and Universal Plywood lived on the circular drive on the point. All the wide back yards ran down to the lakeshore, and every home had its own dock and boathouse at the water's edge. Great old pine trees soared toward the sky all the way down the sloping lawns to the shoreline. About half a mile out into the lake the sun was setting behind the little piles of rock called Danger Island. It was all very beautiful.

'I was being mean about your family,' Billy apologized again. 'Your mother was very nice when my sister . . . she was very kind to me when Anne died.'

Poppy held onto his right arm and walked close by his side.

'What I was little,' she said, 'we always had at least one big race out to Danger Island and back in the summertime. For years and years I came last, then, when I was thirteen, I finally won it. And later, as it was getting dark, we'd have a huge bonfire on the beach and roast weiners and marshmallows. I always burned mine to a crisp. I don't know why, but they don't seem to do that anymore. Daddy always organized it—'

'Naturally,' Billy interrupted, but except for a dig into his hip with her elbow Poppy ignored him.

'I guess he thinks some of the younger men should take over now that we're all grown up except Rachel.'

'Good old Edgar's teaching them a lesson, huh?'

They sat on the dock next to one another and Billy opened one of the Budweisers. It was warm but it was beer.

'How about me?' Poppy asked. 'May I have one? I promise I won't tell on us.'

Billy opened a can and passed it to her. 'No, but I bet you'll brush your teeth mighty fast when you get into the house. I am going to smoke a joint to see if I can unwind the mechanism.'

As he was getting a joint out of his cigarette package, the

boathouse floodlight came on and illuminated the entire dock like a stage set. Edgar Richardson's voice boomed down the long lawn from the patio. 'Are you kids down there?'

'He found us,' Billy said.

Poppy shouted back, 'Daddy, we want to be alone for a while, so would you please turn out the light before every bug on earth shows up on the dock?'

'Oh.' Edgar Richardson sounded doubtful. 'Well, okay, out she goes. It's cooling down fast.' He meant hurry up.

The floodlight went out as abruptly as it had come on. The night seemed much darker than it had before. Billy lit up the joint and took a deep drag on it.

As he exhaled he watched the sun make its dignified descent into the east. Both the lake and the sky were calm plates of gold.

'How about it, Popsy?' he asked. 'Want to get stoned with me and watch the light dying out of the day?'

Poppy had been smoking up with Billy since the night they first met, when he had tried to teach her how to inhale without coughing. She had developed her own method of taking tiny little puffs one after another. Billy passed her the joint, laughing as she went to work on it.

'I think it's so cute the way you suck on a joint,' he said. 'You go suck, suck, suck in little wee breaths as if it were a lollipop or a nipple.'

'Oh, suck, suck yourself, Billy Mackenzie,' Poppy retorted.

'I can't,' Billy said, 'and, believe it or not, I actually used to try. But I saw a guy suck himself off in a dirty movie once. He must have been a gymnast.'

'Honest to God?' Poppy took her last puff.

'Honest to God, he did. Rocky thought it was perverted but I thought it looked like fun.'

'You would.' Poppy handed the joint back to him. 'That's enough for me.'

Billy dragged the smoke in deeply and swallowed it, then

held the tail end of the joint out to Poppy.

'Go on,' he encouraged, 'one more suck before it's too late.' But Poppy shook her head no. 'I'll do it for you then,' Billy said. 'All you have to do is kiss me and go suck suck on my lips and I'll blow the smoke down your throat.'

He filled his mouth with smoke and blew it into Poppy's mouth slowly while they kissed. Then he swallowed what was left of the joint and lay back on the uneven planks of the old dock, his arms folded under his head.

'It is getting chilly,' he observed. 'It's August already. In about two minutes, I think I'll feel tolerable. How about Popsy?'

'You know perfectly well I'm stoned. I feel just dandy.' Poppy lay down beside Billy and cuddled against his body.

'I want to know how dandy.'

'Dandy, dandy, dandy,' Poppy repeated. 'You know, I love getting stoned with you. I don't even feel guilty about doing it anymore. I can't help it if it's bad.' She rested her head on Billy's chest and brushed her long hair back from her face.

'Oh, shit,' Billy said, 'damn near everything's bad that makes you feel good. I'm going to tell you a secret. I've often had this desire to get your whole family stoned and see what happens. I figure some good hash oil in spaghetti sauce would do the trick. Jesus, would I love to see them all wondering what was going on when it finally hit them.' He giggled. 'Especially Jack, oh, boy, I'd love to see Jack stoned. Ah, well, it's a good thing I've never had the guts to do it.'

'Billy,' Poppy asked suddenly, 'what were you and my father talking about while you were helping him cook up the steaks on the barbecue tonight? You both had such serious faces.'

'Can't you guess? What do we ever talk about? We talked, or I should say Edgar talked, about my future. But you must understand he doesn't mean my future, he means his past and Jack's future because Jack's future is *the* future. And of course he's thinking of your future, because he's scared to death you do love me.'

'Daddy knows I'm in love with you, Billy, they all do. I haven't made any secret of that.'

'He must be scared shitless.'

'I don't care if they're scared or not, and they know that too. Billy, I get awfully tired of the way you think I'm nothing but a Xerox duplication of the rest of my family. I do love them, and I always will. But it is no big secret to me that my father is—'

'He's a fucking tyrant,' Billy interjected.

'Now I just agree, right? Or do I get to pick my own words?'

'How about Jack? What's your word for Jackie, the golden boy?'

'Jack is a stuffy old man at twenty-five.'

Billy smiled in the darkness. 'He's a prick.'

'Jack was a prick when he was ten years old.'

'Man, do the men at the plant hate Jack. I think they hate him more than they hate your father.'

'My father does mean well, Billy, he really does.'

'Billy,' Billy intoned solemnly in a fair imitation of Edgar Richardson, 'Billy, I mean well, I really do. A lot of people talk down our little northern towns, but this is God's own country, the north. The trees have been here since time immemorial, and with our modern scientific reforestation techniques they will be here forever unless those crazy damn Russians start throwing their missiles around. The Chinese seem to have come to their senses, but the Russians have always been crazy, you never know what they'll do. I've been in trees and tree products all my life, Billy, and it's been a very good life. People will always need toilet paper, Billy, because they have to wipe their assholes every time they go for a crap. Why, at any given moment, every Goddamn second of the day, countless millions of people are unrolling hundreds, no, thousands of miles of toilet paper. And they waste it, too.

They waste it because they're scared! Billy, people are scared of shit, especially their own! They do not want to get their own shit on their fingers! Toilet paper is power, Billy, power!'

Poppy was pressing her face hard into Billy's chest to smother her laughter and beating with her fists at his head as he laughed himself.

'Stop it!' she begged. 'Stop it, you're too mean!'

'He actually said that – toilet paper is power. Then he gets onto Delsey and a sort of glow comes over his face.' Billy resumed his imitation of Edgar Richardson. 'And Delsey, Billy, Delsey is the undisputed queen of the toilet tissues, because Delsey is the *best*, the best on the market! Dear God, I'd like to have just one penny for every roll of Delsey that's been flushed down the toilets of the world! I'd be rich! And we haven't even considered Kleenex, Billy, oh-ho-ho-ho-HO! Just let your mind focus in on Kleenex. People hated blowing their noses back when they had to use handkerchiefs. All that mucus and snot drying out and getting stiff in their pockets all day long! All those germs! All those stuck-together snotrags to wash and iron by hand. Now people blow their noses out of habit whether they need to or not, and why? Because they don't have to use handkerchiefs, because they have Kleenex! Billy, let's get down to the nitty-gritty. You're going into your last year of high school, you have to make some big decisions and soon, and I want you to think, just think, about taking your degree in forestry. Just look at Jack – why, he's set for life, not a worry in the world! Billions and billions of human beings who haven't even been born yet will be wiping their assholes with Delsey and blowing their noses into Kleenex long after Jack retires. No, Billy, there is no better future than forest products. All I ask is that you give it some serious thought.'

Billy groaned.

'Honest to God, Poppy, if your father's told me once to consider a degree in forestry, he's told me a hundred times during the past year. Just look at Jack, just look at Jack, just look at Jack, just look at Jack.' He leaned up on his elbows and looked down into Poppy's eyes. 'You know what I see now whenever I do look at Jack? I see millions of assholes and noses, and Jack's wiping every one of them.'

Billy shook his head and said, 'Toilet paper is power. Shit. I wish I hadn't done that, I've fucked up my buzz.'

After a long silence, Poppy asked in a quiet voice, 'Billy, why are you so afraid to let me love you? You are, you know.'

'Why? Because it frightens me, and because I feel guilty about it. I should never have let you love me, and I know it. That's why. Poppy, I don't want Jack's future. I don't want any of the futures I'm supposed to want. I don't want another ordinary, manufactured life, I'd sooner be dead – like Anne.'

Poppy sat up and placed the palm of her hand against his cheek. 'Don't say that, darling. That's very wrong to say. Anne didn't want to die.' Poppy insisted passionately, 'She didn't, Billy, she didn't want to die.'

'Oh, yes,' Billy whispered, tears glistening in his eyes. 'Oh, yes, she did. Believe me, Poppy, Anne did mean it. I'd like to think she didn't, then I wouldn't have to feel so guilty about it. I do, you know, sometimes I feel so guilty about it I want to kill myself too. But I'm too selfish to do that. While we were driving back tonight, you warned me not to judge other families by my own, but I do, I do. I said earlier I wouldn't change my parents if I could, and I mean that, because they've given me a precious gift – they've *been* what they *are*, so I'm free to hate them, and I do. In a way, they've made my life into a story. I'm like somebody in a story, so I can do what I want and feel what I want. I *can* hate my mother and father. Nobody will ever know how much I hate them for what they did to Anne. I owe them nothing, nothing, so I can wish them dead for what they did and I don't have to feel guilty about it, not one bit. I used to fear I did feel guilty for hating them. I used to think, shit, they'll get the last laugh when they die because I'll feel guilty about that too, but not anymore. I still feel pity for them at times, but I'm getting rid of that too.'

'I don't think I understand you,' Poppy said, 'I want to, but I don't.'

'Why should you? I keep telling you, I'm different, honey. I keep warning you. That's why I'm afraid to have you love me, because I feel guilty about that. I shouldn't have let you love me. It was wrong, very wrong. But I couldn't make myself stop you because I wanted you to love me and maybe stop the hate and the pain. To tell you the truth, I don't understand how you could possibly wonder why I'm afraid to have you love me.' Billy threw himself down on his back and let go a single laugh that bounced across the tranquil lake like a skipping stone. 'This isn't fair of me,' he said, 'it's not your problem. Not yet,' he added.

Poppy removed her blouse and used it to wipe the tears from his face.

'I have one last joint,' Billy said, 'and I think I'll smoke it now if you don't mind.'

They both sat up, and Poppy said, 'You're right, it's almost cold now. I think there're a couple of old sweaters here in the boathouse for when we go sailing. I'll get them.'

'Why bother? It's time I went home anyway.'

'No, don't go, I don't want you to go yet.'

Billy lit up his last joint and smoked it while Poppy went off into the dark boathouse. She returned in a few moments with a couple of bulky sweaters and put one around Billy's shoulders. He offered her a toke but she shook her head in refusal.

'I'd be staggering,' she said.

When he had finished the joint, Billy flicked the tail end out into the dark water and lay down again. Poppy put the other sweater on and lay down too, her head resting on his stomach. He caressed her long, soft hair.

'You were so pretty that night,' he murmured, 'so pretty in

the moonlight. You looked like you were floating on the moonlight, not on the water at all. I'll never forget it. I knew you were the most beautiful girl I would ever see, and I thought I would die watching you. I really did.'

'I knew that,' Poppy said. 'I tried to look beautiful for you. You'd spent the whole afternoon and half the night showing me how beautiful your body was – everywhere I looked, there you were, posing away like mad in your Speedo, doing Mr America with your muscles.'

Billy laughed. 'I did not,' he objected.

'Oh, yes, you did. You did everything but tell me you were the best stud alive and don't you dare deny it. You're a terrible showoff. There must have been a dozen girls at the beach that day, but I knew you were zeroing in on me. But it was me who said I'd like to stay for one more swim when all the other kids were heading for home. And it was me who took off my bathing suit in the water, Billy, so I could pop up naked and take you by surprise.'

'You did, too,' he grinned. 'I have to admit it.'

'Some people might even think it was me who seduced you that night, but I promise never to reveal that fact.'

'All that was after I got you to smoke up. I deliberately persuaded you to get stoned so you'd let me make love to you. You didn't know me, what a cold, scheming bastard I can be.'

'You weren't afraid that night, were you? You didn't seem to feel guilty then, not to me anyways.'

'No, I didn't, but I should have.'

'Bullshit. You loved peeling off your Speedo while I watched. Admit it, admit it or I'll tickle you.' Poppy walked her fingers up Billy's chest toward his armpit and he rolled, giggling, out of reach.

'I admit it, I admit it.'

Poppy leaned up on her elbow and gazed into Billy's stoned, shining eyes.

'Just what is it you know, Billy Mackenzie – or think you

know – about yourself that I didn't know then and don't know now?'

'Poppy, not ten minutes ago you said you don't understand me.'

'I don't, but I want to. That's what makes you so interesting. Do you honestly imagine I *ever* thought you were the same as all the other boys in school? Do you really think I am that stupid, Billy? So just what is this fabulous secret you imagine I don't know? I've admitted I don't understand you, so that doesn't count. Once and for all time, I want to know why you think I shouldn't love you. Not, of course, that it can change anything now.'

Billy tried to think for a few minutes before he replied, but he was too stoned so he gave up. 'I just don't fit into the world the way other people do, and I can't make myself want to. I only pretend to belong to it. I pretend to think like other people. I pretend to feel like other people. Shit, Poppy, I have been pretending now for so long, so *long*, I don't even know when I'm doing it anymore most of the time. That's why I like getting stoned, so I can be myself for a little while, so I can feel unreal for a couple of hours. And maybe even happy, though I've never been sure of that.'

'Are you pretending when we make love?'

Billy was silent.

'I think I must have a right to know that much,' Poppy protested. 'Are you pretending then, while we're making love?'

'No,' he said finally, 'I think that's real.'

'You think,' Poppy repeated, 'you think that's real.'

'I guess I think those are the only real experiences I've ever had in my life. Okay?'

Poppy sat back and hugged her knees tightly and sighed. 'Now you only guess you think. I guess *I* think I'd better quit while I'm ahead, before you start wondering who I am and what my name is. Next, you'll be telling me you're always stoned when we do make love, so it doesn't count.'

Billy sat up too and looked across the lake past Danger Island to where the ends of the sky were still shimmering with pale pink and orange reminders of the sun that was beyond the horizon. The new moon had appeared from nowhere.

'Jesus,' Billy said, 'I hate these conversations about love!'

'Why?'

'Do I hate these conversations about love,' he repeated. 'You know I hate them, too. Poppy, I don't *know* things the way you seem to think I should know things, so I can never say what you want me to say.'

'I want you to say what *you* want to say, not what I want you to say!'

Billy turned his head around to stare through the darkness into Poppy's eyes.

'I do not *think* about loving you *ever*! I just love you when I say I love you. Even when I'm buying you a present as a surprise, I am not *thinking* about loving you. When I'm up in Thunder Bay, I just go and buy you the damn present. I guess I assume I love you, I haven't the faintest idea. I don't know.'

'Well, I do think about it,' Poppy said softly.

'Then stop.'

'I think about it a whole lot, and I know it's all counted for me.'

Billy saw fat teardrops sliding down across the contour of Poppy's high cheekbones as she tossed her hair back over her shoulders.

'Don't cry,' he whispered, brushing away the tears with his thumb.

'It's all counted for me,' Poppy repeated in a small, choked voice. 'And now you are all I have to care about in the whole world. You're why I get up in the mornings. If I've got you, that is. What do you guess you think about that one?'

'See what I mean about these conversations? You can't *talk* about love. I thought this was going to be a love scene, and look what it's turned into now. I still think you're the most beautiful girl I will ever see. I still want you to love me. I think I would die if you stopped. So I guess you've *got* me, if you're crazy enough or dumb enough to want me. Do you see why I hate these conversations? Because I really don't know what I'm supposed to say. Hell, I don't even know what I'm supposed to feel – what you want me to feel. When I say I love you, Poppy, I am not *thinking* I love you, I'm not thinking at all. But you talk as if I'm supposed to be *thinking* that I love you every minute of the day. I get the idea I'm supposed to feel the same way I feel when we're making love even when I'm pumping gas at Chuck's garage. But if I said that I do, I'd be lying. Or look, let's say I'm taking a piss at seven-thirty-two in the morning, right? You talk as if I'm not thinking I love Poppy while I'm pissing, then I don't really love you. If that's the way it's supposed to be, then it's not the way I am. What I do when I'm pissing is watch my piss hit the water. Period. I don't believe our love disappears as soon as we stop thinking about each other for a split second, and I think that's a weird way to think. I love you when I say I love you. I have never said I love you to you without meaning it. It has never been a lie, not once.'

'So what you're talking about is when we're making love, am I right? I mean, about my body and your body, and what I let you do to my body with your body. That is what you're talking about. Sex.'

'You left out what I let you do to my body,' Billy said, 'but yes, I guess that's what I mean.'

'But even that's just guesswork.'

'No, I mean it. I love you when we're making love. I love you most when we're fucked right out of the world. I can't help it if that's when love is realest to me. In fact, I don't want to help it – that *is* when it's real as far as I'm concerned. I also love you when I'm looking at you – at your throat – or your eyes – or your breasts – and I start to imagine our lovemaking.

Right this second, I'm looking at your lips and the edges of your teeth peeking out between them. If we weren't buried in this asshole conversation, I'd probably be kissing you by now and saying I love you. Instead we're *talking*. Personally, I think fucking's more fun.'

Poppy made a face. 'Why did you have to choose my lips? You know I've always hated my lips. They're too big and squashy.'

'I know *you* think they are,' Billy laughed. 'That's why you don't put your lipstick out to the edges of them, so they'll look smaller.'

'You aren't supposed to notice that.'

'Really? Really and truly?' he grinned. 'I noticed that before you even knew who I was – the first day I saw you in grade nine. So, does that prove I love you, I wonder? My keeping it a secret?'

Gently, Billy touched her lips with his fingertips. 'Poppy, I don't think it's wrong or strange that I should know how much I love you when we're making love, I really mean that. Then is always for me. I thought you knew that. Then is my always.'

Poppy placed her hands on either side of Billy's face and searched his eyes with her own. 'You say pretty things, Billy Mackenzie. I love you for saying that.'

'I can say it because it's true. You are my now – you are my always.'

Wordlessly, she leaned forward and kissed him.

'I love you, Poppy, I love you,' he whispered, taking her into his arms. 'I do wish we were someplace else.'

'Why? We can make love here.'

'Right here on the dock? Oh, I don't think so, honey. That floodlight could be whammed on any second, then what would we do?'

'I guess we'd tell them to turn it off again,' said Poppy with a smile.

CHAPTER SEVEN

Except for a few days, August was cool and the skies were cloudy as often as not. It rained frequently and the north winds promised that colder weather would soon be on its way. On Saturday, the eighteenth of August, Billy Mackenzie turned nineteen.

Agnes Mackenzie had once been told by a fortuneteller to beware of a dark and dangerous man who had been born under the moon of the Dog Star, Sirius. During bitching battles, she often reminded Billy that he had been born under the Dog Star's moon.

He woke up that morning from a terrifying dream at a quarter past six, after only two hours sleep. In the nightmare, he had been riding on a bus across a flat, featureless landscape. He seemed to be the only passenger, and he wasn't even sure the bus had a driver. Abruptly, the bus slowed and stopped at what was presumably some sort of crossroads in the middle of nowhere. Through the dirty window beside his seat, Billy saw an abandoned, ramshackle garage. There were no human beings in sight, and no cars or vehicles of any kind, but a large, beautiful gray dog was limping aimlessly around the gravel grounds of the service station in slow agony. One side of its sleek body had been eaten almost entirely away – the flesh was gone, the white bones were exposed. Somehow, Billy knew the dog's flesh had been torn off its body and devoured. The dog made no sound as it lurched about on the gravel, but Billy could see the pain in its enormous eyes and was overwhelmed by pity and sorrow. He wanted to help somehow, yet he did not seem able to leave his seat. Just before he wakened, he realized the dying dog was himself.

He lay there, damp with perspiration, possessed by a paralyzing dread, listening to his own breathing. Of all the dreams he had been able to remember when he woke up, this was the worst. He knew it was full of important meanings, but the dream kept its secrets. He tried to decipher its code, but he couldn't. He could almost hear heavy gates crashing down one after another, locking the meanings of the images beyond his reach.

Then, as it so often did, the memory of Anne intruded and took over his mind. On Billy's birthdays Anne had always gotten up early and come to his room to wish him a happy birthday and give him her present. She would not be coming today, she would never come again. To drive that thought away, he decided to get up and make himself a pot of coffee. Perhaps he had been thinking of that, of the fact that Anne would not be waking him up this morning, when he left Rocky the night before at the Gold Fever and drove alone to Nugget's dismal little cemetery. The graveyard was now located next to a new water tower that was under construction. Beyond it lay the wasteland of bush that stretched in all directions for hundreds of miles. He had gathered a handful of wild flowers and ferns and laid them on Anne's grave. Then he had sat down beside her and remembered her long into the night.

In the kitchen he found his mother seated at the little table drinking a cup of tea.

Billy said, 'Good morning.'

Agnes Mackenzie said, 'Wonders will never cease.'

Billy filled the automatic coffee pot he had bought for himself with water. 'What's the wonder, Mother?' he asked while he got the coffee going.

'You got up so early. You didn't get home till four o'clock in the morning.' She poured another cup of tea. 'It's Saturday so

I figured you'd be sleeping it off until it was time to clear out again.'

Billy sat down with her at the table. 'A nightmare woke me up,' he explained flatly.

She made no comment, but a minute or so later, she inquired in a studiously disinterested voice if he planned by any chance to be home for supper.

'Of course,' Billy replied.

His mother put out one cigarette and lighted the next. 'You can ask that Richardson girl for supper if you'd like. Unless I'm mistaken, it is your birthday. I could take a roast out of the freezer.'

'Poppy's not at home, Mother,' Billy reminded her, though he was sure she hadn't really forgotten. 'She's gone on a trip with her parents and Rachel, I told you about it, didn't I? They go somewhere every summer. I guess they're in California by now.'

'Oh,' said Agnes Mackenzie. 'Well, if you told me I'd forgotten. Or maybe I thought I was hearing things, you're not exactly the talkative type around here anymore – when you're here at all. I remember when I couldn't shut you up. Yap, yap, yap, you never stopped talking.'

'Anyway,' Billy said, 'it was a nice idea.' He couldn't stop himself from adding, 'You could call her Poppy, you know, that's her name. I've been going with her for two years.'

'Oh, God, I've offended the resident expert on good manners again, I beg your pardon!' His mother bowed her head in apology. The coffee pot burbled noisily into the silence.

'Mother, you know perfectly well you call her "that Richardson girl" and "what's-her-name" to irritate me on purpose.'

'I think we both know how often you bring her around here,' his mother said. 'Maybe I don't feel I know her very well. It's so long since I've seen her now I'm not dead sure I know what she looks like.'

Billy spread his hands in the air in a gesture of surrender. 'I think we also both know we're heading for a blow-up. Let's not, okay?' Billy got up and went over to the sink. He took the mug he liked from the cupboard and waited there while the coffee pot came to the explosive conclusion of its cycle. After he had filled his mug, he said, 'I could ask Rocky to have supper with us. He wants to take me out tonight to celebrate my coming of age.'

'Ummm,' his mother replied, 'I can guess how he plans to do the celebrating. At least after today you can get plastered legally. Ask him if you want to. I gave up a long time ago trying to stop you from hanging around with that dope addict bum.'

'Let's just skip the invitations. You didn't have to worry anyway, he wouldn't have come. He knows just how welcome he is here. So does Poppy. You don't exactly keep your opinions of my friends a close secret, Mother.'

'I don't open my mouth around your friends.'

'That's precisely what I mean, you don't open your mouth. You don't have to, Mother, you have a wonderfully expressive face. Now let's drop it. I'm quite happy to have my birthday supper with you and Father, by ourselves.'

Agnes Mackenzie lit another cigarette. 'I had thought of making you a birthday cake if you wanted, but I suppose you're above that now,' she said through a cloud of smoke.

Billy sat down at the table with his coffee and lit a cigarette of his own. He knew what it had cost her to bring up the idea of making him a cake. When he looked at his mother's face, he thought he caught a rare glimpse of the desolation that lay behind its usually expressionless mask. His heart was moved spontaneously by a flash of helpless pity.

'Honey—' he began, using just as spontaneously the pet name he had called her when he was a little boy, but he got no further.

'Don't call me honey,' Agnes Mackenzie ordered, staring at him with eyes suddenly gone as flat as painted cardboard. 'I'm not your honey any more, she's your honey now.'

'She?' Billy repeated. Shaking his head, he smiled and put out his cigarette in the ashtray. 'Okay, I give up. But I do think it's very thoughtful of you to want to make me a birthday cake. You still make the best chocolate cake in the world.' He poured himself another mug of coffee and walked back to his bedroom door. 'I'm going to relax and read in bed for a while. Maybe I'll be able to fall asleep for a few hours. I'm tired.'

'Well, that's no big surprise, considering what time you got home.'

'Maybe that's it, Mother, maybe it is. Or maybe it's just because I worked hard all week. If you're interested, I went out to the cemetery about midnight and spent a few hours with Anne.'

Agnes Mackenzie looked up at him sharply. 'I've asked you not to say her name, is that too much to ask? Go back to bed. I'm used to being alone.'

She got up to boil more water for another pot of tea. Billy lingered in the doorway, but his mother kept her back pointedly turned to him and waited for the water to boil.

'I can stay and talk if you want to,' Billy offered. 'I'm not leading the world's most exciting life these days, so I don't have much to say.'

'We both know it's a long, long time since you've had anything to say to me.'

'Mother, let's face facts,' Billy said quietly, 'none of us has been much inclined to talk since Anne died because you won't even let us mention her name. You complain because I don't talk, but that's what I think about most of the time, so what can I do about it? I'm not interested in talking about Nicaragua, or Lebanon, or that crazy asshole that runs Iran, or how the French are taking over Canada – I don't give a shit about that crap. I am full of sorrow, Mother, sorrow. I am so full of sorrow it feels like a heavy stone in my chest, I cry every night—'

Agnes Mackenzie turned to confront him as she interrupted. 'I don't think about it, of course, I don't cry.'

'I'm sure you do,' Billy said gently. Tears dripped down his face. 'I'm sure you do. All I'm saying is that if I can't talk about Anne, I have nothing right now to talk about. Frankly, I think you're right, I think it's wiser if we don't talk about Anne – we can't change what she did by talking about it. We'll each just have to learn to accept it in our own way, we can never know what went on in her mind.'

'She did it to hurt me,' whispered Agnes Mackenzie, 'that's why she did it. She always hated me.'

'That isn't true, Mother. It was herself she killed – you might keep that in mind.' Billy was filled with rage by the ghastly selfishness of what she'd said. He knew he should get out of the kitchen before he let go. He should get out fast, very fast.

His mother's eyes shone like shellac, hard and unbreakable. 'I know what I know,' she said cryptically, the words falling from her lips like stones.

Get out, get out, the voice in his head shouted, but it was too late. 'What is it you think you know, Mother? What is it? What is it?' His voice was shaking.

'I know what I know,' Agnes Mackenzie repeated, her eyes not meeting his. 'She hated me and now you hate me. Go and read your books and leave me alone. I like to be alone, it's better that way.'

Before he could say whatever was coming next, Billy stepped down into his room and shut the door. He shot home the bolt and leaned against the door, breathing hard and fast. In the kitchen he could hear his mother making the tea and a few minutes later the TV in the living room came blasting on. He threw himself onto his bed and lay there panting, waiting for the fury in his soul to burn itself out.

Eventually he must have fallen asleep despite the continuous noise of the television, because the next thing he knew it was twelve-thirty and Rocky Barbizan was banging on the door that opened directly from Billy's room into the small back yard. His room was hot, airless, stifling. It felt like a tomb. He opened the door for Rocky and pushed the outer storm door back against the wall of the shed-like back porch that had been converted into his bedroom when the Mackenzies moved into the house fifteen years earlier. He blocked it open with a rock he kept on the top step for just that purpose. Beyond the back lane lay one of the several empty lots that fronted on Main Street and were littered with disintegrating, rusted-out cars, trucks and other vehicles. Two ancient school buses and the rusty hulk of a small mobile home had been rotting into the muskeg in this particular dumping ground for as long as Billy could remember. The rest of the lot was packed with cars and trucks in various stages of ruin and decay.

Rocky Barbizan had walked into Billy's bedroom and seated himself on the end of his bed. 'It's a good thing I woke you up, Billy-boy, it's like a fucking inferno in here. You could suffocate to death.'

'It was cold last night.'

'It ain't exactly warm out now but at least that fuckin' rain went away. Come on, get some clothes on, birthday boy, I came to give you a birthday-present you'll never forget. I been waiting a long time for this, let's go!'

'For Christ's sake, Rocky,' Billy protested, 'I'm not even awake yet. Gimme a few minutes will you?' He went and sat on his bed, bunched up his pillows so he could lean against them, and lit a cigarette. The mug of coffee he had brought in with him hours earlier was sitting on the box that served as a bedside table. The coffee was cold but he drank it anyway.

Rocky looked at him thoughtfully. 'You look like hell, what's wrong?'

'Nothing. I told you, I'm just waking up. After I finish this coffee I'll take a shower.'

'Where's Medusa and creeping Jesus?' Rocky had picked up the nicknames from Anne. Billy could remember the night she had explained to Rocky who Medusa was and how she had had the power to turn men to stone with her stare.

Rocky had been fond of Anne and kind to her always. A few times he had taken her to the movies while Billy was pumping gas and out to a restaurant for coffee after the show was over; they were the only dates Anne had ever had. Once, after a lot of cunning persuasion, he had even managed to get Anne to go to a school dance with him. If there had ever been any chance of Billy's feelings for Rocky Barbizan fading out with time, that danger had been extinguished forever by those actions. Rocky's sweetness to Anne had deepened Billy's affection for his friend into a love that nothing could destroy. Billy Mackenzie knew that for Rocky Barbizan he would give up his life without a second thought. Thinking about all this brought tears to his eyes again.

'Aw, Billy, don't start bawling today,' Rocky said softly. 'Can't you be happy just for today? It's your fuckin' birthday, for God's sake, I wanna show you a good time.'

Billy wiped his eyes. 'Just ignore it, I'll be okay in a few minutes.'

'You shouldn't've gone out to that creepy cemetery alone like that. That's what you did, isn't it?'

Billy nodded. 'How'd you know I went there?'

'I don't know how I knew, I just knew. Why didn't you ask me to go with you instead of just disappearing? You know I'd'a gone along.'

Billy smiled. 'I know, Rocky, I know. I wanted to go by myself, I guess. I'll go take that shower now.'

Ten minutes later he was back in his room with Rocky, dressed and ready to go. 'Okay,' he said, back to his normal self. 'I'm ready. Now just what is this present I'll never be able to forget?'

'You'll find out,' was all Rocky would say as they walked out to his car, parked in the narrow back lane.

He drove south along the lane to Macklen Street and turned left past the dilapidated shack that had been decomposing into the weeds on that corner since before the Mackenzies moved into their bungalow. Sticking up out of the tall weeds and young trees that had sprung up from the gravel was a For Sale sign so old the words had faded into a blur. Nugget was disfigured with dozens of places just like this, collapsing ruins abandoned in the fifties and sixties after the gold mines were shut down. Many others in much the same condition were still inhabited by old people who had stayed behind to die and hadn't yet managed to do so. Every once in a while, one of them was actually sold to a young couple with grandiose plans for wholesale renovations that usually petered out into paint jobs and new panes of glass in the broken windows.

Rocky pulled up at the corner to wait for a break in the stream of Saturday traffic that was rolling north and south on Main Street. While they waited, Rocky shoved a tape of Bruce Springsteen into the slot and turned it up loud. Springsteen was Billy's favorite singer; he felt he was one of the few songwriters who talked about the real world.

Ironically, the tape had taken off toward the end of 'Darlington County'. Bruce Springsteen was singing about seeing his friend, Wayne, 'handcuffed to the bumper of a state trooper's Ford' as Billy and Rocky stared through the steady traffic at the solid brick bulk of the Ontario Provincial Police building. It was one of the few buildings in town, excluding a few dozen recently constructed private homes, that had been made to endure. The other structures in Nugget that, as a little boy, Billy had classified as *real* buildings were the post office, the three schools, the district hospital, and the government strongholds from which laws were administered.

In a nutshell, the real buildings were those into which people were put whether they wanted to be put there or not, or buildings that served as centers of surveillance, control, and coercion. Like every other OPP station Billy had seen in northern Ontario bush towns, this one had a token front lawn bordered by rows of petunias and marigolds. He couldn't imagine who they thought they were kidding. He personally knew several young men who had been viciously beaten with fists and truncheons somewhere inside those brick walls – so much for the petunias and marigolds.

Rocky became impatient while Springsteen started singing 'Working on the Highway' and whipped into a right turn that forced the driver of a half-ton truck to slam on his brakes. A long honk of his horn was followed by two shorter blasts. 'Go fuck yourself, buddy!' Rocky yelled as they headed south toward Highway 11.

The traffic was slow. They passed the Fleur de Lis restaurant, which stood opposite the OPP headquarters in its own little island of gravel and dust. They passed another of the empty lots in which old cars and trucks were decaying into the swampy weeds and bush-choked depths like prehistoric beasts. They passed several of the derelict shanties that looked as if they'd been dropped into the dense bush around them from outer space. They passed two once-prosperous garages that had gone out of business during the most recent phase of the depression; both had a few unsold secondhand vehicles stranded in their gravel wastelands, mementoes of the town's heyday. Then came a succession of large new homes whose owners had filled up their sixty-six feet of swampland with hundreds of tons of gravel to prevent their kids from drowning in the basements. The houses were perched about three feet above street level as if on a series of stages. After the last of these homes, another long strip of primeval bog waited under the low, gray clouds. In the middle of it sat an old school bus, almost hidden from view by the bush. Its glassless windows stared out at the street from the undergrowth like the hollow eyes of an angry skull. Next to that, someone a long time back had set a jumbo house trailer up on pedestals of cement blocks. The pedestals that had once supported the front end of the trailer had sunk under its weight into the quagmire and buckled, and the whole front end had lain smashed to the ground ever since. According to two faded signs, the place was still both for sale and for rent.

Across the street from the trailer home that had taken a nose dive, the Gold Fever Motel was still thriving, despite the fact that except for a fancy new neon sign it looked ripe for demolition. Directly next to the Gold Fever was Billy's favorite of all the old hovels in Nugget. It was a tiny box of a house that had a huge hole in its front wall as if a bomb had been exploded inside it. The hole had in fact been put there only a few years back by a drunk driver intent on out-racing the cops. His truck had flown at sixty or seventy miles an hour off the ice-covered roadway, still unpaved in those days, and plowed through the flimsy wall into the living room. The old couple who had expected to finish off their lives in the little house had been moved into the Senior Citizens' complex to die. For reasons Billy could not even guess at, nothing had been done about the damage, and every winter for the past four years the living room was hip-deep in drifted snow.

About two hundred yards farther south they passed the Princess Hotel, presently the most popular of Nugget's three bars. Originally a miner's hotel, the old two-story structure had been bought two years earlier by a flamboyant young Frenchman from Quebec. His name was Jacques but everyone called him Jocko. Jocko had done a superficial renovation job on the Princess and converted its first floor into one enormous room. He turned a judiciously blind eye to a lot of underage drinking and to indiscriminate dope smoking, and he provided live entertainment by touring rock groups.

Naturally, Jocko had been doing a sensational business ever since he opened the joint. All the bands, even those whose young musicians seemed to have some talent, used the same apparently sure-fire techniques to bludgeon the audiences into submission and occasionally even token applause. They flashed colored spotlights on and off in repetitive patterns, dressed like thugs of one kind or another, tried to look like coldblooded killers, and used enough amplification to wake the dead. From about nine o'clock to one o'clock in the morning, you could hear the monotonous thudding of the top forty for blocks in every direction.

Inevitably, the Gold Fever had been compelled to adopt the same policies in order to stay in business, and the competition between the two bars had become open warfare. Conversation in either bar was impossible while the bands played their sets, so everybody sat, drank, and smoked or got stoned while they stared through the haze at the entertainment that was being pumped at them through walls of stacked amplifiers that were often eight feet high. In between songs whose lyrics might have been written in Swahili for all anyone knew, the singers, usually female, shouted things like 'Save me some of that shit, man!' That week the group at the Gold Fever was called Pimples. All the groups got progressively louder as the night passed, and by the time Billy had left the previous evening the noise Pimples was manufacturing had been excruciating. Tonight, for his birthday, Rocky was taking Billy to the Princess to hear a group called Switchblade.

As they left the Princess behind them he shouted at Billy over Springsteen's music, 'That Switchblade is one fuckin' fantastic band, Billy-boy, you'll love 'em.'

'Will I be able to hear them?' Billy shouted back.

'You better believe it, man, they got the biggest Goddamn amplifiers you ever saw. They got a record deal comin' up soon in Toronto. I was talkin' to the singer on Tuesday night, she's got tits like fuckin' volcanoes.'

If Rocky was right about the amplifiers, Billy thought as they crossed the bridge that spanned the narrows, maybe Switchblade would be the group that would literally bring down the house.

As soon as they had crossed the bridge, Rocky slowed and put on his left-turn signal. A moment later he turned onto the narrow road that wound along the south shore of the lake through the bush toward Buchanan Point.

Billy turned down the volume of the music. 'Where the hell are we going?' he asked.

'Up, up, in the air,' Rocky grinned. 'I'm takin' you for a little spin in Charlie's Beechcraft.'

Billy was stunned. 'In Charlie Buchanan's plane? How in hell can you do that?'

'Don't worry, I'm not stealin' it. Charlie knows all about it.'

'You mean Charlie Buchanan said you could use his plane?'

'Any time I want till he gets back with his old lady. I already took her up a few times so I'd be ready to take you up today, and I'm tellin' you – this is one beautiful fuckin' airplane.' He brought his car to a stop outside the locked gate in the stone fence that ran around the Buchanan property from the narrows at one end to the open lake at the other.

'Rocky,' Billy said, 'what's going on? I don't understand why Charlie Buchanan would give you his plane to use.'

Rocky Barbizan smiled at Billy as he opened the car door. 'What can I say, Billy-boy? People take a likin' to me once in a while, can I help it? Come on, let's get goin'. Didn't I tell you I was gonna make this one birthday you'll never forget?'

The flight with Rocky in Charlie Buchanan's plane was Billy's first experience in the air. It was interesting and fun, but he had been told he was supposed to find it the thrill of a lifetime so he pumped out as much enthusiasm as he could dig up. They were in the air for almost two and a half hours, flying in a wide, generally circular route over all the lonesome little bush towns of which Nugget was the hub. They flew east to swoop down low over Lac du Bois, north to swing over the even smaller railroad town of Banner, which for years the Canadian National Railway had been effectively threatening to close down but never did, west as far as the old, tiny settlement of Kanoka on Highway 11, and then did a close inspection of Kanoka Lake Lodge, where Rocky was employed as a pilot. After that was over, they flew back to Nugget following the twists and turns of the highway.

Actually, Billy didn't have to say much because Rocky talked incessantly, as he always did. He explained the intricacies of the instrument panel, and gave Billy an exhaustive account of the plane's specifications and a quick lesson on the basics of how to fly a small plane. Billy didn't listen attentively to the flood of statistics and instructions his friend poured forth, but he did appreciate that Buchanan's plane was a beautifully made machine. It was worth a small fortune and looked it, even to someone as uninitiated as Billy.

The experience of seeing what the place he'd spent his entire life in looked like from thousands of feet in the air was Billy's chief source of pleasure. It looked like what it was – bush and rock from horizon to horizon and beyond in every direction. The vast and forbidding wilderness was punctuated by small chains of frigid-looking lakes and crisscrossed by logging roads, many now out of use for the time being, which wound into the bush camps from the main arteries that linked the towns together. In grade eleven Billy had plowed his way through a grueling two months of local geography; gazing down at it from the plane was rather like looking at a huge blow-up of all the maps he had been compelled to memorize.

Most intriguing of all, though, was flying over the town of Nugget itself. He was struck with the impression that from high in the air it looked solid and purposeful, ordained to be what it was and where it was. What you saw from the sky was an orderly gridwork of streets lined with houses. When you were down on the ground and living in the town, Nugget felt temporary and insecure, like an accident or a mistake, something that shouldn't be there any more and would eventually be disposed of. For that matter, all the little towns possessed an appearance of necessity from up in the sky; they seemed more real. They also looked cleaner and neater, not at all like the shabby, thrown-together dumping grounds they were, oppressed by the resignation, unemployment, and debt-haunted anxiety of the settled family people and seething with the frustrations and boredoms of the young. From up there, you might wonder why the alcohol consumption rate in northern Ontario towns was forty per cent higher than the rest of the country's. You didn't wonder when you were putting in the days in Nugget with your feet planted on the ground and your eyes wide open.

On the drive back into town, as they rolled past the assortment of abandoned, boarded-up buildings that lay rotting into the swamp directly north of the bridge, Billy knew he had come down to earth.

As was usually the case now, supper with his parents was uneventful, but Anne's absence from her side of the small table still persisted. It was like eating with a ghost who didn't need a plate. After Billy blew out the nineteen candles, they ate the chocolate birthday cake Agnes Mackenzie had made. Billy ate twice as much as he wanted and raved about it. His parents gave him a shirt and sweater, and he tried them on at once to show his appreciation. Then he insisted on cleaning up the mess and washing the dishes while his mother drank tea and smoked cigarettes and his father read bits and pieces to her aloud from Friday's *Toronto Globe and Mail*, a ritual that had been going on for years. That night he read of the most recent complications in El Salvador, of the impossibility of predicting the economic future except to warn that it was likely to be unstable, and page after page of political speculations about the upcoming federal election. By the time

Billy had washed the dishes and tidied up, they were ready to move into the living room to watch an hour of TV reportage on the election campaigns and a news broadcast from Vancouver.

At eight-forty-five Billy announced that he had arranged to pick up Rocky at nine o'clock and got up to go. After thanking his mother again for a lovely meal and for his new shirt and sweater, he said he was looking forward to eating another big slice of cake when he got home.

Agnes Mackenzie looked up at him with that same empty expression on her face. 'Well, it's been nice to see you again,' she said. 'Stay longer the next time.' Billy pretended not to hear her as he left the room.

Once he was at Rocky's, they smoked a couple of joints in Rocky's bedroom and drank a few bottles of beer. After they were stoned, Rocky said, 'How's that for a California gold rush, Billy-boy? That's the best damn grass we've had for a long time.' Then he gave Billy an ounce of the California pot as a birthday present. Billy protested, but Rocky insisted and stuffed the plastic bag into the pocket of his jacket.

They talked about De Lorean's acquittal, and Rocky showed Billy an article he had torn out of the Saturday *Times-News* from Thunder Bay. It was headlined 'John De Lorean Is One Hot Item', and reported that the glamorous De Lorean was indeed 'beseiged by offers for films and books on his life', and that the very recently born-again Christian intended to devote the rest of his life to spreading the Gospel. Billy got a good laugh out of that, and Rocky reminded him that he had predicted De Lorean would make a new fortune out of his cocaine adventures.

Rocky had yet another article to show Billy, one bearing the headline 'Tropical Tree Blossoms Sensuality'. It was about the discovery of a chemical called yohimbine that was derived from the bark of some African tree. After two years of testing, yohimbine had produced what the California researchers referred to as 'a bunch of sex-crazed rats'. They were now ready to test the new chemical on human beings, and the program's director was quoted as saying, 'Not surprisingly, we have an ample number of volunteers'.

'They'll make the fuckin' stuff fuckin' illegal,' Rocky predicted. 'Billy, if we could bust into that lab and steal the fuckin' formula we'd be fuckin' millionaires overnight!'

They were both high by the time they left for the Princess, where they spent the rest of the night watching and listening to Switchblade do their thing. Their thing was noise and plenty of it, so the Princess was packed. Billy and Rocky ended up sitting with the same bunch of young, single dope-smokers they always ended up with. Everybody was either getting drunk or was drunk already, and the dopers were all stoned; so the big crowd seemed to be having a whale of a time. At about eleven-thirty they started dancing on the miniature dance floor. Since the men outnumbered the women by at least two to one, there was no woman who wasn't dancing, except the one who couldn't stand up. Rocky was busy hustling Annette, one of the young waitresses. She was new in town and married to a truck driver she couldn't stand the sight of. Her husband looked congenitally sour and crabby and spent almost as many nights in the Princess as Annette did so he could keep a jealous eye on her. They had two kids who, as far as Billy could determine, seldom saw either of their parents. Whenever Annette served their table, she stood at Rocky's elbow and his hand played over her ass and up and down her thighs with explicit expertise, so Billy guessed her husband had good reason to be jealous.

Joints were openly being passed around the table but Billy just passed them on. When Switchblade finally took a break, Rocky slipped out one of the joints he had tucked into his cigarette package and said, 'Billy-boy, it's time you smoked with me, you're losin' your buzz, I can tell. You started thinkin' already.'

'Okay, okay,' Billy agreed, 'but only in the can.'

'Who the hell cares? Who's watchin'?'

'Everybody's watching, Rocky, everybody's watching every minute. You ought to know that by now. Let's go, I need a piss anyways.' He got up, slipping on his jacket so nobody could steal the bag of dope Rocky had given him, and headed for the men's toilet.

Behind him Rocky shouted, 'You're not the man you used to be, Billy,' but he followed him nonetheless.

The men's john had not been renovated and looked and stank like what it was, a cramped corner hole containing two toilet stalls, three cracked and stained urinals, a filthy ancient sink that sagged from the wall, and forty years of urine soaked into its rotten wood floor. Billy unzipped his fly and stood at one of the urinals between two other guys. Rocky burst through the door, saying, 'Now I gotta piss too, I think it's the stink in here.' He stood at the urinal next to Billy's as soon as it was vacant, lit up a joint before unzipping his fly, took a couple of deep drags, and passed it to Billy. Billy zipped up his fly and went to lean against the drooping sink in the corner. The California dope was fast-working and by the time they had finished it both of them were feeling the effects. Billy had started thinking about Poppy. He missed seeing her already, and the Richardsons did not plan to be back from their trip to Mexico until the end of August.

Rocky draped his arms across Billy's shoulders and leaned his forehead on Billy's forehead. His blue eyes blazed.

'That's good stuff,' Billy said. He could feel himself beginning to relax at last, as if his mind were a gigantic ship secured to a wharf by thick ropes and the ropes were coming undone one by one – soon he would be sailing on an ocean as blue as Rocky's eyes. 'Where'd you get it?'

'I didn't. Kazdan made a big buy in Toronto last week. He brought back three pounds and got scared with so much on his hands so I bought half of it.'

Kazdan was a young doctor who had come to Nugget four years earlier from Toronto, straight out of medical school, and had quickly become notorious because of his frequent indiscreet references to the medicinal virtues and recreational joys of marijuana. He soon learned to keep his mouth shut except in congenial company, but by then his reputation as a crusading dopehead had invested David Kazdan with the charisma of scandal.

The noise of the music had started again and Rocky said, 'Let's go drink some beer.'

Billy was stoned but good, and the next time he looked at his watch it was a quarter to one. He had been drinking steadily, anything Rocky had been buying, and somehow more than an hour had disappeared. He wanted to go home to bed, but he stuck it out for Rocky until about one-fifteen, when they began kicking out the ones who didn't want the night to end. He and Rocky staggered out with the bunch that left by the rear door. There were quite a few guys lounging about and looking for rides in the gravel parking lot behind the motel. A vicious fight had broken out between two young men, and one of them was banging his opponent's head against the hood of a parked truck. Rocky lit up his last joint and he and Billy smoked it just outside the door under the bright floodlight that shone above the exit.

'This is fuckin' just crazy, Rocky,' Billy said, but he was too far gone to even act on this knowledge and move out of the light into the dark. Then, suddenly, two cruisers whipped into the parking lot out of the deep dark of the back lane. Luckily the fight was still in progress and drew the attention of all four OPP constables, who leaped energetically from the cruisers. This gave the hangers-around a chance to disappear quickly and silently in all directions. Billy and Rocky ended up out on the corner of Main Street under a street light. A crowd of about twenty young men and a few girls were talking loudly in between the cars and trucks that were still parked in front of the Princess. There was going to be a party someplace; there nearly always was on Friday and Saturday nights. Naturally, Rocky wanted to go to it. Usually Billy went along, but this night he meant to stick to his guns and go home despite Rocky's considerable persuasive powers. He failed.

'Just wait one fuckin' minute, will you,' Rocky said loudly, holding tenaciously onto Billy's arm. 'We've had a good time today, right?'

'Right,' Billy repeated, 'but I still wanna go home.'

'You're fuckin' right we did!' Rocky declared belligerently. 'You can't just fuckin' go home on me now.'

'Rocky, I'm tired, it's past one-thirty, it's cold, and it's a long walk, so why can't I go home? I'm also stoned and I'm drunk, I'll be lucky if I get there.'

Rocky yanked Billy toward him by pulling on his jacket, and pinned his eyes on Billy's. 'You don't love me no more.'

'I do so love you.'

'Not really, you don't love me really.'

'I love you, I love you, for Christ's sake, what d'you want me to do, kiss you under the Goddamn street light?'

'You really really love me?'

'You know I do, Rocky.'

'But will you always love me? I wanna know, I just wanna know.'

'I'll always love you,' Billy promised.

Rocky smiled at him and pulled him even closer so he could whisper, but it was a loud whisper. 'That's why you can't go home, because you're the only fuckin' human being that loves me and the only one I love back. I love you, Billy, I don't have no fun except with you because I love you and you're the only person I trust on the whole fuckin' earth, on the whole earth, Billy-boy.' Rocky jabbed Billy's chest with his finger to emphasize his point. 'I don't give a fuck for anybody else.'

'You love your grandmother and she loves you.'

'Fuck she does. You know who she loves, she loves that

fuckin' Polack Pope that's comin' over here next month.' Rocky giggled and stumbled into Billy. 'She's been babblin' about that fuckin' Pope ever since she found out he's comin', Billy. She's goin' with that busload of old assholes to Toronto so she can see him. I told her a thousand fuckin' times she won't see nothin' but a guy ridin' inside a plastic bubble, but she thinks, she *thinks* she's gonna get to kiss his magic fuckin' ring.'

'Rocky, are you going to pass out?'

'I never passed out in my life,' Rocky said proudly, 'not once, never.'

Billy tried to step back but his friend hauled him closer still.

'You know why I love you, Billy? I was always dumb in school, and you was always smart, but I ain't so dumb I don't know I was dumb and that means I'm not so fuckin' dumb, don't it? I know my life don't add up to a pile of fuckin' dog shit and it never will, but you got brains, Billy, you got brains and you're *my* friend. You'll never know what it meant to me to have the smartest fuckin' bastard in the school as my best buddy. Everyone of those cocksucker teachers knew you picked me, Billy, they knew *you* picked *me*, and I loved you for that, Billy, I just fuckin' loved you for that! They couldn't figure it, I could see it in their faces, and every time I saw it I loved you more.' There were tears in Rocky's eyes, the first Billy had ever seen, and he could hear his own heart pounding. Rocky stood back then and beamed at him. 'I never told you before, did I? I never told anybody else that I love them, 'cause there ain't nobody else. That's why you can't go home. Because I don't want you to.'

'I won't go home, Rocky,' Billy said, 'but let's get out from under this fucking street light before we get picked up.'

'Besides,' Rocky said, 'look what I got, the coop da grass, I saved it for you and me.' Out of his jeans pocket he pulled a small amount of cocaine carefully folded into Saran Wrap and held it up before Billy's eyes.

'Jesus fuckin' Christ, Rocky,' Billy hissed, 'put it back in your pocket! There's cops all over the fuckin' street! Come on, come on!' He hurried into the darkness of the side street in the direction of Rocky's grandmother's house without looking back.

Behind him Rocky grumbled, 'Fuck the fuckin' cops.'

Billy glanced over his shoulder and saw that his friend was following him. 'You fuck the cops if you want to, Rocky,' he called back.

They were halfway down the block when the headlights of a cruiser came round the corner of First Street East and crawled slowly toward them. 'Just look sober and keep walking,' Billy said softly under the crunching of their feet on the gravel. The cruiser passed them by but it seemed to take forever. Not until they had reached the corner and were starting south on First Street East did Billy look back; the cruiser was pulling out onto Main Street.

He let out a sigh. 'You know, Rocky, I fuckin' hate it when you talk about my brains, but I did try to teach you one thing. You do not *ever* get to fuck the cops, not ever! They fuck you, Rocky, they fuck you! If you could just learn that, you might get to the end of your life.'

'Who wants to, Billy-boy, who wants to? Are we goin' to my place?'

'We sure as hell are, I want to get off the streets.'

At its southern end, First Street East dribbled off into the bush. Three very short streets opened onto First Street East before it ceased to exist and stretched about a block into the bush; Rocky's grandmother's shack was the last house on the third street. Behind and beyond it there was nothing but bush and swamp, through which paths led to the reed and bulrush-choked shore of Nugget Lake. They went in by the back door, staggering through the little kitchen in the dark to Rocky's bedroom. On the way, Rocky picked up half a dozen cold beers from the refrigerator he had bought his grandmother for

Christmas. Billy sank onto the waterbed Rocky had bought for himself only recently, and listened to it gurgle as it undulated beneath his body. The cool night air, the fear of being picked up and jailed, and the exercise of walking had somewhat cleared his mind. He had already decided he was staying for the night. Rocky opened two beers and gave one to Billy, then put a new Rod Stewart cassette into his elaborate sound system and turned it up loud. The old lady was deaf.

'For God's sake,' Billy exclaimed. 'I'm tired of shouting.'

'Okay, okay, okay, okay, okay.' Rocky turned down the volume, then he got down on his knees and set about the business of forming the cocaine into four lines on a corner of the table beside his bed. Billy drank his beer and watched.

'Where'd you get it this time?' he asked, but Rocky was too absorbed to reply.

When the lines were ready, Rocky got two tiny straws from a pile he had saved from many nights in the bars and gave one to Billy. The rush was electrifying. Billy felt glorious as he fell back on the bed. Rocky crossed his legs beneath his body on the floor, which made him look like a delirious guru. 'Ooooh, I love that fuckin' dust,' he crooned happily. 'Now we gotta find that party and get us some pussy.'

Billy leaned up on his elbows. 'I am going no place, period. Shit, I feel happy.' He sat up and leaned against the wall so he could slug at his beer but it was empty. He opened another bottle. 'Where the hell did you get it,' he asked again, 'from Kazdan?'

'Charlie's place. He'll never miss it.'

'You mean you broke into the Buchanan house?'

'I don't have to fuckin' break in,' Rocky grinned. He leaned forward, opened the drawer in his bedside table, pulled out a leather key case, and dangled it before Billy's eyes.

'How in hell did you get keys to Mrs Buchanan's place?' Billy asked incredulously.

'I'm lookin' after it, checkin' it out every coupl'a days,

something about the insurance.'

'You've been lying to me,' Billy said. 'Half an hour ago I was the only guy you trust, remember? What went on between you and Charlie Buchanan? It doesn't make sense. He meets you once by accident and he gives you his plane to use and the keys to his old lady's house. What'd you promise him? What's Buchanan gettin' from you? I don't give a damn what it is, I just don't want you to do it.'

'I didn't promise nothin', Billy, honest I didn't.'

'You're lying.'

'I already told you, for fuck's sake. He might need a pilot.'

Billy took a slug of beer and laughed. 'Might, might, it don't sound like might talk to me, baby.'

Rocky sat forward and leaned on the bed. 'For one night, Billy,' he said with a grin, 'for one night's work I'd get fifty thousand dollars if he does use me.'

'And if he does, you're going to do it, aren't you?'

'I didn't promise, and that's the truth.' Rocky stretched out on the floor. 'Fifty thousand Goddamn dollars – I could buy me a fuckin' Porsche!'

Billy howled with laughter. 'What are you, fuckin' crazy or what? You can't just come rollin' into town in a fifty-thousand-dollar car! How the hell are you going to explain where you got the money, you picked it out of air? I mean, shit! It's a fuckin' miracle that cruiser didn't pick us up tonight, me with a wad of grass in my jacket and you with that Goddamn cocaine in your pants!'

'I'll figure it out, I'll fuckin' figure it out.'

'The cops already know you've been selling dope for years—'

'The cops don't *know* fuck-all about me,' Rocky interrupted. 'You got that? They don't know nothin', nothin', nothin'!'

'Okay, so they just think it. They'll start thinking a lot harder when you show up in your Porsche. Maybe you should get a Rolls instead so they won't notice it. You can tell 'em the

Pope gave it to your granny.'

They both started laughing and couldn't stop. Then Rocky lined up the last of the cocaine, and after they did it he turned the cassette over and started dancing by himself. 'I swear to God, Billy,' he said, 'it was nothin' but an idea he got, but even if he does want me, it's nothin' dangerous.'

'It's fifty thousand dollars dangerous.'

'I wanna tell you, you know.'

'I know you do. It doesn't make any difference anyway, Rocky, you already told me too much. You told me too much when you told me you were talking to Buchanan at all. He'd kill you for what I already know. I'd bet on that.'

'What do you know? What did I tell you?'

'I know he's bringing something in that he wants to fly out, and I don't guess he wants it flown up to Hudson's Bay. You're flying dope across the border into the US.'

'You got it,' Rocky said. He opened two more beers and climbed over Billy onto the other side of the waterbed. 'So here it is,' he said, beginning to talk excitedly. 'One day in September, I go to the White Birches Inn over in Lac du Bois early in the morning while it's still dark. I go up into the bush behind the motel and watch, I just watch all day to see that nothin' funny's goin' on. If I see anything unusual, it's all off. But if everything looks right, some guy shows up at eight o'clock at night in a black Toyota with Alberta plates. He's got a room reserved at the back of the motel where it's quiet and he parks the Toyota there. At eleven o'clock another guy shows up, comin' from the east. He's drivin' a 1981 two-tone blue LTD with Ontario plates. He's got a reservation at the back, too, so he parks the LTD outside his room and locks the doors. At midnight, a third guy shows up in a tan 1980 Mercury from Saskatchewan and books into number forty-two, that's the last room at the right end of the motel. At one-thirty, all three of these guys sneak out the back door of the motel and get into the Toyota and head east. In ten minutes I slip out of the bush and go to the LTD. I open the door with a key and there's a metal tackle case on the floor behind the driver's seat. I take the tackle box and put it in the Mercury on the back seat. Then I get in behind the wheel and slide down out of sight and wait. In a few minutes this big nigger Charlie calls Rio Mickey shows up and I move over and he gets in behind the wheel. He drives me to the Lodge. I'm booked to fly him up to the camp on Oshegoon Lake. Instead, I fly southwest to Whitefish Bay. I land the plane fifty kilometers south of the town of Whitefish Bay, in Michigan. These guys slip out to the plane in a rubber boat and Rio Mickey gives 'em the tackle box. They test the stuff right there in the boat, they give him the money in a metal tool box, and I fly the plane back. That's it. Six hundred kilometers round trip, fifty thousand dollars.'

'There's no 'if's and 'might's about it, is there?' Billy asked. 'You're going to do it.'

'You bet your sweet fuckin' life I am,' Rocky said. 'So, what d'you think?'

'What is there to think? But it ain't my sweet fucking life you're betting, Rocky, it's your own.'

'Right you are, Billy-boy, it's my own. Nobody else ever wanted it. I found that out a long time ago.'

That was the first and the last allusion to his parents that Billy ever heard from Rocky Barbizan.

For a few days, Billy worried about Rocky's apparently deepening involvement with Charlie Buchanan, but there was nothing he could do to stop it. Twice he tried to talk to Rocky about it, but all his friend was interested in was the image of himself cruising around in a Porsche. Then, by pure chance, Billy happened to notice a report in the District Briefs column of the Thunder Bay newspaper. It concerned the arrest of four men on drug importing charges at a resort only a hundred kilometers from Thunder Bay, and spoke of more arrests to come as the police stepped up their crackdown on narcotics smugglers. Billy showed the report to Rocky, but Rocky's only comment was that he could spot an undercover narc a mile away.

CHAPTER EIGHT

The last two weeks of August went by. The days got shorter, the nights got cooler, the winds got colder, and the skies got grayer. On the last few days of the month, the threat of early frosts required the gardeners to protect their more vulnerable floral displays with sheets of plastic that flapped and snapped in the winds. The idea of returning to school seeped more and more often into the forefront of Billy's mind. Because of timetable conflicts in the second semester of the previous year, he still needed four grade thirteen credits, and he could only pick up three of these subjects in the first semester of the coming academic year. That meant he had to drag himself through to the following June.

The prospect of faking his way through another ten months of a system he regarded as a fraud and a charade made him feel physically ill. It seemed to him now that he had always been puzzled in school by the way all the other people behaved, teachers and students alike. What he experienced as an act, a studied performance that everyone conspired to put on, they seemed to really believe in. During his adolescence, the puzzlement had given way to a mystification that bordered on awe, a state of permanent amazement. The monotonous sequence of virtually identical performances appeared to be the true substance of reality to everyone else, while Billy floated through them in slow motion as in a ceaseless, surrealist dream. Everyone else barged across the surface of the days with an assured confidence that everything they said and did mattered; to Billy, each day was another carbon copy of an original he had yet to live.

This year would be no different, and now he wouldn't even have Anne to chat with when they passed in the hallways on the way to their respective classes. Thanks to his spurious popularity – for which, as Anne had told him, he was himself responsible – every day would consist of the same false actions. A hundred hellos, hi-theres, and how-are-yous; thousands of auxiliary nods, smiles, routine grimaces, and simulated laughs at things he didn't think were funny; assorted expressions of commiseration and sympathy he didn't feel at all; and a whole lot of keeping his mouth shut when he wanted to argue or make a protest. Every sixteen-hour program faultlessly executed you called another day and buried in the graveyard of sleep. Without calendars and clocks, Billy was sure he couldn't have distinguished any particular day of the past five or six years from any other, or from fifty zillion possible days to come. The thought that his entire life was going to be disposed of like so many timecards punched into oblivion a day at a time had now become intolerable.

The curse of his popularity only deepened the mystery of it all. He never spoke honestly to people, either because he didn't know what they wanted him to say or because he knew exactly what they wanted him to say and he didn't want to say it. His conversations had been gradually reduced to a skimpy and cryptic repertoire. The response he used most often was the single word 'really'. Sometimes it was a question, sometimes an exclamation, but most of the time it was a fill-in-the-blank-yourself expression. The other two phrases he used most frequently, when more than a 'really' was called for, were 'Well, I guess so!' and 'You could say that'.

The fact that these responses were both evasive and insincere didn't make him feel like a phony; he considered them to be genuine insincerities. Sincerity or truth would just scare the shit out of people anyway because they weren't in the script. Billy assumed that behind this facade of universal deceit there must lie the real thing, actual life, but he had no idea what the real thing would turn out to be should it ever be revealed to him. He often entertained the possibility that behind the curtains lay nothing, nothing whatsoever, not even a stage. More often he was convinced that if the great lie ever collapsed, it would collapse to disclose an anarchy in which the power of money was the sole prize and everyone who imagined he already had a share in that power would kill to keep it. The ensuing blood bath would be a policeman's paradise. The whole world would become a concentration camp, run by the tyrants with the money and managed for them by a secret police force of spies and informers and an army of hit men.

In time, and Billy thought it quite likely he would live to see it, crime as it was now understood and defined would cease to exist. It would be converted into another function of government, like sex, education, injustice, and war. Independent entrepreneurs like Charlie Buchanan and the big shots of organized crime would become government flunkies, like parents, teachers, cops, and scientists already were. Rocky would be an employee with a desk in the Dope Tax Control Board – the DTCB.

Whenever Billy let his imagination fill in the details of this alternative to the way things were, he understood why ordinary people preferred a lifetime of groveling and sucking ass to the prospect of annihilation. So did he, at least for the time being.

Poppy sent letters from San Francisco, Los Angeles and Mexico City, and a steady stream of postcards from what seemed to Billy like every town they stopped in long enough to fill up the gas tank. She wrote the same thing every time, that she missed him and wished she were back home. Billy was glad he couldn't reply because all he would have had to say was I told you so. She hadn't wanted to go in the first place, but had been incapable of saying so to her parents because it would spoil the whole vacation for them and she would never hear the end of it. They didn't get home until Sunday, the second of September, early in the evening. It was about eight-thirty at night when Billy answered the phone to hear her voice, and almost nine-thirty by the time he got to the Richardson home.

Billy was surprised when Poppy came running from the house before he was able to get out of his truck, and even more surprised when she got into the truck to sit beside him and told him to drive somewhere as soon as the first kiss ended. They often went for coffee in the restaurant at the White Birches Inn, so Billy headed for the highway, but Poppy burst into tears as soon as he had turned the corner out of Pine Point Crescent. Billy pulled over and stopped, wondering what in the name of God had happened. Poppy had turned away from him and was sobbing with her forehead resting against the window.

He pulled her around into his arms. 'Poppy, what's wrong?'

Poppy whirled violently to look at him. 'I'm pregnant.' She threw herself against him and sobbed into his chest.

For what seemed a long time he said nothing. Then he said, 'Jesus.' After another stretch of silence he asked, 'Are you sure?'

Poppy sat up then and told him she was sure, that her period was more than a month overdue. She had never missed a period before since she had started to menstruate when she was twelve years old. Then she began crying again.

'Let's get out of here for a while,' Billy said.

He drove out to Highway 11, and decided there to go to the Provincial Park where he and Poppy had first met. After they had crossed the bridge over the Lac du Bois narrows and passed the Indian reservation, he said, 'Look, honey, even if you're right, it's not the end of the world, but women miss a period without always being pregnant. The first thing we have to do is get you to a doctor for a test. I'll try to get in touch with Kazdan tomorrow and arrange for you to see him on Tuesday, but it's a long weekend so he might not even be at home. You can't carry on like this for two days. If I have to, I'll go over to the hospital Tuesday morning and catch him there while he's doing his rounds and he'll do the test that afternoon. They always let us out at noon on the first day of school so there's no problem with that.'

Listening to him talk appeared to calm Poppy down a little. 'Maybe he won't be able to fit me in,' she said in a little girl's voice.

'He'll fit you in, don't worry. He likes me, we smoke dope together at his place every once in a while. We've had some good times. But you have to hang onto yourself until we know for sure one way or another.'

He drove along the winding road through the park until it came to its end, and stopped the truck. They sat in silence, staring through the windshield across a grassy slope that went down to the lake.

Finally Poppy said, 'It's my fault. I should have gone on the pill.'

'Honey, let's not start that routine. It never ends and I've had enough of routines that never end. You didn't want to use the pill so I agreed to use safes. Sometimes I didn't, what with one thing and another. Anyway, if you're right, it's too late to worry about those things now. You want to walk down to the lake? It's sort of cold out.'

'Not really.'

'Then why don't you move over beside me. Come on, cuddle up and try to relax.'

When Poppy moved nearer, Billy put his arm around her and pulled her tightly against him.

'How long has it been since your last period?'

'It's fifty-nine days since the start of my last one.'

'Then you must have been already worried before you even left for Mexico. Why didn't you tell me then?'

Poppy suddenly went limp against him. 'I don't know. I was afraid – I just kept hoping and waiting.'

'You must have had a lot of fun.'

'It was a nightmare. I'm sure Mother knows something is wrong. She kept watching me and asking if I didn't feel well.'

'I just want to light a cigarette,' Billy said softly, before lifting his arm from around Poppy's shoulders. Once he had the cigarette going, he put his arm around her again and said, 'It's me you're afraid of, isn't it?'

After a brief hesitation, Poppy asked, 'Why do you say that?'

'I don't honestly know, it just came out. I guess because I know you've never really trusted my love. We've been over that ground often enough, haven't we?'

Poppy sat up and asked for a Kleenex. Billy reached for the box under the seat and handed it to her. She blew her nose and wiped the tear stains from her face.

'I'm afraid you don't want to marry me, that you'll just do it because you have to do it for me, and, ah . . .'

'Ah what?'

Poppy heaved a tremendous sigh and looked at him. 'And I don't want that, Billy. I'm also afraid you'll say I should get an abortion.'

'It's an alternative.'

'Not for me. I don't want an abortion.'

'Then I guess it's not an alternative.'

'I feel guilty now. I don't want to feel any guiltier.'

'Is that why you want to get married? Because you feel guilty? If it is, we'd be making the biggest mistake we'll ever make in our lives. We should get married because we want to, or not at all.'

Poppy lifted her eyes up to his. They glistened with tears.

'Do you want to?'

'Honestly? Honestly I don't know, and that's the truth. I don't think getting married is going to prove anything one way or the other. I don't think it ever has. It's just another way of cataloguing people.'

'So you would only be doing it for me.'

'I don't think that's fair, Poppy. I was talking about marriage, not about you and me. And I am thinking of you, at least I'm trying to. You could give me that much credit, I think. You're not the only one who feels guilty.'

'I don't want you to feel guilty.'

Billy folded his arms across the rim of the steering wheel and rested the side of his head on them so that his eyes were on Poppy's face. 'Truthfully, I don't feel guilty at all, only responsible. If only I were just more ordinary for you, more marriageable, as they say. I wish I were, but I know I'm not. If I could even believe you'll be happy with me. But I am a problem – I've been thinking a lot about myself recently, but I never get past that fact – I am a problem. I live the most peculiar life, and I'm beginning to think it's not going to change. When I think of spending another year in that bloody reformatory, my mind goes completely blank.' He smiled at Poppy and added, 'Come to think of it, if you are pregnant, I guess I won't have to, will I?'

'Don't be silly!' Poppy objected. 'You can't quit now!'

'We're going to live on love, are we?'

'We'll have to live with Mommy and Daddy, I suppose.'

'Poppy, I don't want to live with anybody's mommy and daddy. I'm sick to death of all mommies and daddies.'

Billy sat up and stretched back his arms and shoulders. 'Anyway, we should end this conversation right now and wait till we know for sure, and that'll be Tuesday afternoon at the earliest. If you want me, I'm all yours, you know that. I've never been anybody else's. Come on, let's walk down to the lake and get good and cold, then I'll take you home to bed.'

To Billy's own surprise, he was grinning happily at Poppy. 'Guess what? I just had a real wish, honey. I wished I could spend the night with you. It's been so long. I'd give anything to do that tonight. So you see? Things could be worse.'

Poppy murmured in a wistful, weary way, 'I wish we could just run away now and never come back.'

'Well, we can't. I mean, I could, but you couldn't. Besides, even if you had it in you, it wouldn't really be fair.'

Billy got out of the truck and waited for Poppy. They walked into the cool wind off the lake down to the water's edge. There they sat on the grassy ledge with their feet down on the narrow strip of sand. Billy put his arm around Poppy's back and tucked his hand with hers into the pocket of her jacket. They listened to the water lap the shore and stared out across the dark expanse of the lake.

'It's going to kill Mommy and Daddy,' Poppy said.

'Poppy, if you'd quit calling them Mommy and Daddy, it might not kill them quite so effectively. They might start thinking of you as yourself, not Mommy's and Daddy's little girl. You could make that a project for the next few days. Call them Mother and Father, just as if you were all grown up.'

'I'm sure Mother knows, or suspects anyways.'

'Then it won't come as a total surprise to her.'

'It's going to be awful, awful, awful,' Poppy whispered.

'Look,' Billy said, 'all you have to do is get through tomorrow. Tuesday morning, as soon as you wake up, you pee into a little bottle, that's what they use for the test. Then you do as usual and get on the bus for school. I'll take the sample over to the hospital lab and use my name. Tomorrow you can spend with me. I'll pick you up as early as you want and get you out of the house.'

'What'll we say we're going to do?'

'It doesn't matter what we're going to do, just say we're going out for the day. You can rush around making a really nice picnic lunch, that'll keep you busy. I'll pick you up at nine o'clock and we'll just disappear. Now, how does that sound?'

'But suppose it's raining?'

'Suppose it's snowing, suppose the first earthquake in history strikes northern Ontario, suppose the sky falls down. Just make us a lunch and I'll pick you up at nine. If it's miserable out, we'll drive into Thunder Bay. Actually, that's not a bad idea. We wouldn't get back until late at night and you could go straight to bed. That's what we'll do, we'll go to Thunder Bay on a little spree before we have to go back to school.'

'Daddy'll say that's crazy, driving there and back in one day for no reason.'

'Daddy can stuff it up his ass if he wants to,' Billy replied. 'I'm picking you up at nine o'clock. Let's go.'

When they stood up, Billy took her into his arms and kissed her. Poppy pressed her head to his chest and whispered, 'Oh, God, I missed you! Sometimes I thought I'd go crazy. We stayed for three days at Disneyland. Daddy absolutely loved it. He must have taken a thousand pictures of it.'

Billy laughed. 'I'm not surprised. I'm sure it's a model of organization and efficiency. He was probably picking up ideas. Maybe he'll reorganize the K-C plant into an industrial Disneyland.'

They did go to Thunder Bay on Labor Day. They saw two movies and had supper at a popular restaurant. Billy ordered a bottle of expensive wine, the first they had shared. As far as he could tell, Poppy's spirits picked up and she calmed down for a few hours. Even when they kissed good night at almost three a.m. in the Richardsons' driveway her body seemed to be fairly relaxed in his arms.

As she was climbing the steps to the front door, Billy rolled down the window and called to her. 'I do love you, you know.' Poppy ran back to the truck and they kissed again through the open window. When she pulled her lips away from his, he said, 'Go to bed now. I'll still love you in the morning.'

On the drive home, he lit a joint and smoked it. He always enjoyed the sensation of driving when he was mildly stoned, especially at night. It was rather like what he imagined space travel must feel like. You seemed to be standing still in a kind of limbo while you were actually hurtling through time and space, as if the highway were a black rubber band being secretly stretched out by playful giants. It was fun.

So Poppy was pregnant. The business he'd used about waiting for medical proof to alleviate Poppy's panic cut no ice with Billy himself. Kazdan had not gone away for the long weekend, and Billy had reached him Monday morning before he and Poppy went to Thunder Bay and made an appointment for Tuesday at two o'clock. But he had no hope at all that she would turn out to be mistaken. Once their certainty had been confirmed scientifically, it would be time for the fateful confessions. The next ten days would be ghastly. He didn't much care what went on in the predictably bizarre scene with his own parents. If he didn't like even the looks on their faces or the first words out of his mother's mouth, he would pack up and leave. He was tired of the work it took to maintain the fiction that living in the Mackenzie home was endurable. It wasn't, and in fact he would be glad to face up to that fact. He may have loved them once, but he didn't love them now. He didn't even like them. The only thing they could do that would be beneficial to him now was die.

The Richardsons, however, were a different proposition. Poppy's parents, both devout Roman Catholics, would naturally be unhappy and disappointed. Her father would hate Billy's guts, and Billy would know it no matter how hard Edgar tried to conceal it for Poppy's sake. She was an extremely attractive girl, she was intelligent, she had always been an excellent student, and they had had high hopes for her future. On the plus side, they appeared to have long ago accepted that he and Poppy might be genuinely in love and that when the right time came along they would marry. So far as Billy could tell, except for Poppy's big brother Jack, the family was fond of him, and he had spent a great deal of time in their company. Whether that fondness would now evaporate like a puff of smoke was unpredictable.

Indeed, his future, as well as Poppy's, had moved entirely into the realm of the unpredictable. Poppy would hate that, but Billy wasn't so sure he did. For a long, long time he had been uneasily conscious that he seemed to be coming to the end of all his ropes. Driving home that night, he felt almost as if he were falling free, plummeting into himself, into his real life, plummeting into something anyway.

Into his mind sprang Miss Copper's exquisite little warning in his autograph book so many years earlier.

Billy had heeded her advice, and now he'd been licked dry. There was no glue left. His future was pure guesswork, and Billy strongly suspected he would prefer that to the officially normal state of affairs, in which the future was pure guesswork disguised as a sure thing.

The worst he had to fear was winding up in the dead letter box, a piece of undeliverable merchandise.

So he was right. Things could be worse.

CHAPTER NINE

On registration day, only the new grade nine students had to be at the school by nine o'clock. Between nine and ten o'clock, they had to sit through the annual assembly staged to indoctrinate each fresh crop of indentured innocents. Students returning for registration in grades ten to thirteen were not scheduled to show up until ten o'clock.

But Billy had to get to the school before eight-thirty so that he would be there waiting when Poppy got off one of the two buses that brought students in from Lac du Bois daily. Poppy needed him to be there, he was sure of that.

He had set his alarm clock for seven-thirty, but he woke up in a cold sweat before six o'clock. As the familiar morning pollution flushed through the canals of his mind, Billy listened once again to the barely audible sounds of his father creeping around like a cat burglar as he got ready for work. The store did not open until nine o'clock, but Alex Mackenzie had always been there by seven-thirty at the latest. During his routine preparations, he sneaked about as silently as possible, ostensibly so as not to wake his sleeping wife. In her dark bedroom, Agnes Mackenzie would be lying wide awake and listening as always, waiting for her husband to be gone.

The second-last thing his father did every morning was breakfast on tea and toast in the kitchen. The last thing he did before he slipped on tiptoe out the front door was make a fresh pot of tea and leave it stewing for his wife on one back burner of the stove over a low heat. And every morning of Billy's life, as soon as the sound of his father's car rolling out of the gravel driveway had faded away, Agnes Mackenzie got up at once. She put on her housecoat, poured herself a mug of strong black tea, and retired to watch TV in the living room as she drank the tea and smoked the first dozen cigarettes of her day. She had always drunk one entire pot. Now she often drank two.

So that morning as usual Billy heard his mother in the kitchen within a few minutes of his father's departure. A long time back, Anne pointed out to Billy that their father must obviously know his wife was only waiting for him to clear out. Otherwise, there was no point to his preparing her a pot of stewed tea every morning. The game was another mutually convenient arrangement, a way of avoiding the high risk of unpleasant discord in the early mornings. The life of the Mackenzie family had been gradually organized into nothing but convenient arrangements – none of them openly acknowledged – that served as safe passages through the minefields.

Billy's back bedroom had come in particularly handy in this respect. He and Anne had been able to leave the house through the door that opened into the back yard and never see their mother except for unlucky meetings now and then as she came and went between the teapot in the kitchen and the TV in the living room.

What a flaky dump of a room it was! As a kid growing up, it had been fun to have a bedroom with a separate and exclusive entrance, though the room had always been too small and was often bitterly cold during the winter months because of inadequate insulation. It had seemed so grown-up and independent to have a room with its own special exit to the outside world, to be able to come and go as he pleased. Later that door had become their escape hatch, and the room itself a sort of fragile haven. The kind of insulation it did provide made shivering a small price to pay. When he was sixteen, Billy had put a bolt lock on the door to the kitchen so that no one could get into his room from the battle zone without his knowledge.

Billy heard his mother heading for the living room where she immediately whammed on the TV much louder than necessary. As she switched from one channel to another in search of the new early-morning yap show to which she was rapidly becoming addicted, Billy could hear fragmented commercials booming and vibrating through the flimsy bungalow walls. Agnes Mackenzie had ears like Watergate bugs; she could hear the faintest squeak of the kitchen floor through even the loudest of commercials. Knowing that, Billy used to be irritated daily by the excessive blasting of such ugly noise. He knew it was a deliberate tactic to make further sleep impossible for anyone – if Agnes Mackenzie was up, everybody should be up. Now he was so accustomed to waking early that it no longer mattered. He did leftover homework whenever he had it to do. When he didn't, he lay there and let his mind wander where it pleased within its ragbag of widely assorted obsessions.

That morning, the hunt was unnecessary. His mind zoomed in on Poppy's pregnancy and stalled.

At ten past eight he heard his mother refilling her mug with tea for the third time. He gave her time to get back to her chair in the living room, then went to the bathroom to shower and shave. He had arranged with Chuck Courtis, his boss at the Texaco garage, to work that afternoon, so he phoned him and told him he had to cancel out because of an urgent medical appointment and that he would be unable to work the following weekend as well.

Chuck was annoyed and wanted to know why, so Billy turned his back to the living room and whispered, 'Because I might be getting married depending on what we find out today. Is that a good enough reason?'

'Shit, Billy,' Chuck Courtis said, 'I thought you were smarter than that.'

'So did I,' Billy agreed, 'but I guess I'm not. I have to go, I'll get back to you about the weekend as soon as I know the score.'

He wore the new shirt and sweater his parents had given him for his birthday and left for school by the front door so he could say good morning to his mother and she could see that he was wearing them. By this time, their estrangement was so complete that Agnes Mackenzie's face almost never betrayed what was or might be going on behind the mask. It was like trying to converse with a stone idol.

'Well, I'm off to school for another year, in my brand-new back-to-school birthday clothes,' Billy announced. He smiled. His mother did not.

'I thought you didn't have to be there till ten o'clock,' she challenged. Billy knew she knew why he was going so early. What she had really said was, 'You'd rather spend the next hour and a half with her than with me.'

Since the only answer to that one was yes, Billy said so long and cleared out.

It took him only a few minutes of fast walking along the barren gravel roads to get to the high school. On the way, he passed quite a few of that year's grade nines, a remarkable number of whom looked like midgets. For the first time, Billy felt like an ass as he walked with them in procession into the ugly brick building to begin day one of the one hundred and ninety-four lawful school days of the year. The heavy doors whooshing shut behind him sounded like the vacuum seals of an airtight tomb sucking into place, locking him in. God help me, Billy thought. Then he bumped into the principal just inside the doors. The general offices, the principal's office, and the office shared by the two vice-principals were all situated in the same hall. Mr Popowski, immaculate in a suit that looked as though it had never been worn before, looked like he was on his way to a summit meeting to solve the first crisis of the year. But he wasn't. When he saw Billy, he stopped, replaced the crisis symptoms with a broad smile, and said heartily, 'Welcome back, Billy! How was your summer?'

'Excellent,' Billy replied. 'I hope you had some time for a little rest. Did you go away anywhere?' Mr Popowski was known for the staggering number of holidays he spent at the school.

'No, just out to the cottage as usual. No rest for the wicked,' Mr Popowski laughed. 'Have a good year, Billy.' The crisis face returned and the principal strode into his private office with executive decision in every step. It was a big day.

Billy set out on the long walk down the main hallway to the other end of the building where the buses from out of town unloaded their students. He figured the new suit Mr Popowski was wearing would be replaced the following Monday by something that had already been broken in. The principal had a reputation for being as tight with his money as he was with school discipline.

The new contingent of grade nines were wandering around with bright, though distinctly apprehensive eyes. Some were clustered in groups for self-protection. Only a very few senior students had already showed up, the ones who had no life except what transpired in school and were relieved to return. Billy said hello to four of these former classmates and to half a dozen teachers as he progressed down the corridor. All the teachers greeted him warmly. Mr Carney, the head of guidance, appeared to have forgotten Billy's aberrant behavior the day he had sung the praises of the New Oxford poster and been so flippant about the computer career printouts. That was good. The teachers seemed very happy to be back at work for another year and marched about their business with bouncing feet and cheerfully eager faces. Even Billy found it hard to believe that all this apparent zest and zeal would give way before the week was out to the drudgery and boredom of discipline and nagging.

Poppy looked miserably unhappy and frightened when she

stepped off the bus in a new scarlet coat, and after Billy kissed her she hung onto him like a little old lady.

'I'm sure mother's guessed,' she whispered. 'I can tell she knows something terrible is wrong.'

'Honey,' Billy said, 'if you've been wearing the same look on your face at home, you don't have to wonder why. It's you who thinks something terrible is wrong. When do you start wailing like a banshee and gnashing your teeth?'

Billy took her hands from his shoulders and into his own. They were cold as ice and trembling. She looked about to start crying any second.

'What a pretty red coat that is,' he commented.

'You can't fool me, Billy, you're angry.'

'I am not angry,' Billy said patiently. 'I simply can't stand that wimpy look on your face. We haven't committed a felony, Poppy. Do we have to wallow in guilt for the rest of our lives because I got you pregnant?' He lit a cigarette, though smoking in that particular doorway was illegal.

'See, you are so angry.'

'I am not angry,' Billy repeated. 'What I'm trying to say is that the next few days are going to be bad enough, Poppy. They'll be even worse if you're going to start bawling about it.'

'Worse! How could they be worse?'

'We could be dying of fifty different diseases. Do you want me to list them alphabetically?'

The rest of the students from Lac du Bois had gone into the school and the buses were pulling away. They were standing outside alone.

'I'm sorry,' Poppy apologized, pulling open the door.

Billy held her back and hugged her to him tightly. 'I don't want you to apologize! Now you're apologizing to me, for God's sake!' He pitched his cigarette away. 'I know how you feel. Do you think I'm not scared? No, strike that, I'm not scared at all. I'm just reading the lines in your script. Is that what you want, Poppy?'

'I'm not playacting, Billy.'

'Are you sure? Look, we don't have to be here until ten o'clock when we go to first period, and there's no point in our wandering around the halls in this mausoleum. Let's go for a coffee, come on, come on!' Billy yanked her behind him.

They walked to the five-block strip of Main Street that constituted Nugget's Times Square and sat in a booth at the rear of the Northern Lights, the dingy little restaurant where students hung out to drink pop and smoke cigarettes.

When the waitress appeared beside their booth she said, 'Hi, Billy. Gee, it's a long time, huh?'

Billy smiled at her. 'Oh, hi, Denise. It sure is. Bring us some coffee, will you?'

Poppy said, 'I don't want any coffee.'

'Drink it anyway,' Billy ordered, lighting a cigarette. 'The caffeine sharpens up the day.'

The waitress brought their coffees, both spilled in the saucer. 'Gee, I guess you're still in school, huh?' she said to Billy.

Billy nodded. 'That's right, one year to go. How long have you been working here now? It must be ages.'

'Oh, gee, yes,' Denise smiled, 'it'll be three years in October. You don't want anything else?'

'Just more coffee when this one's gone. Nice to see you, Denise.'

When she had gone, he said casually, 'I screwed Denise in grade nine.'

Poppy's eyes widened. 'What did you say?'

'I said I screwed Denise back in grade nine. We did it in the back of somebody's car at a school dance. As I recall, she wasn't very good, but in those days I didn't know it. Denise Laroche she was then, but she's married now, I can't remember who to.'

'Billy Mackenzie!' Poppy exclaimed.

'Hah! I figured that might perk you up.'

Poppy was looking at Denise, who was now behind the counter filling up the salt shakers for the day.

'Dumb like you wouldn't believe,' Billy went on. 'She stuck it out in high school for two years, both of them in grade nine. For that matter, she didn't actually get into grade nine. They finally had to transfer her out of grade eight because she was socially out of place. I think that meant she already had those enormous boobs. According to Rocky, she used to jack the boys off at recess over at the Catholic School. Denise told me she fucked her teacher in grade eight, a Mr Desaulniers. I guess he wanted to get rid of her.'

'I don't believe that!' Poppy hissed, her eyes flashing angrily. 'I baby-sit for the Desaulniers all the time! Mr Desaulniers is the principal at St Patrick's over in Lac du Bois now.'

'Don't take my word for it,' Billy said, 'go ask Denise.' He drank some coffee and smiled at Poppy.

'I wouldn't believe her, either,' Poppy declared. 'You told me I was the first girl you ever – ever had!'

Billy signaled for more coffee and Denise came and filled his cup. Her breasts were bigger than ever and quivered with a life of their own, despite the brassiere that showed through her white uniform. After she had gone again, Billy leaned forward on his elbows. 'I told you you were the first girl I've ever loved, and you are. I never told you you were the first girl I'd ever fucked.'

'Billy Mackenzie!'

'For that matter, neither was Denise. She was second.'

'Billy Mackenzie!'

'Poppy Richardson! Poppy Richardson! Tell me, am I going to spend the rest of my life with a woman who's going to be saying "Billy Mackenzie!" to me like that?'

'Like what exactly?'

'With an exclamation mark like a school teacher, that's like what. So I fucked Denise once, so what?'

Billy smoked while Poppy snuck another long look at the waitress.

'She has eyes like a fish,' she said at last.

'She fucks like a fish, too,' Billy replied with a laugh. 'She wriggled the whole time. Mind you, I don't think it lasted more than two minutes.'

'And if I heard you correctly,' Poppy said snippily, 'she wasn't the only one, just number two?'

'That's right. But she did the best wriggling.'

'I'm glad you find it entertaining! Exactly how many were there, or did you stop keeping track?' Poppy yanked a wad of paper napkins out of the metal container. 'I'd like to know how long a lineup I'm at the end of!'

'Not very long,' Billy grinned. 'To be precise, there were five.'

'Is that plus or minus Denise?'

'Plus Denise. So that makes six altogether. Not very impressive, is it?' He inhaled and exhaled smoke. 'For such a famous stud, I mean.'

Poppy was tearing the paper napkins into long strips.

'Oh, I'm impressed if you aren't! I had no idea you were a famous stud, Billy. Tell me, do I wriggle too much too? You must be a good judge of technique, how do I rate?'

Now Poppy was using the long strips of torn napkin to make a latticework pattern on the arborite table top. Billy put his right hand on hers and she pulled it away quickly.

'Poppy,' he sighed, 'what's this Pollyanna shit? You know the girls around here as well as I do. I could probably have had dozens if I'd wanted. Those girls didn't mean anything to me, darling, nothing at all, and you know it. The other five were even dumber than Denise, and that's saying a lot. Now that you've brought it to my attention, they all had eyes like a fish.'

Poppy raised her own eyes. 'That's the meanest single thing

I've ever heard you say, Billy. People can't help it if they're dumb.'

'Hey, come off it,' Billy objected. 'It was you said she had eyes like a fish, not me! But you're right, it was mean, and neither one of us should have said it. I didn't even know those girls, honey, not really. I've never known any girl but you, and I've never wanted to. I love you.' She let him hold her hands this time.

'Do you mean that?' Poppy spoke in a shy tremble.

'Yes, I mean it. But I wish you'd stop making pie tops with those damn strips of paper.' Billy stuck his finger into her coffee. 'It's too cold to drink now. Let's go, it's quarter to ten.'

Billy left two dollars on the table. As they were leaving the Northern Lights, Poppy said, 'Under the circumstances, I think this has been a very strange conversation. I don't know why it came up, now of all times. Do you? I'm just curious.'

'I've no idea,' Billy said as the door swung shut behind him. 'I certainly didn't plan it in advance. But it did change the look on your face. Before you looked like you'd been slugged with a sledgehammer.'

'And what do I look like now?'

'Like a wife,' Billy laughed. 'So maybe that's why it happened.'

By the time they got back to the school it was ten o'clock, and time to begin the rigamarole of registration day.

From ten to ten-thirty everyone sat in the class in which they would spend their first seventy-minute period for the rest of semester one. At ten-thirty, the bell would ring to signify the beginning of a mini-day. The mini-day consisted of all students spending fifteen minutes in three or four of periods two, three, four, five, or six, according to their individual timetables. At the end of each fifteen-minute segment the bell would ring again and they would have five minutes to find their ways to their next designated class. At the end of each five-minute break, the bell rang again and the next mini-period began.

Since only a very few students had more than four assigned courses during a semester, there were always a considerable number wandering around the halls or loitering in the cafeteria waiting for the next bell to ring. At five minutes past twelve, the mini-day ended, and at twelve-fifteen the buses loaded up the out-of-town kids and took them back to their respective towns or one of the several Indian reservations.

Billy's first half hour was spent with seven other students in Mr Agnew's algebra class. That was clearly going to be a long ordeal. He knew all the students present, and at least four of them had been well beyond the limits of their tolerance for mathematics since grade eleven. By the end of grade twelve, they'd passed their pain thresholds. Mr Agnew had been patience incarnate with them in grade twelve; he'd had no choice unless he wished to reduce his class to two or three students within the first two weeks. In order that these dogged sufferers should not be doomed to failure before the grade thirteen course began, repetition and review to the point of physical nausea would be the rule, not the exception.

As a home room teacher, Mr Agnew was a supreme fart and a fiend about punctuality, skipping, and absenteeism. He was at least six foot two inches tall and powerfully built, and it struck Billy as incongruous that such a big man should be so finicky about such petty drivel. Most teachers tended not to send all students who were a minute or two late down to the office for their pink late slips – they sent only the ones they disliked. Nor did they examine too closely the admit slips brought up to their desks by students who had been absent. They knew they would get hundreds of the pink and yellow slips before the year was out, maybe thousands, for all Billy knew.

But Mr Agnew took such matters seriously as modes of discipline. When the bell rang to signify the beginning of period one, he locked the door. Anyone who got to it five seconds late had to trek down to the office for a pink slip. When a student returned after even one day's absence, Mr Agnew studied the reason given on their yellow admit slip with the diligence of a homicide detective. Whenever the reason they had given to Miss Sweet – Mr Sweet's youngest daughter and now the junior secretary who looked after all slips – was stated as 'personal', Mr Agnew always smiled knowingly. He also suspected all requests to leave the room to go to the bathroom as almost certainly deceitful, especially if he knew the student smoked, and he timed the student's absence from class to the second. Period one was going to be excruciating.

The only novelty during his half hour with Mr Agnew came in the form of the new Nugget District High School Calendar, distributed to the class after the lecture on homework. The calendar was twelve pages thick and printed on what looked like very expensive pale orange paper, a costly little novelty indeed. On the cover was a drawing of the school, but any resemblance to the real building had been carefully avoided. Instead of the scenic color photographs usually found in commercial calendars, there were twelve pages of a freshly formulated Code of Student Behavior. The code covered every conceivable aspect of the student's day in or around the school.

After he'd passed the document out, Mr Agnew informed them that all students were expected to study and learn the new code and – significant pause – that occasional random tests would be given to see if they were living up to these expectations. Presumably, Billy thought, that meant they were supposed to memorize the twelve pages of very fine print.

A rapid skimming of the first few pages was enough to give the impression that they were not mere students but inmates of a juvenile detention home. The regulations governing what kids could and could not wear on their bodies took up most of the page adjacent to January. Among the items that were unconditionally prohibited were 'revealing' tank tops and miniskirts, all see-through blouses on girls, 'immodest' necklines, and any kind of T-shirt or jacket that had been imprinted with any kind of reference to sex, alcoholic beverages, mind- or mood-altering drugs, or blasphemy. That would take care of at least fifty per cent of the T-shirts the student body owned. Banned, too, were clothes decorated with the names of any rock groups that were 'obscene or otherwise offensive', or with illustrations of any rock group that were 'in any way salacious or suggestive'. That took care of the rest of the shirts favored by the boys.

Having digested the first page of rules about clothing, Billy found himself raising his hand. Day one, he thought, and I'm already looking for trouble – but he didn't lower his arm.

'Billy? You have a question?' Mr Agnew popped his eyes whenever he responded to a raised hand. Billy had never understood what the popped eyes meant, aggression or defense. Perhaps it was both.

'Yes, yes I do,' Billy said. 'I'm not quite clear on what you mean by occasional random tests.'

'It seems clear enough to me. What don't you understand?'

'Does random mean now and then, or does it mean unannounced?'

Mr Agnew smelled challenge in the air. 'It could mean either or both, I suppose.'

'I see,' Billy said. 'Another thing, what exactly happens if you fail one of these occasional random tests, or all of them for that matter? It would be easy to fail if the tests were sprung on us as surprises. There's a fair amount of material here, isn't there?'

'If you fail a test, you fail.' Mr Agnew gave Billy a coy, teasing smile to let him know he'd picked up the undercurrent.

'Sir, what I want to know is this – do these tests count or not? If they don't count somehow, who's going to waste time memorizing this behavior code? If they do count, how do they count? Surely they can't count as regular term tests in math or physics, that couldn't be legal, could it? What does my knowledge of this stuff have to do with algebra or any other subject?'

As Billy baited him Mr Agnew's eyes had gradually narrowed and he pursed his lips; he didn't have an answer. Obviously, the administration had neglected to provide a failure punishment, a necessity if they were going to threaten the kids with tests on a minutely detailed code.

'Maybe we get detentions if we fail,' Billy suggested helpfully, 'or a three-day suspension? Though that doesn't seem right either, does it?'

Fortunately, the bell rang then, before Billy could do any further damage.

'I'll have to look into this matter, Billy, and let you know.'

'I'd appreciate that, sir,' Billy said, struggling to free his long legs from under the desk. 'I've got three heavy subjects as it is, I won't have any time to waste.' Billy could feel Mr Agnew's eyes sizing him up from behind as he left the room. The wind was up.

Why had he done it? What was driving him? Thinly veiled sarcasm was the prerogative of teachers. Whatever it was had to be brought under control before exercise refined it. Billy determined not to open his mouth. Anything might come out of it.

He met Poppy in the hall and she immediately asked what was wrong.

'Nothing special,' Billy said. 'I can't stand it, that's all. I see you have the new law code, too. Quite a production, isn't it?'

'I haven't really looked at it.'

'We'd better go,' Billy said. 'I'd give you a kiss but I'd rather not till I've checked on the punishment. I love you, honey.'

The same group of eight students showed up in Miss

Farquarson's physics lab. That meant another seventy minutes a day of agony for the entire semester. Billy was sure the whiz kids would find physics even more obscure than algebra. Enduring the deadly tedium would have the usual reward; the slower the class, the higher his own grade would be. Poor Miss Farquarson loved physics, and by the end of a semester she was a nervous wreck after five months of compulsive scolding. She used up her fifteen minutes on another lecture about doing their homework religiously every night if they hoped to scrape up even a bare pass.

The next fifteen minutes symbolized a spare period for Billy. He walked the halls and looked about. He noticed there seemed to be more Indians in the school than in previous years. They were now referred to as 'native students', not Indians, but the new nomenclature did not appear to have changed anything that mattered. Except for the very few who lived in towns and had made white friends, they still clustered in separate groups like outcasts. And, as mysteriously as in the past, he saw the Indian kids were finding themselves in classrooms they had exclusively to themselves. And the classrooms were those in which Basic Level courses were taught. Basic meant dumb. Even back in grade nine, Billy had concluded that some terrible injustice was operating secretly behind the scenes. It had to be impossible that all the Indians who lived on reservations were dim bulbs.

Billy's fifteen-minute mini-spare was nearly over and he was walking toward his third and last mini-period when Mr Cartwright came bursting through the gym doors and stopped to say hello. They exchanged reports on their respective summers. Both were glad to be back.

'I don't suppose you'll reconsider your decision and come out for the senior basketball team,' Mr Cartwright said as they were about to part. 'It's your last year, Billy, I'd like to have you back on the team.'

Billy surprised himself by lying smoothly – maybe he was

getting back into the swing of things. Cartwright was Mr Popowski's pet.

'I've already thought about that, sir, and I'd really love to come back, I've missed it.'

'Terrific!' Mr Cartwright slapped Billy on the shoulder.

'Well, there's a problem I have to sort out before I can say for sure one way or the other. I'll let you know in a day or two. But, actually, it's doubtful.'

Mr Cartwright's professionally personal smile changed to an expression of professionally personal concern. This man cared.

'What's this big problem, Billy?'

'Too big to talk about,' Billy said as the bell rang again.

His third and last preview of coming attractions was Mr Adams' English class. Mr Adams was notorious for giving high marks to sucks, so in his classes everybody sucked. He was a dull man but dependable, and had no kinky wrinkles in his personality Billy could cater to. But he was a rabid patriot, to judge by the course he had planned.

Mr Adams had written on the blackboard the titles of the books they had to buy. As the eleven people in the course wrote down the titles, Mr Adams held up a book and said a few words about each one in turn. They were *A Dictionary of Canadian English*, *A Handbook of Canadian Grammar and Usage*, an anthology almost three inches thick called *A Canadian Anthology*, *A Treasury of Canadian Poetry*, and two fat Canadian novels, one called *Prairie Lives* and another called *Wheat*.

Billy had had Mr Adams back in grade ten and could recall grinding through a variety of Canadian material, but nothing to rival this onslaught. He was dying to ask what Canadian grammar and usage was and how it differed from English grammar and usage, but he managed to keep his vow of silence. Mr Adams told them the course would begin with *Wheat*, which he described as a humorous yet tragic saga of two hundred years on a Manitoba farm. Never had Billy expected to see the day when he would long for Mr Sweet. Alluring smiles, skintight jeans, and stimulating postures could serve no purpose this year. No, patriotic propaganda was the ticket to Mr Adams' heart.

For Billy, the mini-day was over. All he had to do was repeat the pattern five days a week for five months with each fifteen minutes stretched out to seventy, and he would have three more credits. The prospect numbed his mind.

Poppy was waiting for him in the hall outside Mr Adams' classroom. He tried to pep up his face for her.

'Hi, honey, how does it look?'

'Oh, who cares,' Poppy said. 'Let's go, please, Billy, I want to get it over with.'

It was only a quarter to twelve, so they had plenty of time. All they had to do was get Poppy's urine sample over to the hospital laboratory, then they could go someplace for lunch. Billy planned to take her out to the restaurant at the Sleeping Beauty Motel on the highway, a few kilometers east of the junction. They served the best food available in the district, and everyone in Nugget dined there by preference on special occasions. This must count as special.

As soon as they had gotten their coats from their lockers and were outside the building, Billy asked her for the sample. She drew the little glass container out of her coat pocket and gave it to him. Billy had agreed to make the delivery and use his name only. This attempt to keep her identity a secret was almost certainly futile. Billy knew both the lab technicians casually, and they knew that Poppy was his girlfriend – all they had to do was put one and one together. But he hadn't drawn her attention to these facts.

The district hospital was directly across Fourth Street South, and Billy was back at Poppy's side in five minutes. They walked hand in hand toward the Mackenzie home. There they got into his truck, and fifteen minutes later they were seated at a table for two in the lunch room at the Sleeping Beauty.

Poppy said she wasn't hungry, and when Billy insisted that she order something, anything, she said eating would make her sick. He ordered her a strawberry milk shake anyway. For himself he ordered a club house sandwich with French fries and a chocolate shake. When the food arrived he tried to con Poppy into drinking the strawberry shake.

'Billy, stop pushing at me, I don't want it. I feel sick.'

So Billy drank both milk shakes while Poppy sipped at a glass of water.

He had finished his meal by one o'clock, but they had nowhere to go. Billy ordered coffee and smoked his last cigarette.

'I guess this is what it's like to be homeless,' Billy said, 'you sit around in restaurants with no place to go. Awful, isn't it?'

'Do you think they know yet?' Poppy asked. She was tearing up paper napkins again.

'I haven't the faintest idea. We'll know at two o'clock.' He took her hands in his and tried to warm them with a rubbing. Poppy pulled her hands away and put them in her lap.

At one-ten he ordered more coffee and went to the cashier to get change for the cigarette machine. Next to the cigarette machine the Sleeping Beauty had a metal rack for the *Toronto Globe and Mail*, the *Thunder Bay Times-News*, and motel magazines like *People* and *Us*. The *Globe* was plastered with publicity about the Pope's latest pronouncements, so he bought it to look at. He picked up the current issue of *People* for Poppy. His second cup of coffee was on the table when he got back. Poppy was white as chalk and tearing up another napkin.

'Isn't it time we went, Billy?' she asked as he sat down.

'Honey, I've told you three times, they don't even open the office door until two o'clock. What do you want to do? Stand outside Dr Kazdan's office on Main Street for half an hour?'

'No, I don't.'

'Then just sit there.' He gave her the magazine. 'There's a *People*. See what Michael Jackson's doing this week.'

Billy lit a cigarette and read the *Globe*'s most recent love songs about the Pope. The story was continued on page two, but when he opened the paper his eyes fell on a page three headline that said 'Trend of Teen Pregnancies Must Be Halted, MD Says', so he read that instead. Some survey in California – everything seemed to happen out in California – had 'indicated teenagers are experimenting sexually earlier but are ambivalent about birth control'. The fourth paragraph asserted that 'The irresponsible attitude of many male adolescents toward birth control may be partially at fault for the increase in teenage pregnancies, so it is important for health professionals to involve them in sex education and family planning.' Billy read this aloud to Poppy and said, 'See, even the *Globe* says it's my fault.'

'What are you trying to do, Billy? Make me even sicker? It must be time to go.'

It wasn't, but they went anyway. They waited in the truck until David Kazdan's receptionist, who was also the woman he lived with, opened the office door.

Fifteen minutes later, they knew Poppy was pregnant, and Poppy was vomiting into the toilet in the doctor's private washroom.

Billy might have felt more guilty, but he didn't know when.

CHAPTER TEN

Billy had been unable to deceive himself about his own reaction to the news. A massive shock of disappointment had seized his heart and for a moment it seemed to stop beating. Practically speaking, this was catastrophe and he knew it.

Kazdan was very kind and understanding to them. He leaned forward across his polished desk and asked, 'Have you considered an abortion?'

'We haven't considered anything, isn't that fairly obvious?' Billy lit a cigarette and inhaled deeply. Kazdan had to dig an ashtray out of a drawer for him. Though he smoked dope, he was fanatically opposed to the smoking of cigarettes and No Smoking signs were prominently placed on the walls of every room in the little building. Billy went on, 'Poppy doesn't want an abortion.'

Kazdan addressed Poppy. 'An abortion is not the end of the world, you know, Poppy. I know a lot of Catholic girls who've had abortions on their parents' advice.'

Poppy said quietly, 'I can't do it. It isn't just my parents, doctor. It's me, I just can't do it. I don't want an abortion myself.'

'We're getting married,' Billy said. 'It's just, you know, the idea of having to tell her parents that she's pregnant.'

'That's never an easy confession,' David Kazdan agreed. 'I realize that. For what it's worth, my advice is the sooner the better. Get it over with.'

'I just need a little time,' Poppy said. 'I can't go home now,

I'm too sick, I've never felt so sick in my life.'

Billy stood up. 'There's no point in sitting here any longer. Come on, honey, let's go.'

'You can stay here as long as you need to,' Kazdan said. 'I have four other consulting rooms.'

Poppy looked up over her shoulder at Billy. 'I have to phone Mommy. She'll be wondering why I didn't come home on the bus. I don't know what to say – there is nothing to say.'

Billy moved the telephone across the desk and handed the receiver to Poppy. 'I'll dial the number,' he said, 'tell her you're staying at my place for supper.'

'I've never done that before.'

'There's a first time for everything,' Billy said, 'just get it over with.' While Billy dialed the number, Kazdan got up and said there was nothing more he could do now. He asked Billy if he wanted to make another appointment for Poppy, and when Billy said yes the doctor took him out to his reception desk. He made an appointment for two weeks later; by that time, one way or another, things would have settled down. When Billy got back to Poppy, she was just replacing the receiver and there seemed to be a touch more color in her complexion.

He smiled at her and said gently, 'Ready to go now? I've made you an appointment two weeks from today. Here's the card to remind you, though I doubt if you'll need reminding.'

Not until they had climbed into his truck and he reached into the pocket of his jacket for the keys did Billy find the bag of California dope Kazdan had put there. He must have done it while they were in the bathroom. His first impulse was to return it, but he decided not to when he read the note the doctor had wrapped around it: 'This is on the house, Billy. Drop by and let me know what happens.'

Poppy looked depressed and exhausted, and when Billy asked her if she was okay, she said she felt tired enough to sleep forever. 'We'll go to my place,' he said, starting the engine, 'and you can lie down in my bed and have a sleep. My mother has some Librium, you can take one of them.'

'What are they?'

'Just tranquilizers. Maybe we should have asked Kazdan for a prescription for you. I didn't think of it. I'll go back and see him again, in fact I'll go today. You have to eat something, too, Poppy, or you really will get sick. Did you have any breakfast?'

'No.'

Billy backed around and drove through the gravel parking lot next to Kazdan's new prefab office building to the back lane. As he was turning left into the lane, Rocky Barbizan was just turning into the lot. He signaled to Billy and braked his car; Billy stopped and rolled down his window. His friend's piercing blue eyes fixed themselves on Billy's face. They were smart eyes, Billy thought.

'Who died?' Rocky asked.

'Nobody. Do I look like somebody died?'

'You look worried.'

'Really? Well, you always say I spend my life worrying about nothing. This time it isn't nothing. Rocky, I have to go, I'll see you later.'

'I'm going down to the Princess to see Annette, I'll buy you a beer.'

'Maybe later, we'll see. Poppy's staying over till after supper so I don't know.'

Rocky waved and Billy drove out the back lane to Fourth Street South and then to the Mackenzie house. Poppy asked if his mother would be home and Billy remembered then that on Tuesdays Agnes Mackenzie did her weekly stint for the Ladies' Hospital Auxiliary by working for the afternoon in the Tuck Shop. She wouldn't be home until five, and at seven o'clock she had to be at the Legion for the bingo. His father would go directly from work to his Rotary Club dinner meeting. Except for about an hour and a half they would have the house to themselves. That was a stroke of luck he hadn't thought of.

He gave Poppy a Librium and made her eat a bowl of Campbell's Scotch broth and some toast. Then he took her into his room and gave her a pair of his old pajamas. Poppy protested, but Billy overrode her objection. 'For Pete's sake, Poppy, in a few days we'll be married. Just put the pajamas on and get into bed.'

'Your mother'll think it's funny, won't she?'

'I don't give a damn if she does, but if you're so concerned you can get into your clothes when you wake up and she'll never know.'

'I won't be able to sleep, I know it.'

Billy sat beside her. He brushed her hair against the pillows for a few minutes, and then held her hand in his own for a while and talked to her. Over and over, he reassured her that he loved her and would take care of her, and eventually he saw the strain and tension of her terror draining from her face. She let out a tremendous sigh and her body relaxed at last. It was almost four o'clock when she finally fell asleep; Billy left the room quietly and shut the door. In the kitchen he boiled some water, made a cup of instant coffee strong enough to taste bitter, and sat down at the kitchen table to smoke and think.

What he thought about was the Richardsons. For quite a while after he first met them, Billy had thought of them as perfect parents who had raised a happy and loving family with signal success. As he had gotten to know them, however, this fantasy had begun to disintegrate, a process which had yet to reach its bottom line. In his own way, Poppy's father was an autocratic tyrant with a very high opinion of himself and his accomplishments. As long as his son and daughters had done as he wanted them to do, in the home, at school, in the Catholic church, and in the community, the almost mythically happy family had sailed along smoothly like a boat on an ocean as calm as the water in a bathtub with nobody in it. Mrs

Richardson seemed basically not to count, not even to exist, as a person in her own right. He had yet to hear her disagree with her husband about anything that mattered. He golfed, so she golfed; he jogged, so she jogged, even when she was dog-tired. She cooked, she made beds, she cleaned house, she did enough church work for ten women, but at ten o'clock at night, even in the dead of winter, if it was time to go jogging, Ellen Richardson pushed herself up out of her chair, put on her jogging duds, and by God she jogged. And if she was slow getting ready, old man Richardson did not hesitate to show his impatience. Billy had finally come to the conclusion that he had run his family according to the same principles he adhered to as production manager at Kimberley-Clark. It wasn't a family at all; it was a small corporation. As such, it had clearly turned a profit, for until now no one had slipped up or slipped out, which in itself was surely a trifle odd. Poppy's brother, Jack, was a clone of his father, and Billy knew for a fact that the workers at the plant hated his guts. The ones who had been in high school with Jack didn't even say hello to him and would have nothing to do with him in their leisure time. Like his father, he seemed to have no real friends.

One night in particular stood out in Billy's memory as instructive of what really lay under the Richardson family's veneer. They had come to the end of a very long session of Trivial Pursuit and were chatting for a few minutes before Billy left for home. It was close to ten o'clock, almost time for the jogging ritual. Somehow the conversation had turned to the subject of possible careers for Billy, Poppy and young Rachel. Mr Richardson found this subject extremely congenial as it concerned the making of money and the achievement of success. Clearly, as far as he was concerned, Poppy's future had already been decided upon; he spoke confidently of how happy she would be *when* she was a teacher *and* working in Lac du Bois at St Patrick's school. Poppy made some comment to the effect that she would at least like to try acting, that she had always thought she might be a good actress.

Her father laughed indulgently, and Mrs Richardson smiled in amusement and said, 'My goodness, dear, you can't be an actress!' When Poppy asked why, Mrs Richardson went on to explain that all actresses were prostitutes, everyone knew that! They had to sleep with any man who wanted them to get anywhere. Billy knew that Poppy dreaded the idea of ending up as a teacher and was dying to get out of northern Ontario as soon as possible and forever. She had often spoken to him of the possibility of taking her university degree in the performing arts. He was just about to object to Ellen Richardson's assumption that all actresses were whores when Poppy's father announced that it was time to go jogging. His wife hopped up on cue and the evening was over, which was probably just as well.

Now Poppy was pregnant, and had been reduced to a state of abject terror by the idea of having to tell this to her mother and father. Anxiety, even extreme anxiety, Billy could have accepted as natural and normal; sexual revolution or no sexual revolution, he thought almost any girl from a respectable, small-town family would be fearful at the prospect of making that particular confession to her parents. But why the horrific dread that Poppy was experiencing now if Mommy and Daddy were in fact so all-fired loving? It didn't make sense. It didn't make sense at all, not if in her heart Poppy believed in her parents' love. But it made perfect sense alongside the preposterous assumption that all successful actresses were whores. Indeed, Billy realized, what would be more likely than that Poppy was feeling that by becoming pregnant she had become a whore?

By the time he had reached this point in his thinking, Billy could sense the gathering together of many resentments into a consolidated hostility toward Poppy's family. The look on her face, the way she was behaving, were not expressive of an anxiety suitable to the occasion; she had been giving off the signals of someone in positive and imminent danger. Suddenly, in wave after wave, love for Poppy surged through him as if there were too much blood in his veins and arteries, enough to burst his heart open at the seams. The pressure was actually painful. He felt he would kill to keep her from harm, he would kill anybody, without a second thought.

He would have to be careful. Thank God he had some money in the bank.

When his mother arrived home shortly after five o'clock, Billy told her as soon as she got in the front door that Poppy had been taken ill and was sleeping in his room. He said she had been ill ever since she came back from Mexico. She asked if she should warm up enough leftover stew for three, but Billy told her that he wanted to let Poppy sleep until she woke up on her own and that she should just feed herself. If Poppy were hungry when she woke up, he would eat with Poppy before he drove her home to Lac du Bois.

'Suit yourself,' Agnes Mackenzie said with a shrug of her shoulders.

Billy went into his room and found Poppy still sound asleep. He sat in the old wooden chair he had placed beside the bed, drank a warm beer from the case he kept in his room, and smoked a joint while he listened to the sounds of his mother warming up some stew and making a pot of tea.

Poppy slept peacefully until six-thirty, and Billy sat watching her. At six-thirty she either started to dream or reached a point in a dream already in progress that disturbed her. She began breathing through her open mouth in little pants and turning her head from side to side. Then she said quite distinctly, 'Oh, oh no, you don't mean that,' and seconds later she opened her eyes. Billy moved to sit on the edge of the mattress and spoke her name as he stroked her long, tousled hair from her eyes and forehead.

'Oh, Billy,' she said, 'I was dreaming.'

'I know, you were talking in your sleep. You said, "Oh, oh no, you don't mean that." What were you dreaming?'

After a moment Poppy said she couldn't remember a thing except that she had been in danger, great danger of some kind.

'You're not in danger, darling, you're here with me in my room. You've been sleeping for hours. It's almost quarter to seven. Move over so I can lie down beside you.' When Billy had lain down and propped one of the ancient pillows behind his head, he drew Poppy to his side and she rested her head on his shoulder. 'I can feel you tightening up like a spring,' he whispered, 'relax, for God's sake, let yourself go. I love you, you know. I've been sitting in that chair and loving you for ages.'

'You have?'

'Yes, I have. I was waiting for you to wake up so I could hold you like this.' Billy tightened his arm.

'Oh, Billy, I do love you.' Poppy drew in a deep breath and let it out in an audible sigh. Her forehead sank into the place where his neck joined his shoulder, and he could feel her warm breath on his throat.

'I'll love you till I die, Poppy, and I'm glad you're pregnant, I'm glad you're having my baby, I'm glad, I'm glad.'

'How can you be glad, Billy? How can you say that?'

'You don't mean how, you mean why. And right now that doesn't matter, Poppy. What matters now is that it's true, that I mean it. Figuring out why something is true takes a long time, and sometimes it can't be done no matter how long you think about it. If our baby's a little girl, I want one favor, I want to name her Anne for my sister.' There was a pause, and then he added, in a choked whisper, 'You see, I can't even say her name without crying.'

'I hope it is a girl if that's what you want. And of course we'll call her Anne.' Poppy sat up and used the edge of the sheet to wipe the tears from Billy's eyes. 'Please don't cry darling, you know I can't bear it when you're unhappy and so sad.'

Billy looked at her and smiled. 'I'm not sad, honey, I'm sort of happy. It was just the idea of a new Anne, a happy Anne. I know it's a stupid idea, but I like it anyway. Because she will be happy, you know, and she will be free and strong, and she will love us and not ever be afraid of us if we let her be free, if we just learn how to let her be free. I know one thing we must not do, we mustn't think of this child as *ours*. We must never talk about *our* baby, or about *my* son or *my* daughter. It must be very hard to do because nobody does it, it must be almost irresistible, almost impossible. We'll have to be careful. We must be on guard against that starting now.'

'Don't we have to think of her or him as somebody's?' Poppy asked. 'If it isn't ours, whose is it?'

'It's God's. It's God's baby. You know, I've never been able to say I don't believe in God, I must have known He'd come in handy some day and He has. It's God's baby. Isn't that thrilling to know? It's the most thrilling idea I've ever had and I feel like celebrating it so I'm going to smoke a joint on it and think about it all night.'

He reached under the mattress for what was left of the pot Rocky had given him on his birthday.

'There's a bottle of wine under the bed somewhere, behind the case of beer. You find it and we'll have a glass of wine to celebrate God's new baby. Come on, get out that wine. I'm not crazy, I'm just happy.'

Poppy climbed out from under the covers in Billy's pajamas, and the bottoms fell to the floor around her feet. Billy laughed as she reached down to pull them up. 'What's the point of pulling them back up? You might as well leave them there. There are some wine glasses hidden behind that bookcase.' He lit the joint while Poppy found the wine and the glasses. 'Remember how I told you Anne and I used to lock ourselves in here on Tuesday nights and talk? It was just like this, and I can almost imagine she's here now watching us. This wine has been there since before she—since before she—'

'You don't have to say it, Billy.'

'Yes, I do. I have to say it until I can say it without this happening. I can't start bawling every time I think of it for the rest of my life. It's been there since before she killed herself. You look cute in my pajama tops. You can take them home with you and sleep in them tonight.'

Poppy was actually laughing. He poured two glasses of wine and gave one to her.

'I think we should both make a toast.' He clinked his glass against Poppy's and said, 'To God's baby. Now it's your turn.'

'I don't know what to say.'

'Say what's in your heart, just say it, don't think about it.'

'I love you, I love you, I love you, Billy Mackenzie, I love you, I love you. I love you! Why am I crying?'

Billy laughed. 'You're not, you're loving me and I love you for it, I love you back, Poppy Elizabeth Richardson Mackenzie! Now we have to drink the whole glass down together. Down the hatch!'

They drank the wine and Billy set the glasses on the chair to refill them. He left them there and took Poppy in his arms. 'We're all alone, you know,' he said.

'I know.' The room seemed very still.

'Let's make God's baby again. I don't care if it's a boy or a girl, you know, as long as it's one or the other. As long as it's beautiful and smart as a whip.' He brushed his lips lightly across Poppy's. 'Let's make it all over again. God wants us to, you know, He does, He really does.'

He undid the buttons on his pajama top and touched Poppy's breasts.

'I,' he whispered, and kissed the nipple on her left breast.

'Love,' he whispered, and kissed the nipple on her right breast.

'You,' he said, and kissed her mouth.

'Oh, God, I love you, Billy.'

Then Billy took off his clothes and they made God's baby better than they'd ever made it before.

After the loving, they lay side by side and drank a second glass of wine.

'I'm going to say something I've never been able to say before,' Billy said after a few minutes. 'I'm all fucked out. God must be happy now.' He turned his head to look at Poppy. 'I don't give a shit about my family, I don't give a shit about your family, I don't give a shit what anybody on the whole fucking earth thinks of us. I don't give a shit about anybody or anything but you and me and that baby. Tomorrow after school we'll tell 'em all, and anybody who doesn't like it can go to hell.'

'No,' Poppy said. 'I've been thinking. I want to tell my parents myself.' She sat up with her arms around her knees.

'Why all of a sudden?'

'I don't know, I just do. I want to take my share of the responsibility. I'll tell them tonight as soon as I get home, then tomorrow we can talk to them together if they want it that way. You can drive me home after school. What time is it?'

Billy checked his watch. 'Who'd have believed it, it's nine-fifteen.'

Poppy climbed over his legs and began dressing. 'Take me home now before they have a chance to get to bed. I mean to get it over with tonight before I lose my courage. I'm tired of feeling so frightened, and if I wait until tomorrow I'll just lie awake all night and get sick again.'

By the time they pulled up outside the Richardson home, all the lights were out except in Poppy's parents' bedroom. She kissed Billy and opened the door. Before shutting it again she said, 'I'm glad. In fifteen minutes it'll be done with. I'll see you in the morning, Billy. Good night.' She slammed the door and he watched her disappear into the darkness between the high cedar hedges.

During the drive to Lac du Bois they had figured out their combined assets. The Richardsons had been giving Poppy a five-hundred-dollar bond for her birthday every year since her birth; by now they must be worth at least ten thousand dollars. Thanks to the money he had been making that summer, Billy had about six thousand dollars in his bank account. They had enough to get through to the end of the first semester, when Poppy would have enough credits for her grade twelve diploma. Billy was going to look into the possibility of taking a fourth credit by correspondence. If that turned out to be possible, he would be through at the same time. And they had five months to make the decisions about what to do then.

CHAPTER ELEVEN

When Billy got home the living room light was on and the TV was loud enough to be heard from out on the street when he got out of his truck. He was a bit surprised to see his father's Datsun in the driveway since it was only ten-thirty and the Rotary meetings usually kept him out later. He walked up the gravel drive and went into his room through the back yard door. They must have seen his truck arrive. There was no way they could have heard him come in the door through the reverberating din of television noise, but one of them knocked at his door as soon as he had taken off his shirt. He unshot the bolt lock and opened the door. It was his father. Billy said hi.

'Your mother and I wish to speak to you in the living room,' he announced. Billy said sure thing and followed him into the living room. His father turned the television volume down to zero and then sat down beside his wife on the sofa. Agnes Mackenzie was staring at him purposefully. Billy said hello to her and asked how she had done at her bingo.

A lengthy pause ensued before she said, 'I didn't go to the bingo.' She lit a cigarette and exhaled.

Billy took that in. 'Where did you go? It must have been important for you to give up your bingo.' He was still standing in the archway.

'I didn't go anywhere.'

'Oh,' Billy said. He knew then what was coming. He leaned his bare shoulder against the archway and waited. His mother continued to stare at him with stony eyes. She had a large repertoire of patented looks, each one subtly different. The look she was using on him now was her most impassive. Like a reptile, she seemed not even to blink. This look meant You-Are-Not-There-I-Have-Obliterated-You.

'I am here,' Billy said finally. 'I thought you both wanted to talk to me. What's the problem?'

'Tell him, Alex,' his mother said, without moving her eyes.

'After what went on in your bedroom tonight, your mother and I have decided that you are not to bring that girl into this house again.' Having spoken, Alex Mackenzie peeked at his wife to see if he'd read his line correctly.

Billy said slowly, 'After what went on tonight. What exactly does that mean?'

'It means just what it means.' His mother paused long enough to butt one cigarette and light another. Then she swallowed some tea. She really was a consummate actress, Billy thought; her timing was flawless. 'It means don't bring that chippie into my house again. Ever.'

Billy's first impulse was to shout that Poppy was not a chippie, but he stopped himself by grinding his teeth hard together. Chippie was a word his mother used often to describe girls who reputedly slept around, or who looked like they might someday. A few years back, Billy had hunted the word up in a dictionary and learned that a chippie was a prostitute. Agnes Mackenzie saw chippies, tramps, and sluts everywhere. Every girl Billy had dated fell into that category.

He stuck his hands into his back pockets. 'What exactly is a chippie, Mother?' he asked quietly. 'Or am I still too young to know?' She didn't respond except by blowing out smoke. 'Poppy is my girlfriend, Mother. Actually, she's my fiancée.' He knew that word would cut deep. 'She comes from a very nice family and I've been going with her—'

'Going is right,' his mother interrupted.

'—I've been going with her for almost two years, more than

two years, in fact. She is not a chippie, as you know perfectly well.'

'You can call her whatever you like,' said his mother. 'Just don't bring her into my house again.' She drank some more tea.

'We wanted someplace to talk, Mother,' Billy explained, 'and it's too cold to sit outside in my truck because the heater isn't working too well. So we sat in my room for a while after she woke up. Is there something wrong with that?'

'Some talker she is,' Agnes Mackenzie snapped back.

In a voice that shook with his effort to contain his anger, Billy asked, 'What do you mean by that?' He must not lose control. That was what his mother wanted him to do. 'Answer me, Mother, I want to know what you mean.'

'Since when do I have to answer you in my home?'

Exasperation broke through Billy's resolve. His voice, when it came, was almost a shout. 'Since never, Mother! We all know whose house this is! I don't believe this, I'm nineteen years old and I have to go through a KGB inquisition because I had my girlfriend and fiancée in my bedroom for a few hours. I love her, I love Poppy, for Christ's sake! I thought you might have figured that one out by now!'

'I'll tell you what I know, I know what you two did in that room tonight. I don't care how old you are, you're not turning my home into a whorehouse with that little tramp.'

At that point, Billy slammed out of the house by the front door before he lost control entirely. The urge to slap his mother's face had been almost irresistible. How right Anne had been – Agnes Mackenzie would be easy to kill. His father, who had sat through it all without an objection, wasn't worth murder.

Though it was only the fourth of September, the night wind was bitterly cold when Billy stepped out onto the small porch. After his mother's carefully calculated use of the words whorehouse and tramp, his mind had gone temporarily blank. It was amazing that his mother could still get to him. For years he had been telling himself he had stopped caring what either of his parents thought, said, or did, but obviously he was wrong. Agnes Mackenzie was not only still able to penetrate his defenses; she had the power to demolish them and would go to any lengths to do so. Billy's body was jangling all over like a diesel engine on high idle. He felt like he wanted to do some damage, a lot of it. He wanted to break things up.

Instead, he took a joint out of his wallet and smoked it. He sat down on the top step, though he didn't give a shit if they saw him or not. During the first couple of drags, he thought about his father's initial pronouncement, so proper and pompous, so prissy and refined. Instead of calling Poppy a whore or a tart, he referred to her as 'that girl'. In a way, Billy realized, he preferred his mother's naked aggression to his father's civilized cowardice. Agnes Mackenzie's declarations of war unfailingly provoked a response of some kind; you couldn't help but fight back because you knew she meant to liquidate you. The urgent need to assert himself was gathering in Billy now, spreading with the speed of electricity along high-voltage wires. Rationally, he knew he didn't care what his parents did or did not know about what had gone on in his room tonight. It wasn't tonight that was enraging him. It was the sickening sense of having been raised as a criminal, of having lived his entire life under incessant secret surveillance.

Undoubtedly, he and Poppy had been spied on. Usually his father did the actual spying, but his father had not been home while he and Poppy were happily making love in his room. He distinctly remembered having heard the loud slam of the front door at ten minutes to seven – and he'd assumed his mother was gone. He also knew that his mother had not telephoned his father to come home until after he and Poppy left for Lac du Bois; the Datsun had not been in the driveway. It was, of course, possible that Alex Mackenzie had parked his car down the street and sneaked into the house silently, then gone to get it later. Now, there was an assignment that would exert a natural appeal on his father's cowardly and nasty instinct for the acquisition of secret knowledge. Over and over, Billy imagined his father slipping soundlessly into the house in response to a whispered phone call, then gliding like an ethereal snoop across the dark kitchen to eavesdrop at Billy's door. Had he also peeked at them through the half-inch crack that had opened up over the years between the doorjamb and the plasterboard wall? Almost certainly he had, Billy decided. In his mind rose the image of Alex Mackenzie peering through the narrow crack with one pale blue eyeball.

He placed his elbows on the floor of the porch and leaned back on them. Around him, the September night was dark and wild, as if the elements of nature were as overcharged with energy as Billy was himself. Overhead, but pressed close down like a lid, tumultuous clouds were boiling like dirty water in the sky. As he gazed up into that dark and queerly silent turmoil, the clouds in the night sky transformed themselves into a crowd of demented faces with bulging, watching eyes. Across the gravel road and its weed-choked open ditches, the north wind whipped at the tops of the evergreens in the bush that stretched from there to God knew where. The violent sky, the treetops that seemed to be smacking against it like big black tongues, the cold rush of the wind, all were so alive, so alive. The entire universe was pulsing around him like a dangerously inflamed organism about to blow up. Like me, Billy reflected, it looks as dangerous as I feel. The dope had already done its job and he felt a crazy grin opening up in his face like a manhole. He imagined it getting bigger and bigger until he was nothing but a monster mouth screaming 'Fuck off!' at the observers in the darkly moving sky.

The next thing Billy knew he was back inside the house, responding like a trained rat to his mother's challenge, looking for trouble that he intended to find.

In the living room, the TV was once more pouring out the

noise of commercials but the room was empty. He saw the crack of light under his parents' bedroom door; his father had gone to bed. But the kitchen light was on and he knew he would find his mother there, waiting for him. She knew it wasn't over, that the pattern wasn't complete. She was standing at the counter waiting for toast to pop up. Billy knew she knew he had entered the kitchen; he also knew that she would ignore him.

He heard himself saying, 'Mother, I have to talk to you.'

'Then talk,' she replied tonelessly without turning to look at him. 'I can hear you.'

'I'm not going to talk to your back.'

'Then don't talk,' she said in the same monotone.

When she wanted to, which was often, his mother could empty her voice of any identifiable emotion. The sound that came out didn't even sound human; it sounded like it was rising from the depths of an abandoned mine shaft. It was the vocal equivalent of the face that meant You-Are-Not-There. Billy leaned one side of his rump on the edge of the kitchen table and gazed at his mother's eloquently hostile back in stoned amazement. He thought that at that moment the woman actually hated him. Then he asked himself, is it possible my own mother hates me because I had sex with my girl in my bedroom tonight? Surely it was unbelievable that she would feel any more than disapproval. It couldn't be just the sex. His parents had known at least since the day he ate the condom that he was fucking the girls he dated. It had to be the fact that he was in love with Poppy Richardson that she hated.

The toast popped up into the long, long silence. It seemed to have taken forever, but Billy knew that was the effect of the dope. Slowly, slowly, Agnes Mackenzie spread the toast with butter and jam. On the stove, the kettle was just coming to a boil for a fresh pot of tea. When his mother turned to get the teapot she glanced at Billy as if he were an uninteresting intruder.

'I thought you wanted to talk.'

He had won a round.

'I just want to get this business about tonight straight in my mind,' Billy explained quietly.

'It's already straight as far as I'm concerned.' She dumped the contents of the teapot into the sink. Then she turned the hot water on full blast to heat up the teapot while she rinsed it out.

'That's good, now you can explain it to me,' Billy continued sociably. 'As you know, I've always been sort of slow to understand what's going down around here. I mean, you say you know what went on inside my room tonight when I thought you were playing bingo, but I obviously don't know what went on outside my room tonight. Since it's supposed to be my bedroom and Poppy is my tramp, I figure I have a right to know how the hell you know so much!' Without knowing he was going to do it, Billy banged both fists down so hard on the table top that his hands hurt and the table bounced. 'That is what I want to discuss. If it's not too much trouble, of course.'

His mother put two tea bags into the warmed-up teapot and poured boiling water over them. She set the pot on the back burner of the stove to stew the tea. When she had done that, she picked up her plate of toast and set it carefully on the table. Then she lit a cigarette and leaned against the sink counter to stare at Billy while he stared back, waiting.

During the staring contest, which was an obligatory phase of the ritual in every major confrontation, Billy could not deny that what he saw in his mother's green eyes did look like pure hatred. Her eyes looked stuck open and her eyeballs were still as blank and unblinking as a reptile's. It was like gazing into the loaded barrels of a shotgun, and his assumption that she must be certifiable didn't make her any less scary.

'Don't you shout at me,' she warned when she was bored with staring. She delivered each word separately like a pitched stone. 'When Madame Cecile found out you were born under the Dog Star moon, she told me what to expect. She was right, you've been nothing but trouble since the day you were born.' Madame Cecile was a charlatan from Thunder Bay who claimed to be psychic. A couple of times a year she toured around the dismal little towns giving palm readings, holding séances, and raking in a small fortune.

He leaned across the table and spoke softly. 'I wouldn't have to shout, Mother, if you didn't keep that fucking television set turned up loud enough to reach the Goddamned moon.'

Agnes Mackenzie let out a mouthful of contemptuous smoke and tossed her cigarette into the sink. Placing both hands on the other end of the table, she leaned toward her son venomously. 'Look, Mister Big Shot, this is my house, and it's my TV, and I don't have to take any crap from a foul-mouthed punk like you. I don't have to answer any of your questions either. If you don't like the house rules, you know where the door is.'

Billy burst into laughter. 'I love it, I absolutely love it! You've been using that line on me since I was old enough to piss standing up. We need new dialogue for the act, even if this is the last performance. As for my language, I'm proud to say I have never used a word in this house that I didn't learn from you.'

The term 'last performance' had struck home; Billy had seen the muscles in his mother's face twitch, and he smiled at her broadly because he knew she would die before she would ask what he meant.

Agnes Mackenzie said, 'You want to know what I think? I think you're stoned, you Goddamned dope addict. I saw you smoking out on the front steps. I knew that's what you were doing.'

'Did you now!' Billy exclaimed. 'I am stoned. So what? I guess I have no secrets at all, do I? You know just every little thing I do and that is that. That's what always gets to me, Mother, how much you know, and the interesting ways you and your peeping Tom acquire your knowledge. I shouldn't be surprised as often as I have been, of course. I've had nineteen years of living in this fucking precinct house, I ought to be used to it.'

His mother had poured herself a cup of hot black tea and was placing the teapot back on the burner. Billy went over to the door of his room and inspected the crack where the plasterboard panels in both the kitchen and his bedroom had pulled away from the doorjamb. By pressing his right eye against the opening, he could see clearly into his room, though he could only see the bottom half of his bed because it was placed alongside the north wall. He stepped back and studied the door and the wall. Agnes Mackenzie had picked up her plate of cold toast and her cup of tea and was just leaving the kitchen on her way to the TV in the living room when Billy lifted his right foot as high into the air as possible and drove it at the wall. Even he was surprised to see his foot and ankle disappear through both plaster panels into his room. He heard the wooden chair beside his bed topple to the floor. He lifted his leg again, aimed carefully, and drove it with all his strength at the side of the door. The top hinge broke and the door hung crazily in space.

His mother was shouting. 'You'll pay for that, you crazy bugger! Alex! Alex! Phone the police!'

'Why bother with them?' Billy asked. 'You're the Chief of Police in this Hell's Kitchen.'

His father was now standing behind his mother in the hallway in his pajamas.

'He's doped up, Alex, stay out of his way. Tell the police we've got a dope fiend smashing up the house.'

'If you bring in the cops, Mother, everybody in town will know all about it. And boy, will I talk or will I talk. Before I'm through, nobody'll be wondering anymore about why Anne killed herself. Just for the hell of it, I might do some embroidering, and I'm a very convincing liar. But even if I stick straight to the truth, you'll never live it down.'

His father was dialing the OPP.

'Hang up the phone, Alex.'

'I will be more than happy to pay for the damage. I'll get the money from the bank tomorrow, cash, and put it into your hands.' Billy gestured at the jagged hole in the wall and the broken door. 'I am now going to bed to sleep for the last night in your house, Mother. Tomorrow night I will come and get the few things I think of as mine. I may be a bit late because I have to go over to see the Richardsons; Poppy and I are getting married. As you can clearly see without having to peek through narrow cracks, my bedroom has no one in it, I will be sleeping alone. But if you feel like checking things out, feel free to do so as often as you please. I do sleep naked and often kick off the blankets during the night. Don't let that stop you, though, as I'm not the least bit shy, stare all you want. Now, may I please get by you both so I can go to the bathroom? I have to urinate, but I will leave the door open while doing so.'

His parents backed up against the door of Anne's room and Billy went past them and into the bathroom, leaving the door open behind him. He heard them walk into the living room while he was pissing. As he was leaving the bathroom a few moments later, he turned quite spontaneously to the right and walked into the living room himself. He smiled at both of them and went to stand beside the television set.

'Since this is my last night under my parents' roof,' he said, 'I am going to do something I've been thinking of doing for years.'

He turned the volume knob to the right as far as it would go. The noise of the beer commercial that happened to be on at the time made the TV set vibrate. He nodded once to each of his parents and left the room.

In his bedroom, he stripped off his jeans and shorts, took a couple of warm beers from the box under his bed, opened them both, and lay down on the bed to drink them. His body was almost slimy with sweat so he didn't even pull the sheet over himself. Sleep seemed out of the question in his hopped-up state, but perhaps the beer would tone him down if he drank enough of it.

The television set was turned off while he was getting out the beer, then the lights in the living room went out. But only his father went to bed, and Billy lay there thinking of his wretchedly unhappy mother sitting in the dark and smoking, smoking, smoking. Sometime after his fourth beer, he must have dozed off because he woke up at four o'clock to hear the sound of Agnes Mackenzie's anguished sobbing from the living room. Hate him she might, but love him beyond endurance she always had, and Billy knew it. If there was one thing Agnes Mackenzie did not want, it was to part from her son. Billy was her life.

CHAPTER TWELVE

Agnes Mackenzie went into her bedroom a few minutes past five. Billy waited half an hour before he got up and made himself a pot of coffee. When the coffee was ready, he poured himself a mugful and lay in bed to drink it and smoke. His father was late getting ready for work and didn't show up in the kitchen until almost eight o'clock. Billy happened to be up to refill his mug and their eyes met through the open doorway. His father stared at him with a hurt pout on his face and said, 'I hope you're happy now.'

'I don't expect to be happy,' Billy answered, and went back to lie down after pulling the coffee pot plug from the wall outlet. He had drunk the pot dry. His father ate hastily and left for work. Billy put on the same clothes he had taken off, grabbed a binder filled with blank paper, and slipped out the door into the back yard. But it was even colder than it had been the night before and there was frost on the grass, so he went back to get his basketball jacket, which was hanging over the back of a kitchen chair where he'd left it the previous afternoon. At school he went directly to the east-end doors and waited for Poppy's bus to arrive.

She looked tired and pale in her scarlet coat, but she seemed to be under control. Billy walked with her to her locker.

'How did things go?' he asked on the way.

'Not as bad as they could have,' Poppy replied with a grimace. 'I was right about Mother, she was expecting it. She cried all night.'

'And your father, how did he take it?'

'He was horrified. But I expected that. He kept saying "How could you do this to your mother?" '

Billy couldn't help smiling.

'Anyway, we're going over to talk over our plans with them after school. Daddy's leaving work early. I told them we'd be there about three-thirty.'

Billy walked Poppy to her home room and told her what had happened between himself and his parents. Naturally, she was upset, even though he assured her the split had been in the air for years, and that he personally was glad it was over and done with.

At eight-forty-five the bell rang to signify that it was time students were either in or heading for their first period class. When Billy got to Mr Agnew's classroom, his teacher waited until he had sat down before reminding him that jackets were not allowed in class. Billy explained that he had quite forgotten to get a locker the day before.

'Then you'd better do it now,' Mr Agnew said.

'Sir, it's seven minutes to nine, I'll be late for class if I go now. Couldn't I just put it on one of the empty seats for today?'

No, he couldn't. Billy got back up and went down to the office. The final bell rang just as he got there and he had to stand and wait through the Lord's Prayer, the national anthem on tape, and five minutes of announcements. Then he bought a combination lock, walked to the locker, hung up his jacket, put on the lock, and went back to class.

When he opened the door and walked in, Mr Agnew glanced at the clock on the wall and looked expectantly at Billy, waiting for him to produce the pink late slip he had not even thought of asking for. So Billy went back to the office and lined up behind half a dozen other students to wait his turn. Miss Sweet was surprised.

'Isn't this the first time you've ever been late, Billy?' she asked. He said yes. As she made out the slip Miss Sweet said it was a shame he had spoiled his perfect attendance record.

Billy returned to his algebra class only to have Mr Agnew call his attention to the fact that he had forgotten to buy the algebra textbook at the school bookstore.

'If I go to buy it now, sir,' Billy said patiently, 'do you want me to get another late slip or will that one do?' This problem was resolved by Mr Agnew's returning the late slip Billy had just given him and instructing him to have Miss Sweet alter the time notation. The secretary who looked after the sale of grade thirteen textbooks was busy, so it was fifteen minutes before Billy walked into Mr Agnew's classroom for the third time and was at last permitted to sit down and stay that way.

Five minutes later there was a knock on the door and, after a few seconds of waiting, Mr Agnew turned from the door and told Billy he was wanted in the hall. Billy expected to find Poppy but found Mr Cartwright instead. He assumed Cartwright was there to talk about Billy's rejoining the basketball team, though the phys ed teacher was wearing a decidedly somber face.

Cartwright ordered Billy to follow him and led him through the school to his private office, which was located in a narrow corridor that ran along the west side of the gymnasium down to the boys' and girls' change rooms. His former teacher and coach unlocked the door to his office and grimly motioned Billy inside. The first thing Billy saw was his own basketball team jacket lying on Cartwright's cluttered desk. He knew then what was coming; it hit him like a fist. Behind him, the teacher had closed the door of his office with a neat little click.

When Billy turned to look at him, Cartwright was wearing a combination of the standard teacher's You've-Been-Caught look and the I'm-Deeply-Disappointed-in-You look. While Cartwright silently dished up the looks, Billy was thinking. For four years he had been the top student in Cartwright's phys ed classes; for almost four years he had played on the junior and senior basketball teams under this man's coaching. Not once had there been any trouble between them until Cartwright busted Rocky, at which time Cartwright had already selected Billy as Athlete of the Year. They had not been friends, of course; Cartwright's unceasing crusade against nicotine, alcohol, and any kind of dope would have prevented friendship under any circumstances. But they had been friendly. Now the man was trying to terrorize Billy into breakdown and confession as he had done to others so often in the past. But this time Billy could discern a particularly intense shine of triumph in Cartwright's eyes. He had landed a hot one, a top academic student with a previously untarnished reputation. Unexpectedly, Billy started to giggle. The situation had suddenly reminded him of an old TV show called *The White Shadow*. Today it was his turn to be straightened out by the saintly coach-confessor who would show him the way to redemption.

Sure enough, when Billy started giggling, Cartwright promptly dug out of his Rugby pants pocket the plastic bag of dope David Kazdan had put into Billy's jacket the day before. He held the bag of marijuana out toward Billy on the palm of his right hand and inquired in a polite, almost prissy voice, 'When you're quite through laughing, perhaps you'll let me in on the joke? Perhaps you'll also tell me what this is?'

Cartwright had spoken in a well-practiced, Shame-on-You voice, rich with his automatic assumption that his victim would cower in fear and guilt. Now that he was at last the victim, the assumption struck Billy as unbearably presumptuous.

He heard himself saying, 'I'm sorry I laughed, Mr Cartwright, it was just a private joke. As for what's in your hand, you obviously know perfectly well what it is, so I don't understand why you're asking that particular question. I've been caught red-handed, haven't I? Do we have to play games?'

Cartwright lifted his eyebrows half an inch; he was almost as good with his eyebrows as Agnes Mackenzie.

'Games? I'm asking you that particular question, as you put it, Billy, because I found this particular substance in the pocket of your particular jacket in your particular locker. Much to my surprise,' he added after an expertly timed pause, 'much to my surprise.'

The gym teacher's eyes were still projecting sorrowful disillusion, as if Billy had deceived him personally and on purpose. Cartwright was good, there was no doubt about that. Billy might even have believed his feelings were authentic had he not heard the routine so often before, and had Cartwright been able to entirely dissimulate his transparent consciousness of supreme power. But the policeman in his heart had usurped the inner stage, perhaps because he had interpreted Billy's giggling as a form of insolence. In any case, the cop outwitted the concerned mentor.

'Well,' Billy said eventually, 'if you want me to say it that badly I'll say it for you. What you have in your hand is about an ounce of supersonic pot from sunny California. Just the other day I read someplace that it's now a bigger cash crop than Sunkist oranges.' While he was talking, he was wondering how Cartwright had known the stuff was in his pocket. Surely it was impossible the cops had installed secret cameras in Kazdan's office.

As if he had been reading Billy's mind, Cartwright said, 'I saw you talking to Rocky yesterday afternoon in Dr Kazdan's parking lot.'

The teacher waited for a response. When Billy said nothing, Cartwright intoned ominously, 'Nothing to say, Billy?'

'Nothing whatsoever,' Billy answered. 'Everything's automatic now, isn't it? The letter to my parents, the automatic suspension, et cetera, et cetera. Just go ahead and do your duty. May I have my jacket so I can leave?'

Cartwright stared at Billy intently. At last he asked softly,

'Do I detect a touch of defiance perhaps?'

'To be honest, sir, I don't give a damn what you detect. It's not every day somebody opens my locker and goes rooting through my pockets. I can't pretend I like the sensation. Actually, it would never have entered my mind that you or anyone else had the right to do that. I'd have thought it was against the law.'

'We have the right if we have reasonable suspicion.'

'And seeing me talk to a friend for all of two minutes through two windows counts as grounds for suspicion? That's some law.' Billy picked up his jacket.

'Put that jacket down!' Cartwright ordered.

Billy put his jacket on and said, 'I told you I want out of here and I meant it. I have things to do. You want me to feel guilty, but I don't, not one bit. You broke into my locker and took my jacket. Now you've got what you want and I've got my jacket back. All I want to do is get out of this place and you're in my way.'

Cartwright was standing directly in front of the door with one hand on the doorknob. Billy would have to shove him aside unless the man moved. The gym teacher had lost his sanctimonious, priest-like expression entirely; he looked scared and uncertain.

'You're in my way,' Billy repeated, 'and I mean to get out one way or another. Unless, of course, you plan to call in the cops.'

'Nobody said anything about the police, Billy,' Cartwright said. He moved forward and placed his left hand on Billy's shoulder.

'Don't touch me,' Billy snarled, shrugging his shoulder free. He ducked past Cartwright, yanked open the door, and headed up the narrow corridor.

'Billy!' Cartwright shouted behind him. 'I'll see you in Mr Popowski's office! That's an order!'

Billy whirled to look back just before he reached the door

that opened into the main hallway. 'Fuck you,' he said clearly. 'Do I make my feelings perfectly plain? I say fuck you and fuck off.' While he was speaking, his eyes had alighted on one of a row of framed photographs that adorned the walls of the corridor. It was a blown-up photograph of a beaming Jack Cartwright embracing Billy after the Nugget High School senior boys' team won the Northern Ontario championship trophy two years earlier. As Cartwright lunged toward him shouting, Billy ripped the framed picture from the wall and smashed it on the floor. Splintered glass flew across the fake marble. 'And fuck your buddy-buddy act while you're at it,' Billy said before he walked through the doorway.

When he reached the west end of the hallway, he found himself confronted by Mr Popowski and Mr Slago, one of the vice-principals. Cartwright must have contacted the principal's office via the intercom system.

Mr Popowski said quietly, 'Please step into my office, Billy, where we can discuss this problem in private with Mr Cartwright. He's on his way down.'

'There is no problem, I've quit school and I've already said all I have to say to Cartwright.'

He stepped around Mr Popowski and pushed open one of the inner doors. The principal took his arm and said, 'Billy, you know you don't want to quit school now with one semester to go.'

'I know you don't want me to, Mr Popowski. You've been talking for years about all the money I can win with grades like mine when I get my honors diploma. But I sure don't want anybody giving their lily-white money to a dope addict like me.' By then, both Cartwright and Mr Thurston, the other vice-principal, had joined the palace guard.

Mr Slago said in a low voice, 'Nobody is calling you a dope addict, Billy, we know you are not a dope addict.'

'I'm calling myself a dope addict, Mr Slago, because that's how I've been treated.' He could see the pain and confusion in all the mens' eyes as they darted perplexed and unhappy glances back and forth rapidly. His intransigent hostility had taken them by surprise. In some way that was more important to these men than all they sincerely believed he was throwing away, Billy had won. They didn't know what to do with their faces.

'Please don't do this, Billy,' Mr Popowski pleaded.

Billy detached his arm from the principal's grasp, smiled at them, and said, 'Goodbye.'

He walked for the last time out of the school in which he had been a source of general pride. Everybody's darling had thrown himself out on his ass. No doubt it was a big mistake, but he knew he would never return. The four men would now hold a private conference in which they would attribute his bizarre behavior to the evil effects of smoking dope, and thus restore order to their necessary version of the universe. It wouldn't take five minutes.

Billy walked home to pick up his truck. His father's Datsun was parked in the driveway; Agnes Mackenzie must have summoned him to come home. Billy drove straight to the bank and withdrew two thousand dollars in hundred, fifty, and twenty dollar bills from his savings account. Before he drove back home, he telephoned the school and left a message for Poppy that he would pick her up at lunchtime. He parked his truck out on the street in front of the Mackenzie bungalow and went into the house through the front door. All the drapes were drawn and the blind was down on the window of his parents' bedroom; his mother had worked up a migraine; one of her real marathons. He was not surprised to find the bedroom door shut.

His father was in the kitchen. The sink was half full of cold water into which all the ice cubes had been dumped. A couple of small hand towels were soaking in the water; Alex Mackenzie was nursing his wife's migraine by putting cold cloths on her forehead and beneath her neck. At the moment he was waiting for the kettle to boil for tea. He looked at Billy reproachfully as his son walked across the kitchen into his room but said nothing.

Billy emptied the contents of the three drawers in his small bureau onto his bed and realized he had nothing to put them in. All he could think of for the purpose were the large green plastic garbage bags that were kept in the cupboard under the kitchen sink so he went to get them. The tea had been made and his father had disappeared with the cloths that had been soaking in the cold water. Billy could hear his mother moaning as he returned to his room with the package of garbage bags. It took him only a few minutes to stuff the clothing he had piled on his bed into two bags and tie the tops securely. With one in each hand, he stepped up into the kitchen to see his mother shuffling into the room in her housecoat. His father was following behind with his hands full of wet towels. Billy set the garbage bags down and waited until his mother had lowered herself into a chair at the table. Then he took the wad of money out of his pocket and counted ten hundred dollar bills onto the table.

'There's the money to fix the door and the wall with,' he said. 'That should be plenty, but if it turns out to be more you can let me know.'

His father had put the towels back into the cold water and was looking at Billy. 'Is that all you have to say to us?'

'I think we've said everything there is to say about as often as it needs saying. It'll take me a few more minutes to clear out the rest of my things.'

He picked up the plastic garbage bags.

'Is this supposed to mean you're leaving for good?' asked Agnes Mackenzie.

'That's the general idea.'

'And you're marrying Poppy Richardson?'

'Yes.'

Agnes Mackenzie tilted her head back to look into Billy's

eyes. Her own eyes radiated pain. 'How do you expect to finish school? You'll find you have to pump a lot of gas to support two people.'

'We'll manage, Mother. I've already quit school. They don't approve of me either. You'll be getting a letter from the principal which I'm sure will explain everything.'

'You're quite the independent hotshot all of a sudden, aren't you?' Agnes Mackenzie gestured toward the damage Billy had done. 'After nineteen years, you kick down doors and smash your feet through walls and then walk out of here like it was some kind of cheap rooming house.'

Billy thought for a moment and smiled at her. 'Not cheap, Mother. Don't ever think it's been cheap. You got your money's worth out of both of us.'

His mother flicked her eyes at the money that lay on the table and said, 'You think a thousand dollars pays for nineteen years?'

'I wasn't referring to the money, Mother,' Billy explained. 'The money is to pay for the repair of the damage I did. I hadn't realized I was obligated to pay for the nineteen years. But believe me, if I ever have the money to do it, I will. You can make out an itemized bill in the meantime and send it to me.'

'You are a nasty little bugger, aren't you? You don't give a damn about your father or about me.' Tears were gathering in Agnes Mackenzie's eyes.

'Mother,' Billy said quietly, 'I know you don't want me to leave like this, I know it's the last thing in the world you want. But I have to go, I'd have to go even if Poppy and I weren't getting married. I'm sorry about everything, but I just can't take it any more.'

He walked the few steps to the hallway door.

'Why don't you say what you mean?' his mother demanded behind him. 'You love that girl more than you've ever loved me!'

She broke down then and began sobbing. As he turned to look back, Billy felt tears in his own eyes. Agnes Mackenzie had thrown her head down into her cupped hands to weep. His father had moved to stand beside his wife, and placed his hands on her heaving shoulders to comfort her. But he was staring at Billy intently.

'I hope you realize what you're doing to your mother,' he said. 'You're breaking her heart.'

'I've got my own heart to worry about, that seems to be about all I can handle right now.' Billy was about to say that he would come back for the rest of his things when Agnes Mackenzie suddenly jerked back, whirled to face her son, and got to her feet.

'Let the ungrateful bastard go, Alex,' she commanded in a terrible, ragged voice. 'He isn't worth keeping.'

'You're right,' Billy agreed promptly, 'I'm not worth keeping. I probably never was. Neither was my sister. I have to come back for the rest of my things, but I'll say goodbye now. Goodbye.'

He was lugging the garbage bags out the driveway to the street when he heard the front door open and Agnes Mackenzie shouted, 'You! You with the garbage bags! You forgot something I don't want in my house!'

Billy turned to look back as he reached the gravel road. His mother's face was puffy and ravaged with the rage of defeat.

'You think I want your Goddamned money?' she shouted, stepping out onto the tiny porch as her husband appeared in the open doorway behind her. 'You think it's that easy to pay me off and kiss me goodbye?'

She raised her right arm high above her head. Clutched in her fist Billy saw the money he had left on the kitchen table. His father moved quickly to try and stop his wife from carrying out her obvious intention, but with a vicious thrust of her elbow she pitched him back against the open storm door.

'I wouldn't wipe my ass with your money, you rotten son of a bitch!'

With a beautifully executed sweep of her arm, Agnes Mackenzie threw the ten hundred dollar bills over the railing of the porch. The cold wind caught them and blew them off to the south across the neighbor's yard. Alex Mackenzie was already plunging down the steps to run after the money. Some of the bills were several houses away and were still whipping along across driveways and lawns. Billy had never seen his father move so fast. He had to restrain the impulse to laugh. Instead he looked back at his mother, who was now leaning with straight arms on the porch railing, her face proud and unyielding. Billy realized that he preferred the mad magnificence of his mother's theatrical gesture to the image of his father bobbing and ducking to scoop up the bills as he caught up to them. Had she been on a stage, the curtain would now descend to tumultuous applause and a standing ovation.

'You were always right about one thing, Mother,' Billy shouted, 'he is a cheapskate. Look at him go!'

Her eyes bright with crazed triumph, Agnes Mackenzie screamed, 'I'm glad I told the school about that dope I found in your pocket! Did you hear me? I said I'm glad I phoned the principal this morning!'

Billy stood gazing at his mother. She was panting with the thrill of having shocked him with her deliberately delayed revelation. Now Billy knew why Cartwright had searched his locker for dope. A telephone call from a distraught and concerned mother would certainly constitute grounds for reasonable suspicion.

Alex Mackenzie had returned with the money in his hand and was turning his head back and forth from his wife to his son, trying to figure out what had or had not been going on. He was out of his class, there was no doubt about that.

'So am I, Mother,' Billy replied at last, 'I'm just as glad as you are.'

He tossed the green garbage bags into the back of his truck and got in behind the wheel. His parents were still watching as he drove away.

During the few minutes it took to get to the school, and while he sat waiting with the engine idling for Poppy to come out the door, Billy thought over the apparently climactic scene that had just been played out. He was under no illusion that it was actually a real ending; this play never ended. Over the years, there had been countless farewell-forever speeches and stormy exits by one or another of the Mackenzies, but everybody knew the inner logic of the plot required a return engagement. Even Anne's suicide, while it had effectively precluded her physical return to the stage, had failed to remove her from the action. She had been present all along in the locked door to her room, in the empty chair at the table, in Agnes Mackenzie's prohibition of the mention of her name. Anne wasn't dead. She was just offstage.

The look on Poppy's face as she was crossing the road warned Billy that she had lost any ground she had gained. Guilt had bleached her white and she was trembling as she climbed in beside him. She said nothing about it, so he presumed she had yet to hear that he had quit school. When he asked how the morning had gone, she said, 'I couldn't concentrate, I keep thinking of poor Mommy and Daddy.'

Billy stamped on the clutch pedal and jammed the lever into first gear. 'Poor Mommy and Daddy,' he repeated, 'poor everybody except us! Jesus Christ!' Gravel flew as he took off.

'Don't be angry, Billy, please. That's all I need.'

'I apologize,' Billy said as he turned the corner toward Main Street. 'I have three further developments to report, maybe they'll get your mind off poor Mommy and Daddy. One, I quit school; two, I've left home; three, I'm hungry, where do you want to eat lunch?'

CHAPTER THIRTEEN

In the end, they didn't eat at all, they parked outside the Simpson-Sears catalogue office and Billy gave Poppy an account of his morning. His having left home did not much interest her; he would have been leaving in any case in a few days at the most. But she was frantic about his quitting school and his adamant refusal to even consider going back to talk things over with Mr Popowski that afternoon. Soon they were arguing.

'As if we don't have enough problems,' Poppy said. 'I don't understand why you have to make such important decisions now! Today of all days.'

'It wasn't a decision,' Billy said, 'or if it was, it was made a long time ago. I can't explain it, Poppy, I just wanted out. I want out of the life I'm in. I can't take any more of it right now! So just drop it!'

'Billy, you can't just drop everything! Or maybe that's what you want, maybe you want to drop me too. Is that it?'

Billy lit a cigarette and looked out the window at the phony fronts on the old buildings. 'I don't think that's fair, Poppy. I've always tried to be honest with you. I don't think I deserve accusations like that one.'

'No, you don't,' Poppy admitted. 'I'm sorry I said it. It's just that I thought we had everything planned, that we would both finish off this semester.'

'Maybe we will,' Billy answered. 'I can go back to school any time I want, honey, all I have to do is take a week's suspension. If you get right down to it, though, I don't want to go back because I don't know why I was still there in the first place. I haven't really wanted to be there for a long time.'

'What will you do?'

'Work for a while,' Billy said. 'I think I'd like that, actually. I'd have some time to do some thinking instead of just filling up my days preparing for a future I hate the very thought of.' He looked at his wristwatch. 'It's time to take you back to school.' He started the engine and headed his truck back toward the high school. A light drizzle filled the air and he turned on the windshield wipers. Minutes later, he pulled up on the gravel shoulder at the end of the sidewalk that led to the west doors.

'Before you go, I want to ask you a question,' Billy said suddenly. 'How'd you like to move to Toronto?'

Poppy stared at him. 'You mean just leave?'

'Yeah,' Billy said, 'I mean just leave. I think it would be a good idea if we cleared out of here, I think it would solve a lot of problems. You can finish off your diploma there. There's nothing to stop us, you know, nothing at all.'

'Is *that* what you want to do?'

'I think it's a good idea, yes, I do. I wish you could see the look on your face, Poppy. You'd think I'd asked you to move to Venus.'

'For God's sake, Billy, I'm just surprised! What do you expect me to look like when you spring things on me out of nowhere? Am I supposed to just say yes to everything, or do I get to think too? I have to go now or I'll be late.' Poppy opened the door and then turned to look at Billy again. 'Do you love me?'

'You know I do.' Billy leaned over to kiss her. 'I'll pick you up right here.'

'Don't be late.' Poppy slammed the door shut and ran up the sidewalk and into the school.

The only thing Billy had to do during the next two hours

was pick up the rest of his clothes and whatever else that was his at his former home, so he decided he might as well get it over with. When he got there, his father's Datsun was gone, so presumably he had gone back to work. He backed his truck into the driveway and went directly into his room through the back yard door. Agnes Mackenzie had heard or seen him arrive and timed her entrance into the kitchen accordingly. Their eyes met through the space above the broken door as Billy walked in.

'Back so soon?' she asked without pausing on her way across the kitchen.

'I won't be long.' The box of plastic garbage bags was still on his unmade bed. He took one out and opened it and lay it on the bed. He took his one suit, his tweed sports jacket, his two pairs of wool slacks, and his three dress shirts from the hangers in the closet. He folded them as neatly as he could and placed them carefully in the plastic bag. On top of the shirts he lay the only tie he owned that he liked. Into another bag he placed his electric coffee pot, his alarm clock, and his portable cassette player, along with the cassettes themselves. His mother stood watching all this with inscrutable eyes through the hole he had kicked in the wall. Billy carried the two bags out to his truck and put them with the others in the back. On his way back to get the only thing left, his bulky winter parka, the one coat he owned, he remembered the small amount of dope he had stashed under his mattress. While he was stuffing the parka into a bag, he managed to locate the dope with his left hand and slip it into the pocket of his jeans. He had no doubt his mother knew it was there and would check for it as soon as he was gone. He slung the bag containing his parka over his right shoulder and took one final survey of the room in which he had been sleeping since the Mackenzies moved into the house when he was five years old. It looked like he had never been there, which was in a way the truth – the he he was now never had. Billy was just about to leave when he recalled the key to the back door. He set down the bag, removed the key from his keyring, tossed it onto the bed, and walked out.

He still had an hour and a half to wait before he had to collect Poppy at the school. He drove to the beer store, bought a case of Budweiser, and drove out to the cemetery. The temperature was dropping and the drizzle had almost turned into a freezing rain, so after he had stood for a few minutes beside Anne's grave, he got back into his truck and sat there drinking beer and smoking. After the third beer, he couldn't think of a good reason for not getting stoned so he rolled what was left of Rocky's birthday present into five joints and smoked the fattest one. Things were happening for the first time in his life, and no matter how crazy it might be, Billy was glad. At some point, he even began to wonder if maybe he was authentically happy in his real heart. He couldn't be sure because he had no experience in happiness.

He felt bubbly, almost jaunty, as he drove to the school at two-thirty to pick up Poppy. He arrived there a few minutes before the students were dismissed from their fifth period. It occurred to him that a little music might suit the occasion and he popped Bruce Springsteen into his cassette player and lit a cigarette while the gaiety of 'Darlington County' bounced around him like dancing feet. But he couldn't sit still. He walked up the sidewalk to the doors to wait impatiently. From inside the school he could hear the principal's voice droning through the daily afternoon announcements. At last they came to an end and the halls swarmed with students on their way to their lockers. Most of them were free to leave at this time since there were relatively few sixth period classes; they all did their damnedest to avoid taking courses that were scheduled into the last period. Moments later they were flooding through the doors and past him. Watching anxiously for the sight of Poppy's scarlet coat in the crowd, Billy saw Mr Popowski looking at him through the glass and waved to him sociably. As the principal waved back, Billy caught a glimpse of Poppy's coat. When she came through the door, he pulled her into his arms and kissed her hard. 'I love you and I love that new coat,' he said as their lips parted.

The kiss had taken Poppy by surprise. She was just about to say something when Mr Popowski came through the door and joined them.

'You two look very happy,' the principal said.

'We are,' Billy grinned, 'we're getting married.' He took Poppy's hand and held it tightly. The principal looked astounded. Billy smiled at him and said, 'So long!'

Billy and Poppy had turned to head out the sidewalk to his truck before Mr Popowski spoke.

'Billy, don't you think you and I should have a talk about that business this morning? You must know you're making a big mistake.'

Billy let go of Poppy's hand and told her to go on.

She held on to his sleeve. 'Billy, you don't have time now, we have to go.'

Billy kissed her again. 'I won't be five minutes, honey, just get in the truck.' He went back to Mr Popowski.

'Sir, I don't have time to talk now, but I appreciate your caring about what I do. As for the big mistake, all I can say is it doesn't feel like a mistake. It wasn't a snap decision, it's been coming for a long time. I don't really think it had much to do with your finding that dope in my jacket at all, and right at the moment . . .' Billy paused to give the ugly building a once-over. 'Right at the moment, Mr Popowski, you couldn't pay me to come back.'

'I see,' the principal said thoughtfully. 'I assumed of course that your decision to quit was the result of your anger. You do understand that we have no choice but—'

'Indeed I do,' Billy interrupted, 'I definitely do, sir, and that's why I quit, because what I was being trained for was a life without choices and I don't want it. Look, I really do have to buzz off now, the Richardsons are waiting for us, but I'd like to ask you one question. Didn't you find it a trifle odd to get a phone call from a student's mother turning in her own son like that?'

'I did wonder, Billy. It's never happened before.'

Billy smiled. 'Well, at least you wondered. I guess that's a kind of choice, isn't it? And you didn't haul in the cops, I owe you for that. Well, I'll be seeing you.'

The principal was still watching as Billy pulled away and headed for Lac du Bois.

While they were driving south on Main Street toward the highway, the rain began again. Poppy said nothing until he had made the left turn onto Highway 11 when she warned him to stick to the speed limit.

'You smell like a brewery,' she said, 'so I assume you drank all six bottles yourself.'

'Counting the empties,' Billy said with a grin. 'And I thought you were above that, too. I have my toothbrush right here in my pocket, Popsy, and I'll slip into the bathroom as soon as we get there and come out smelling like toothpaste, okay?'

It rained all the way to Lac du Bois. Billy turned up the music and they listened to Bruce Springsteen. When the tape got back to 'Darlington County' Billy sang along on the choruses. Poppy looked at him and smiled.

'You really are happy, aren't you?'

'You know, I was wondering about that earlier myself,' Billy smiled back. 'I think I must be. I know I should be, after all, I've got the number one prettiest girl there ever was or will be in the world. And the finest of ladies, I might add. Yes, I'm scared even to say it, but I'm happy. Let's hope it's a virus, maybe you'll catch it.'

But a few minutes later, as Billy turned the corner into Pine Point Crescent, his happiness began to evaporate. There were far too many cars parked outside the Richardsons' house. The last in the lineup was his father's Datsun, license number PEV 707.

'Goddamn it!' he shouted as he hit the brake pedal and stalled his truck on the road. He looked accusingly at Poppy. 'I thought we were coming for a private talk with your mother and father! It looks like a fucking convention! Shit!' He banged his right fist on the dash.

'Don't glare at me! I'm just as surprised as you are.'

Billy lit a cigarette. 'Jesus Christ! You know, that father of yours needs his fucking head examined, and I mean it!'

'I am just as angry as you, Billy, there's no point in shouting at me. I don't understand why he's done this!'

'You don't? Well, I do! He saw a chance to do some Goddamned organizing and he couldn't fuckin' resist it!' He waved toward the parked cars ahead. 'Who the hell's he got in there, anyway? I recognize my parents' Datsun and your Goddamned brother's station wagon. Whose is the black Lincoln, the hearse?'

'Father Xavier's,' Poppy said. 'He's our new priest. He seems to be very nice.'

'He seems to be very nice,' Billy mimicked, 'he seems to be very nice. I don't believe it! I know your father's an asshole but I cannot believe even *he* would do this to us, to his own *daughter*!' He shook his head and laughed. 'Shit!'

'There's no point in having a fit about it,' Poppy said, 'we won't go in, that's all. I'll phone from the White Birches and tell him to get rid of them.'

'Balls to that! We sure as hell will go in!'

Poppy said, 'No, I don't want a big scene.'

But Billy had started the engine and was parking his truck on the gravel shoulder behind his father's Datsun.

'I mean it, Billy, I'm not going in there! You want to cause trouble and I know it! I can't stand it and I'm not going to! I don't want to sit there so your bitch of a mother can stare at me like – what are you doing!'

'I'm lighting up a joint. If I have to go in there alone I might as well enjoy it.'

'Billy, you wouldn't!'

Billy opened the door and jumped down. 'I wouldn't, wouldn't I? You bet your sweet fanny I would, maybe you're scared of those fools but I'm not. They're a bunch of Goddamned assholes is what they are!' He banged the door shut and took off across the neighbor's lawn towards the Richardsons' front door. Behind him he heard Poppy get out of the truck. 'Billy,' she called, 'wait for me, please!' When she had caught up to him she said, 'We have to go back out to the street, we can't get through the hedge.'

'I'm going to the back door so I can ask that asshole *daddy* of yours some questions before I join the party.' Billy took one last deep drag and popped the roach into his mouth. 'Who belongs to the little Ford anyway?'

'Aunt Margaret, Mother's sister.'

'An aunt even,' Billy muttered as he exhaled. 'I wonder if there'll be room for us to sit down. Come on, let's go and get it over with.'

He took Poppy's hand and they walked alongside the hedge, around the garage, and up the grass to the back door. Billy knocked loudly and pushed the bell button at the same time. Poppy's Aunt Margaret opened the door, obviously surprised to see them there.

'Oh,' she said uncertainly, glancing over her shoulder.

'Hello, Aunt Margaret,' Billy said politely. 'Could you get Mr Richardson for us please?' He and Poppy stepped inside and Poppy's aunt retreated up the three stairs into the kitchen.

'They're waiting for you . . .'

'That was our understanding, too, but they seem to have unexpected company.' Billy followed Poppy up the steps into the kitchen as Aunt Margaret disappeared through the swinging door into the dining room. They had just removed their coats when Edgar Richardson came in.

'What are you doing out here? We're all in the living room.'

Poppy moved past Billy quickly. 'Daddy, what are all those people doing here? Billy's very angry and I don't blame him, so am I! Good grief!'

Billy stepped forward and looked down at the bald top of Edgar Richardson's head. He took Poppy's hand, which was frigid and trembling. 'Our idea was that we were going to have a little talk with you and your wife, just the four of us. In private, you know, all by ourselves. We weren't expecting a tea party.' He flicked his eyes meaningfully at the tray of neatly quartered sandwiches Poppy's aunt had prepared.

'Tea party? I don't think any of us has the occasion confused with a tea party, Billy. By no means.' Inside Edgar Richardson's voice Billy heard murderous longings straining at the seams of his civility.

Mrs Richardson pushed through the swinging door and looked from one face to another.

'Hello dear,' she said to Poppy. 'Hello Billy.'

Mrs Richardson's face looked as if it had been well boiled; the flesh seemed ready to fall off the bones of her skull. Her tremulous smile was funereal, her voice damp with wept tears.

Edgar Richardson whispered grimly, 'I did what I thought was best under the circumstances, Billy. It seems to me the sooner we get this emergency organized and off the ground the better!'

'You might have checked out the circumstances first,' Billy retorted. 'If you had, you might have thought twice about dragging my Goddamned parents over here! As it happens, Edgar, we just had a big showdown a few hours ago, which ended when I left my home *and* my parents, hopefully forever. So their being here is a trifle awkward for both of us.'

'Naturally, I talked to your father,' Edgar Richardson said. 'He didn't say anything about trouble at home to me.'

'Naturally, he wouldn't!' Poppy dug her fingernails into the palm of Billy's hand to shut him up.

'We really must go in and join the others, please?' Ellen Richardson whispered anxiously.

'I'll come with you, Mother,' Poppy said, and followed her mother through the swinging door.

Billy grabbed Edgar Richardson by the arm and held him back. 'I won't forget this. Once we're married, you stay out of our lives. We won't be needing a stage manager.'

Edgar Richardson yanked his arm away as soon as Billy loosened his grasp. 'You've ruined my baby's life, you filthy little bastard!' he hissed. 'You think that gives you the right to boss me around in my own home?'

'Fuck you,' Billy said, and pushed through the door. He almost hit Mrs Richardson and Poppy; they had evidently been waiting just inside the dining room for the two men to join them.

Billy and Poppy followed her parents into the living room. Poppy spoke through a taut, radiant smile, 'Hello, Mrs Mackenzie. Hello, Mr Mackenzie. Hello Father Xavier.'

Billy smiled broadly around the room as they crossed the carpet to the love seat in front of the picture window and sat down. The priest had stood up and was looking at them expectantly. Poppy rose at once. 'I'm sorry, Father Xavier, you haven't met Billy, have you?'

Billy got up and went over to the priest with Poppy.

'Father Xavier, I'd like you to meet Billy Mackenzie. Billy, this is Father Xavier.'

Billy shook the priest's extended hand. 'How do you do, Father Xavier, it's a pleasure to meet you,' he smiled.

'Indeed, indeed,' said Father Xavier. Instead of relinquishing Billy's hand after the usual amount of pumping, the priest folded it inside both his own and gave a firm, fleshy squeeze. As he squeezed, he peered professionally into Billy's eyes, smiled and nodded, and finally said, 'So this is Billy Mackenzie.' The room was silent.

'Yes, this is me,' said Billy.

'Well, well, well, well,' Father Xavier repeated on a descending scale, as if he were making unforeseen discoveries as he stared into Billy's eyes. Billy waited for the fifth 'well', and after an apparently satisfied sigh it finally came, 'Well'. Only then did he let go of Billy's hand. 'We might as well be seated, I think,' the priest said.

'I would think so,' Billy agreed with a nod. 'That's quite the handshake you've got there, almost scientific.'

'Ha, ha, ha,' laughed Father Xavier as he sat down.

Billy returned to sit beside Poppy on the love seat before the window. His parents were seated on the sofa, which was directly across the room. The silence of the universe settled into the Richardsons' living room like invisible cement. Billy smiled at Poppy and spoke in an undertone, 'Are all priests as rude as this one? I think he was actually sniffing as well as staring.'

Poppy ignored him.

Ellen Richardson abruptly rose from her chair. 'I'll just get the coffee and tea now, I think,' she announced. She glanced from face to face and took off for the kitchen as if she were on the lam.

Billy had noticed the little stacks of cups and saucers on the embossed silver tray on the coffee table in front of the sofa on which his parents sat. He recognized the china as Mrs Richardson's best. Next to the cups and saucers were a silver creamer and a silver bowl filled with cubes of sugar. When Billy lifted his eyes and smiled at his parents, Agnes Mackenzie delivered her You-Are-Not-There look and dragged on her cigarette. His father checked out his wife's face to see what he should do with his own. He came up with an effeminate simper that made Billy want to puke. Billy beamed at them both as he wondered if he would ever succeed in dissolving them from his memory. He moved his eyes over to Jack Richardson, who was seated next to the Mackenzies on the sofa, and said, 'Hi, Jack.'

Jack Richardson nodded to him stiffly and said hello.

Edgar Richardson had brought a chair in from the dining room and was seated on it midway between the priest and the sofa. Billy took out his cigarettes and said, 'Today, Mr Richardson, I think I'll be needing an ashtray, if you don't mind.' He smiled at Poppy's father.

'Of course, of course!' Edgar Richardson exclaimed loudly, and hurried into the dining room in search of another ashtray.

Billy turned his smile back to Poppy and murmured, 'Your father is not only stupid, he's downright cruel, and I'm speaking of deliberate cruelty. I presume you recognize a trial when you're one of the accused?'

Poppy replied through the smile that had been frozen on her face since they came into the room. 'It isn't a trial, it's just a mistake.'

'So was the Spanish Inquisition.'

Ellen Richardson returned with two silver pots. 'Here's the tea and coffee,' she announced, and set the two pots on the silver tray as Aunt Margaret arrived with a tray of sandwiches and Edgar Richardson with an ashtray.

'There you are,' he said as he handed the ashtray to Billy, 'have yourself a cigarette, Billy.'

'Thank you very much, sir, I intend to.'

'Let me help you, Mother,' Poppy said as she leapt up to cross the room. Through the smoke from his own cigarette Billy saw his mother scrutinizing Poppy. She had put on her society face but her eyes were flat with undiluted hatred as she watched Poppy moving about. They served Father Xavier first, then his parents, then Jack. Ellen Richardson looked across the room at Billy and said, 'You take your coffee black, don't you, Billy?'

'Yes, ma'am, I do, but I'd rather have a drink right now if that isn't too much trouble.'

Poppy flung him a warning glacial smile. 'Billy, you know

my parents don't drink alcohol.'

'I'd still like a drink,' Billy said in his most friendly, ordinary voice, turning his head to smile at Edgar Richardson. He knew Poppy's father kept a few bottles of liquor in the dining room buffet.

Edgar Richardson stood up and said, 'I believe we do have some whisky left over from last Christmas, Billy. If you would really prefer it.'

'Whisky's my drink, Dad,' Billy replied pleasantly, 'and it's more than just a preference right now, it's a need.' He smiled at Father Xavier, whose bright black eyes were trained on Billy like microscopes. 'Disciplinary action always unnerves me, Father.'

Poppy's father laughed four hollow 'ha's and said, 'I'm glad to see you haven't lost your sense of humor, Billy, but I'm sure none of us is thinking of our gathering as a disciplinary action, ha, ha, ha.'

'I am,' Billy said, 'so I guess it's all in my mind. Let's hope the whisky blows it away.'

Edgar Richardson's face reflected his struggle to control strong words of some kind. He said, 'Under the circumstances, I'm sure we all understand how you must be feeling. Did you want ice in your drink, Billy?'

'No, sir, just the whisky.'

Mr Richardson asked if anyone else wanted a drink, but everyone said no. '*One* Scotch and water coming right up,' he said on his way into the dining room.

'Skip the water too, sir, I prefer my Scotch straight from the shoulder like everything else. No thank you,' Billy said to Poppy's aunt, who had just reached him on her tour around the room with the sandwiches. Edgar Richardson returned with a crystal tumbler and a bottle of whisky that was almost empty. He handed Billy the tumbler and poured about an inch of liquor into it.

'Why not kill the bottle,' Billy said. 'There's not enough left to make the bottle worth the space it takes up, is there?'

Poppy's father emptied the bottle into the glass in silence. Billy looked around at everyone and spoke to the room in general. 'I guess this is what they mean in novels when they talk about a heavy silence. Well, bottoms up, folks.' He lifted the glass high, nodded a toast into space, and downed the Scotch.

Jack Richardson spoke for the first time. 'You find the silence heavy, do you, Billy?'

'I do, yes, I do, Jack. Let's face it, some pretty heavy business is coming down at this little torture party. That is excellent Scotch, Edgar,' he added as he handed the empty tumbler back to Poppy's father. Then he took a last drag on the joint he had been smoking before pinching out the roach and dropping it into the ashtray on his knee. Edgar Richardson was sniffing the air in utter disbelief and eyeing Billy's amiable grin.

'That is very pungent tobacco, Billy,' he observed, 'very unusual. What brand do you smoke?'

'Player's,' Billy said, 'but you're quite right about the pungent odor. I just finished a joint.'

'A joint?' Edgar Richardson repeated. 'Did you say joint?'

'A joint, a joint, my kingdom for a joint!'

'Goddamn it!' Mr Richardson shouted. 'Are you telling me you just smoked marijuana in my living room?'

'I'm afraid I am.'

Jack Richardson was plunging across the room. He pushed his father out of the way and grabbed Billy's shirt.

'Who do you think you are, you dirty little son of a bitch?' he shouted wildly, drawing back his right arm to strike.

'Don't do it, Jackie-boy,' Billy warned, 'don't even try, unless you want your fucking jaw broken. And take your hand off me, I don't like it.' He ducked as Jack Richardson's fist came toward his face and brought his own fist down on the hand that was pulling at his shirt. Jack cried out in pain as

Billy jumped to his feet. The priest had moved swiftly across the room to keep Edgar Richardson from attacking Billy. Jack was coming at him again with bared teeth. Billy drove his left fist into Jack's gut and heard him grunt as he folded. By the time Jack's head came up, Billy had squared off for the kill. The blow he landed on Jack Richardson's jaw sounded like the blow of an axe that would fell a tree. Billy's own head was swimming as he watched Jack Richardson fall unconscious to the floor. Blood trickled from his mouth. Somebody screamed.

'Get out!' Edgar Richardson shouted. 'My daughter is not interested in marrying an animal like you.'

'That's up to Poppy,' Billy spat back. It took him a few seconds to find her; she had collapsed onto a leather hassock beside the chair Father Xavier had been sitting in.

'Sorry about this, honey, but it looks like you have to make up your mind fast. I'm heading out, are you coming with me or not?'

Poppy turned towards her father, tears streaming from her eyes. 'I love him, Daddy!' she sobbed.

Billy shook his head in an attempt to clear his mind. 'If you love me,' he said, 'why are you apologizing to Daddy? Your daddy just ordered me out and I'm on my way.' He started for the kitchen where he had left his jacket, tripped over Jack Richardson's feet, and barely managed to avoid pitching himself into his mother's lap by reaching instead to grab at the archway into the dining room. His mind was flashing like a city under bombardment and his own lunatic laughter resounded in his ears like machine-gun fire.

'It's your own fault, Daddy, it's your own fault, Daddy, it's your own fault, Daddy, it's your own fault, Daddy, it's your own . . .'

Billy felt his knees buckling as Poppy's voice circled around him. He was trying to find her face to look at as he slid down the wall. His knees hit the floor with a thud. Where was she?

'Billy, I'm coming, Billy, I'm coming, Billy, I'm coming,

Billy, I'm coming, Billy, I'm . . .'

Now her voice was whirling and leaping inside his head. Then he found her face right in front of his eyes and felt her arms around his shoulders, her hands gripping his arms.

'Please get up, darling, we have to go, please get up, darling, we have to go, please get up, darling, we have to . . .'

'Will you shut up for Christ's sake, I right now, I right now, right now, right now . . .' It was his voice now.

'Right now?'

'Right now I seem, I seem, I seem to be . . .'

'Billy? Billy? Billy? Billy . . .'

'Going to the dogs, the dogs, the dogs . . .'

As he was blacking out and toppling backwards in very slow motion while Poppy's face floated off, Billy heard Agnes Mackenzie say, 'He's all yours.'

CHAPTER FOURTEEN

When Billy came to his senses, he was still lying on the carpet in the archway between the living and dining rooms of the Richardson house. But though his mind was as translucent as a crystal ball, he wasn't immediately sure where he was, only that he was somewhere comfortably dark and quiet. Not until he turned his eyes to the right did he see the faint light cast by a street lamp through the sheer curtains that hung across the Richardsons' mammoth picture window.

Someone, he guessed Poppy, had put a sofa cushion under his head as a pillow and covered him with a woolen afghan to keep him warm. When he lifted his right hand up before his eyes to see what time it was on his wristwatch, he became conscious of stabbing pains in his hand and remembered the blow he had delivered to Jack Richardson's jaw. He rejoiced at the memory; he must have really connected. That made the pain bearable. It was ten-thirty according to his watch.

Billy flexed his fingers and then stretched them, wincing at the fierce pain that seemed to be concentrated in his knuckles and his thumb joint. But he came to the conclusion that no bones were broken inside the puffed-up flesh of his hand.

'Poppy,' he called, 'are you there?'

'Yes, Billy, I'm right here, darling. Are you okay?'

Her voice had come from just behind and above his head. Billy tipped his head back on the cushion and saw her indistinct form seated on the leather hassock in the dark. Poppy reached down to stroke his forehead.

'My hand is sore. The knuckles are stiff and my fingers are swollen.'

'What did you expect?' Poppy asked. 'I hope it isn't broken anywhere. You fractured Jack's jaw and broke off a couple of his teeth. His face was swelling up into a pumpkin when he left for the hospital with my father.'

'Oh, that's good.'

'Jack was very proud of his teeth,' Poppy observed. 'Very.'

'I know. He told me once his wife, what's-her-name, thinks he looks like the guy on *Magnum, P.I.* He seemed to agree with her.'

Billy double-checked his hand to see that none of the bones were broken by squeezing all the knuckles with his left hand. The pain was intense under the pressure and the flesh was badly swollen, but it did seem to be in one piece. He placed both hands down flat on the carpeted floor and pushed himself up into a sitting position, angling his body on his rump at the same time so he could look at Poppy. He drew his legs up and folded his arms across his raised knees.

'So,' he said, 'here we are. What went on after I so elegantly passed out?'

Poppy sighed and thought for several minutes before she replied. 'Nothing much, really. Everybody went away. Father Xavier was the first to disappear, I found that interesting. He said he had some parish meeting to go to and took off like a shot. Aunt Margaret stood around for a while holding the tray of sandwiches, then Mother told her she might as well go home. And then your parents left. And as soon as Jack came to—'

'How long was he out?' Billy interrupted eagerly.

'Not that long, I guess, but it seemed ages.'

Billy smiled to himself. 'Then I really did knock him out cold?'

'Do you have to sound quite so pleased about it?'

'I am pleased about it. I didn't know I had it in me.'

'Anyhow,' Poppy continued, 'my father drove him to the hospital over in Nugget. They had to wait around for a doctor and didn't get back until about nine o'clock.'

'Where're your parents now, in bed already?'

'Already! What do you mean by already? Billy, it's almost three o'clock in the morning!'

'It is?'

Billy checked his watch again; the hands were still at ten-thirty.

'My watch has stopped,' he said, giving it a shake. 'The battery must have died. I just had this damned battery replaced last month at that skinflint jeweller's.' He took the watch off and stretched to place it on the little end table that sat next to the arm of the sofa.

'You have broke the good meeting in most admired disorder,' he said out of nowhere. He was smiling again as he said it.

'What?'

'It's a line from *Macbeth*, more or less. Lady Macbeth says that after the poor bugger spills the beans at his big coronation bash. You studied Macbeth in grade eleven, you should remember. We read the whole play aloud together down in your rec room. I played Macbeth and you read Lady Macbeth's lines. You were pretty good, too.'

'I remember now. She says that after he sees Banquo's ghost.'

'That's right. I always loved Macbeth. I figure I must see some similarities in me. I could never understand how they could both be so smart and so dumb at the same time. They should have poisoned the old king with henbane.'

Now that his eyes were accustomed to the near darkness, Billy could see that Poppy wasn't seated on the hassock. She was perched on the largest of three suitcases that stood neatly side by side next to the leather hassock. Poppy's new scarlet coat lay folded and draped across the two smaller suitcases.

'What do the suitcases mean?' Billy asked.

'What do suitcases usually mean?'

'You look like you're sitting at a bus stop.'

He saw Poppy looking forlornly around the big room filled with furniture and shadows. 'I guess I am sitting at a bus stop,' she said. 'I just never knew it before.'

'Those are your mother's suitcases, aren't they?'

'Yes, she gave them to me. I've packed most of my clothes, all the things I really wear. I'm going with you. Wherever that is,' she added. 'We have to go somewhere.'

'Is that what you want to do?'

'Yes. That's what I want to do.'

'So we're just going to take off like this, with your parents in bed? No goodbyes, no nothing?'

'There's nothing to say that hasn't been said.'

Billy looked at Poppy hard. 'Poppy, I want to know what went on tonight. I also want my cigarettes and lighter and an ashtray.'

'I put them in your shirt pocket and there's an ashtray on that end table.'

Billy lighted a cigarette and put the ashtray on the floor between his feet. Poppy came down on the floor and sat close to him.

'Now, tell me,' Billy ordered.

'Well, while Daddy was over in Nugget at the hospital with Jack I had a long talk with my mother. She thinks we should just leave. She asked me to apologize to you for what went on today, all those people being here, Father Xavier, Jack, Aunt Margaret. Mother doesn't blame you at all for being so angry.' She caressed the back of Billy's head and the nape of his neck. 'Your hair's getting long again. And she told me how much she likes you, Billy.'

'Did she really?' Billy asked. 'Has she ever said that to you before?'

'Not the way she did tonight, but I always knew she liked

you. Actually, I've never talked with Mother the way we talked tonight. It was distressing, but I'm glad we talked. She was very critical of my father, especially of the way he just automatically takes charge and plows ahead arranging everybody's life for them. She knows you can't stand my father or Jack, that was news to me. I thought you'd done a pretty good job of hiding it, but you didn't fool her.'

'I'm not really surprised. I always sort of wondered what was going on in your mother's mind.'

'A lot,' Poppy said, 'a whole lot. I felt very sorry for Mother tonight, Billy. She made herself sound so used, as if she hasn't mattered at all since she quit teaching and married my father and had all those babies. It was very – it was sad, and I was crying. In fact, I could cry right now just thinking about it.'

'I believe you,' Billy said. 'What did she say about me?'

'Oh, that she thinks you're very different.'

'Different how?'

'She thinks you won't try to own me. Really, that's how she put it, that you won't try to own me. That's why she likes you. She also apologized for carrying on the way she did after I told her I was pregnant. She said she doesn't really give a damn, that she's been putting on an act for my father for so long that sometimes the act takes over all by itself. I was *horrified* when she said that, just horrified.'

'It is horrifying,' Billy agreed, 'no wonder you cried.'

'You know what I told her? I told her you said we have to think of the baby as God's baby, I told her everything you said that night in your room. Then Mother started crying. God, Billy, it was awful, awful! It was *awful*. She told me Cheryl is absolutely miserable with Andy and thinks she never would have married him if my father hadn't pushed it so hard. And Mother can't stand Jack's wife and she's sick to death of the way they're always over here with the baby. Mother didn't *say* it, but I don't think she likes Jack either.'

Billy said, 'Your mother told you a hell of a lot, didn't she?

She must have felt happy getting all this shit off her chest.'

'She came into my room with me while I was packing and we were still talking in there when my father got back from the hospital. Oh, and I told her you thought we should go to Toronto, and Mother says that sounds like a good idea.'

'I didn't mean we *should* go to Toronto,' Billy protested, 'but as you said, we have to go somewhere. I do think we should get away from here, but we can go wherever we want. It won't be any different no matter where we go, every place is one place now. But at least Toronto's the biggest. You can hide out better in a big crowd.'

'I like Toronto,' Poppy said.

'I've never been there. I've never been anywhere but Thunder Bay.'

'If we do go, Mother said she'd look after sending the rest of my things once we have someplace to live. Tomorrow she's going to meet me at the bank so we can get my savings bonds converted into cash and have the money transferred. She even offered to give us her own money if we need it. She still has the money she had saved up from teaching all those years ago, before she married my father. He didn't want his wife to work.'

'It figures.'

'But I told her you'd be too proud.'

Billy had lighted another cigarette. He choked on the smoke. 'Proud!' he exclaimed between coughs. 'I'm not proud that way! Take the money, for God's sake! Your mother's right, we'll need it.'

'Are you sure?'

'I'm sure. That's very kind of her,' Billy continued sincerely, 'I've always suspected I could like your mother. But she's right, she's a sort of phantom now. She reminds me of my poor father in that way. They're both like occupied countries, but at least your mother still has an active underground resistance. My father's a collaborator. And while we're on the subject, your old man has a lot in common with my mother. They'd have made an ideal couple. Speaking of your father, do I take it you haven't talked with him?'

Poppy sat up and sighed. Then she hugged her knees with her arms. 'I tried when he got back from the hospital. But he went stomping off into his bedroom when I told him again that what happened today was his own fault. Then he and Mother started fighting in the bedroom, but I couldn't hear what they were saying. A few minutes later, he came stomping out again, dragging an old quilt. He went downstairs to the rec room and I haven't seen him since. I went in to see if my mother was okay and nearly fainted. She was lying in bed smoking a cigarette! And she had three or four more on her bedside table. She took them out of your package. I didn't know she'd ever smoked, but she told me she'd been smoking since she was fifteen, until she quit for my father.'

'That was her first mistake,' Billy said. 'And her last, too, I guess, the beginning of the end. She shouldn't have quit her job either.'

'Anyhow, she'd already taken a sleeping pill. I didn't know about them, either, but she's been using them for years. My father doesn't believe in pills—'

'He wouldn't, he's the one that causes the pain.'

'—so she hides the bottle in her Tampax box.'

'Jesus.'

'Billy, you have no idea how sorry I feel for my mother. All those years of . . .' Poppy couldn't find the words.

'Lies and suckholing,' Billy said. 'Let's get back to old Edgar. He can't be asleep down there in the basement, his sky is falling. You aren't going to say goodbye to him? Or at least good night? He does love you, Poppy, you know he does.'

Billy watched the first tears sliding out of her eyes.

'Does he?' she choked. 'He has a funny way of showing it.'

She wasn't looking at Billy. Her eyes were focused dead ahead at the picture window behind the love seat, but she wasn't really looking anywhere. The warm shimmer of her tears streaked her cheeks. She licked salt from her lips.

'No,' she said softly at last. 'No, I am not. I've had nothing to do but think all the time I've been sitting here, waiting for you to wake up. I don't see why I should go down there and beg him for his absolution. If he wants to pout, he can pout till the cows come home as far as I'm concerned. I'm very angry with my father, and listening to my mother tonight didn't help any, I can assure you of that! I could have understood Father Xavier being here, and even Aunt Margaret. But he had no *right* to bring Jack over here today! And he certainly had no right to phone your father and invite your parents over without talking to us first. And I mean *us*, Billy, not just you. I've never said it, but I hate that bitch, I hate her. The idea that he would *dare* drag that hateful, nasty woman over here infuriates me, more than it does you, too.'

Poppy covered her face with her hands and shook her head. 'God, do I hate that mother of yours. What's so funny?'

Billy tried to stop laughing. 'The idea your father had to drag her here. Drag? Poppy, my mother wouldn't have missed that opportunity if she'd been on her deathbed once she got the word from the old man. I watched her today. When she wasn't busy beaming her magic death rays at you, she was shopping through the room with her eyes, pricing everything in sight. She even checked out the bottom of her saucer just after your father threw the hairy about my smoking a joint in *his* living room, when she thought nobody would notice. I hope to God it's the most expensive fucking china pattern on earth! Ours is catalogue stuff, made in Taiwan.'

Poppy's lips curled into a smirk of delighted vengeance. 'Is it expensive? Oh, Billy, that stuff is expensive plus! My mother's been collecting it for as long as I can remember, and she still doesn't have the big serving dishes. I'm so glad you told me that.' She looked at her watch. 'Billy, let's go, please. It's almost four o'clock. I don't want to be here when my father decides to come upstairs.'

She stood up and collected her scarlet coat to put on. Billy pushed himself to his feet. He picked up his watch again; it still read ten-thirty. He laid it back on the table. He would buy a new watch, the cheapest Timex he could find.

'I can't believe that damn battery's dead. It must have been ready to expire when they sold me the thing. You know, every time something like that happens to me, I think of Willy Loman in *Death of a Salesman.* Remember? We watched it on TV on the late-night movie one night last spring. He was right, every bloody thing you buy is designed to fall apart or wear out before it should. It's quite the system. I tried to get a copy of the play, but they don't have it in any of the libraries, not even at the school.'

Poppy had taken up the smallest of the three suitcases.

'That reminds me,' she said, 'your mother said to tell you you forgot your books. She's putting them out with the garbage.'

'My books!' Billy cried involuntarily. 'Damn it! I did forget them. Did that bitch really say she was putting them out with the garbage? Tomorrow's garbage day on our street.'

'That's what she said. Would she actually do it to you?'

'You have to ask? She'd do anything. And she knows how much I care about my books. Poppy, where's my jacket?'

'Don't snarl at *me*,' Poppy said. 'I put it right there on the hassock.'

'I didn't mean to snarl.'

'Well, you did.'

Billy shrugged into his jacket and lifted one suitcase in either hand. His injured hand hurt like hell. Poppy had walked to the front door and was waiting.

'Poppy,' Billy said, 'are you sure about your dad? He can't help what he does, you know. It wouldn't kill you just to go down and say goodbye, but it might kill him if you don't. I meant it when I said he loves you.'

'Billy, I'm pretty well used to your direct way of speaking, but there's one thing you say that I really don't like. You say it all the time, too. Now I'm going to say it for the first time in my life, because it's what I feel. He can shove his love up his ass. Okay? Can we please get out of here? I don't belong here any more.'

Outside, they discovered that the skies had cleared and the air was almost warm. It would be a sunny day. Poppy stood gazing up at the stars that blazed above them as Billy placed her three suitcases carefully in the back of his truck. He covered them with a sheet of plastic. When Billy went to open the passenger door for her, Poppy took hold of his left arm tightly.

'Look,' she whispered, 'look at the stars, darling. I know you don't believe in omens and things like that, but I can't help it. I feel they wanted to be there tonight just for you and me. And they do look like diamonds sometimes, don't they?'

'When did I ever say I don't believe in omens?' Billy inquired. 'I don't remember ever saying that to anybody.'

'Billy, you always say there's no such thing as an accident.'

'But Poppy, that's why people *do* believe in omens. You couldn't have omens in a universe of accidents. Come on, get in the truck, I thought you wanted to get away from here.'

'First, I want you to kiss me, the way you've always kissed me when you brought me home. Now you're taking me away, and who knows if we'll ever come back? Kiss me because I love you.'

Billy kissed her, and then Poppy held him close and pressed her face into his chest.

'I love you,' Billy said. It had come out freely, without any thought, so he said it again while the going was good. 'I love you, Poppy, I love you.'

He looked up at the starry sky and saw the Pleiades, the seven daughters of Atlas, and thought of Blanche Dubois.

'Poppy,' he said, 'look, there, those are the Pleiades, the

seven sisters. But you can only see six of them without a telescope, the seventh one is shy. She's a home girl.'

He hugged Poppy to his side. She was a home girl too.

Poppy said, 'I love the way you know all these things. You know so many *things*.'

'No, I don't. I had a book about the stars when I was a little boy. I used it so much it was falling apart, I loved it. My mother threw it out one day while I was at school and I was heartbroken. All it needed was some tape. When I read *A Streetcar Named Desire* last year, I went outside and found the Pleiades. It was about this time of night, too. What Blanche says about the Pleiades when she's looking up at the sky is so lonesome it's unbearable.'

'You read it to me, but I can't remember what she says.'

'Well, she's on her way out with Stella and she looks up at the sky full of stars, the way it is now. Then she notices the Pleiades, and she says to Stella, "Oh, look, there they are, the seven sisters on their way home from a bridge game." Then she says something about how beautiful the sky is on a starry night, and laughs, and jokes, "I ought to go there on a rocket and never come down." '

'That is sad,' Poppy murmured, 'but it's pretty too. It makes you want to go with her, to keep her company.'

'And all that asshole Mr Sweet had to say about Blanche was that she's really a man in drag. I swear to God, I still don't believe it. Let's go, honey. Even remembering it makes me feel like screaming.'

They were both quiet as Billy wove his truck along the silent empty streets of Lac du Bois. Billy was imagining the vindictive satisfaction his mother must have taken when she discovered that he had forgotten the books he loved. He didn't have many, but he had read all of them over and over. Just before they reached the highway, he pulled over onto the gravel shoulder of the exit road, the engine running.

'Poppy,' he said, 'I can't get my mind off my books. I want

to go and get them. I can't bear thinking of them in a garbage can with stinky potato peelings and tins of congealed fat and dozens of old soggy tea bags.'

It was true, he had to get them. They weren't just books to Billy – they were people he loved. Jean Brodie was more real to him than all the teachers he had ever known put together. And all the others were real as well – David Balfour and the noble Alan Breck, Blanche Dubois and Stanley Kowalski, Macbeth and his lady of sorrows, Fabrizio, the Prince of Salina, and Kim, Jim Hawkins and Long John Silver, Robinson Crusoe and David Copperfield, Peter Pan and Tinkerbell. Jesus Christ, it was genocide. Fuck that.

'I have to go, that's all,' Billy said. 'Besides, I have to say goodbye to Rocky.'

'Then why are we sitting here?'

'You mean you want to come with me?'

'Of course I'm coming with you. What else would I do?'

'I thought I could book you a room at the White Birches so you could grab some sleep.'

'I'm not sleepy. I'm just dead beat. I have nothing to do until I meet mother at the bank at eleven-thirty. She wanted to go right at ten o'clock, as soon as the banks open. But I said she had to get some sleep, especially since she'd already taken that pill.'

Billy put the truck in gear and pulled up to make the left turn onto Highway 11, heading for Nugget for the last time.

'I have to go to the bank, too,' he said, 'I'd forgotten that.'

'I hadn't,' Poppy said. 'Billy, you can turn any time, there's nothing on the highway. Once we get your books, we'll have to wait until the bank opens so you can arrange to have your money transferred.'

'Balls,' Billy said. 'I'm taking it with me. I'll buy traveler's checks with it and you can keep them in your purse. I don't want anything left behind me – absolutely nothing. I've got nothing but loose ends ahead of me, Poppy. What's behind me is a big, tangled fuck-up, and behind me is where it's going to stay. I mean that.'

'You like that idea, don't you? The idea of life as loose ends.'

'I guess I do,' Billy said, 'at least they're my loose ends. I've had the other kind of life, tied up in knots. That's okay for the stars, but not for people, not me anyways. I'll go wake Rocky up to say goodbye as soon as I get my books, then we can find something to eat while we're waiting for the bank to open. I'm starving.'

They drove in silence most of the way to Nugget.

Suddenly a low-profile sports car glittered in the sunlight behind them as they were making the last long turn to the north. It caught up to Billy's truck like a bullet and pulled out into the eastbound lane as if to pass. But instead of passing, the driver honked his horn to get Billy's attention.

Rocky Barbizan grinned and waved to them. The window on the passenger side of the dazzling silver Porsche he was driving slid down as smoothly as melting ice. Billy wound down his own window so he could hear Rocky shouting as they sped side by side.

'Hey, Billy-boy,' Rocky screamed, 'is this some beautiful fuckin' machine or not?'

Billy stared at the silver Porsche for a second. 'It's beautiful, Rocky,' he shouted back. 'It's beautiful!'

And beautiful it certainly was, its sleek silver splendor glowing pinkly in the beams of the rising sun.

'Where you goin'?' Rocky yelled.

'Away,' Billy screamed. 'Toronto. Meet us for breakfast at the Northern Lights.'

'What?'

'The Northern Lights,' Billy hollered as loudly as he could.

'Okay, but you better slow down, Billy. You'll get a ticket up at the motel.'

The silver Porsche dropped back swiftly and pulled into the

westbound lane behind the truck. Billy soon left it out of sight.

'I couldn't hear what he said, could you?' Billy asked.

'He said you'll get a ticket if you don't slow down.'

Billy laughed. 'Honest to God, he got the Porsche. I'll be damned, but I feel so good for him I might even be happy. You've been quiet. What have you been thinking about?'

'Loose ends,' Poppy said.

'And?'

'It's a scary idea, but I've always known you were scary, Billy. Now I know why.'

'Does that make me less scary or more scary?' Billy asked as they zipped past the Sleeping Beauty Motel.

'I haven't a clue,' Poppy said, 'and please, don't give me one. If loose ends are what you want, I guess they must be what I want too. As long as I'm not one of them.'

Poppy looked at Billy, who was still smiling about Rocky's dream machine. 'I'm not, am I?'

'Honey,' Billy said, laughing, 'you'll never know.'

But Poppy thought she did.

She definitely knew that Billy was speeding faster than ever, and was about to get a ticket from the cop in the cruiser that had pulled slyly out behind him as his truck sped past the infamous Sleeping Beauty speed trap Rocky had warned him about. The cop was holding off to see how far over the speed limit Billy would get before he spotted his nemesis behind him.

Rocky warned him, Poppy thought, and far be it from me to play watchdog.

Loose ends?

Two could play at that game.